i never expected

You

STEFANIE JENKINS

This is a work of fiction. Names, characters, places, and incidents either are the product of the author's imagination or are used fictitiously. Any resemblance to actual persons, living or dead, events, or locales is entirely coincidental.

**I Never Expected You
Copyright © 2019 by Stefanie Jenkins**

Editing by One Love Editing at https://www.facebook.com/OneLoveEditing/
Proofread by CPR Editing https://www.facebook.com/cprediting
Cover Design by Ya'll That Graphic at https://www.facebook.com/yallthatgraphic/
Interior Book Formatting by authorTree at https://www.facebook.com/authortree

All rights reserved. No part of this book may be reproduced or used in any manner without written permission of the copyright owner except for the use of quotations in a book review.
Independently published.

To Amanda, BJ and Claudia,
Zach wouldn't be who he is today without you guys.
Now go enjoy some chicken wings.

"Love enters your life when you least expect it. It barges in. Soothing fears you never knew existed... Breaking down barriers and laying claim your heart. Oh, when love comes... You'll know." - Phoenix Mode

PROLOGUE
ZACH

"I can't believe you're going to eat all of that," Haylee, my sister Danielle's best friend, says as she takes a seat beside me at the picnic table.

My sister sets the tray piled high with food down in front of her. She takes a seat across from us next to Emmett, her boyfriend, who also happens to be my best friend and Haylee's older brother. Emmett and Dani have been inseparable since they were thirteen. It might be weird for other people to watch their sister and best friend be together, but for me, it would be weird *not* to.

Dani grimaces and looks down at her thin body. "Umm, no. Most of this is for Em and this jackass in front of me..." She points to me, and I hold my hand to my chest as if offended by the nickname. "...who claimed he didn't want anything, but I know him better than he does, so I got extra."

I laugh because my sister is exactly right. Although now, I want to prove her wrong.

"These, however..." Dani holds up a plate full of curly fries covered in cheese, and her eyes light up. "...are for me." She grabs one of the fries and dances as she brings it to her mouth and lets out an over-the-top moan as she chews, forcing us all to laugh.

"You're adorable with how you get with your cheese fries."

Emmett places a quick kiss on her lips before reaching for one of the pit beef sandwiches, a staple when coming to a Maryland carnival.

My mouth instantly waters at the smell of all the delicious food.

"Take a picture, Zach. It'll last longer. Or take that other sandwich off the tray because there's no way I can eat them both. You know you want to."

He doesn't have to tell me twice. I inhale the sandwich. I'm not even sure I taste it as I shove it in my mouth. I crumple the wrapper and place it back on the tray. My stomach now thanks me for filling it.

"I can't believe this is our last carnival together," Dani says in between bites.

Summer will be ending in a few weeks, and Emmett and I will be heading off to college at the University of Pennsylvania. It's only a two-hour drive from where we live in Annapolis. Dani and Haylee will begin their senior year, and if all things go as planned, my sister will join us at UPenn next fall.

"It's not like we all won't be back together next summer. We'll come back. Coming to these carnivals is tradition." Carnivals were never really my thing, but I enjoy the company. The four of us have been coming to the local firehouse carnival for as long as I can remember.

"Dani's right," Haylee adds. "It just won't be the same. Everything will be different."

She shrugs. Life might change, but we will always have each other.

I reach over to snag a piece of funnel cake off Haylee's plate, and she smacks my hand away. "Uh-uh, Mr. I'm Not Hungry. Go get your own. I didn't wait in that line for this just to share."

I roll my eyes at her. The girl takes her funnel cake seriously. Haylee takes a massive bite of the sweet treat and gets powdered sugar everywhere.

"Hey, Hails?"

She turns toward me with a mouth full of food. "Huh?"

A puff of powdered sugar smoke escapes her mouth.

"You got a little something there." I move my hand in a circular motion all over my face.

"Real attractive there, sis," Emmett jokes from across the table.

"Thank you," she mumbles in between chewing. "I plan to make some lucky man very happy one day."

Lord help the man who plans to marry her. I'd say he deserves a gold medal.

"So, what next?" Haylee asks, throwing her empty plate in the trash. It's rather impressive that she ate the entire funnel cake herself.

"We can go ride some rides," my sister suggests.

"Ooh, how 'bout the Zipper," I call out. That ride is my favorite.

All color has drained from Haylee's face, and her eyes are wide. "Oh, hell no. You know I don't do heights."

There are not many things this girl is afraid of, but heights are at the top of her list.

"What about the Tilt-A-Whirl?" Haylee rubs her hands together in excitement.

Meh, that ride always makes me dizzy.

"Why don't we play some games? They have the water gun balloon game over there. That's always fun." Em points over his shoulder in the opposite direction.

"Oh look, there is a new fun house this year," Dani shouts.

"Those things are stupid. They're so easy to get through." I sigh. A fun house? Those are for kids.

"I bet I could beat you through there." Haylee stands up straight with an intensity in her eyes that I see when she gets competitive.

Now, this just got interesting. Haylee and I are never ones to back down from a dare or a bet, and she knows I can't refuse.

I step up to Haylee and stare down at her. "Oh, it's on. Winner gets to pick the ride, and *when* I win, we will be going on the Zipper."

Haylee extends her hand, and I take it.

"Deal," we both say at the same time.

"Here we go again." Dani rolls her eyes.

"Oh, this is gonna be good." A mischievous smile comes over my best friend's face as he tugs my sister's arm, pulling her closer to his chest.

Haylee and I both take the positions at the fun house entrance.

"The first one to the finish line wins," Haylee explains. "Ready. Set. Go."

Seventeen minutes later, Dani and Haylee are in one cart, and Emmett and I have crammed into another on the Zipper. I love my best friend and all, but I don't think I need to be *this* close to him. As the ride begins to take off and the carts begin to spin, I hear Haylee's screams from the cart in front of us.

"I hate you, Jacobs!"

"You know she's going to knock you on your ass when the ride is over, right?" Em says, shaking his head.

"Yup," I say in between my laughter.

It was so worth it.

CHAPTER 1

Haylee

The sound of "Fix You" by Coldplay, my brother's favorite band, plays through my earbuds to drown out the silence that fills my house these days.

It's been five weeks since my brother, Emmett, was killed in a car accident in Philadelphia. He was on his way back to his apartment from the library to meet Dani, who had driven up there to surprise him for the weekend. However, he never made it back home.

The funeral is over. The people are gone that have been filling my house the past few weeks delivering food, giving their condolences, and keeping us company. It's not death that's hard; it's what comes afterward, the silence, that is deafening. How am I supposed to move on from life without my brother?

I'm lying on my bed staring at the ceiling. It's been a struggle to get out of bed lately. What's the point? If I do have the strength to get out of bed, I'm in my best friend's bed, grieving with her.

I close my eyes and allow the lyrics to consume the hole in my heart. Alone in my room, I don't have to hide my pain and sadness. I don't have to be strong for my parents, best friend, and others. I allow the tears to freely flow down my cheeks.

I have so many questions racing through my mind, but the biggest one that will never get answered is, *"Why?"* Why him?

Why did my brother have to die at only eighteen? He had his whole life ahead of him.

I STOOD IN FRONT OF THE CROWDED CHURCH, MY GRIP TIGHT on the paper as I laid it flat against the stand. I blinked back the tears. I needed to get through this. Why did I tell my parents I would give the eulogy?

"Emmett Hanks was..." I paused at having referred to my brother in past tense. I wasn't sure that was ever something I would get used to.

I began again. "Emmett Hanks was a son to two of the best parents anyone could ask for. He was a big brother, a boyfriend, and a best friend. Em was a strong athlete. I used to joke with him saying he was born with a lacrosse stick in his hand. When he loved, he loved with all his heart."

I looked in Dani's direction, but thankfully, she was looking down at her hands. I knew if my eyes connected with her and I saw how broken she was, I would lose it.

"It was something I admired so much about him. Emmett wasn't just my big brother; he was my teacher, my hero, my protector. He fought off the boogeyman, kept away the monsters under the bed, and even chased away the boys he said weren't ever good enough. He held my hand in the dark and walked with me by my side. I know he will do that still. I just won't be able to see him."

A twinkle of color caught my attention, and I stared above the crowd at the reflection of the sun shining through the stained-glass windows illuminating the church in bright, bold colors, just like my brother had in a room. His smile was infectious.

He was here.

A happy memory hit my brain, and I completely forgot about the rest of my speech.

"One summer..." A smile hit my lips as I remembered it clear as day. "We were out riding bikes with Zach and Dani, and there was this big hill in our neighborhood. I think we were maybe seven and eight. When I drove past the hill the other day, it was just a tiny bump in the road, but to a little kid, it was a mountain. The four of us just stared at the hill. Zach and Dani, both fearless, raced down the hill first. I held back—I was terrified. Emmett looked over at me." I closed my eyes and could hear my brother's voice in my head. "He said, 'Be brave and fearless, Hails. I'm right here beside you.'"

How was I supposed to be brave and fearless without him here?

"I adjusted my helmet and began to pedal. As soon as we reached the bottom, he jumped off his bike and ran to hug me. 'You did it. You're so brave.' He may have thought I was brave, but it was only because I had him there."

I caught my breath and gave one last look around the church. "When you see a beautiful sunset, or the wind blows, or maybe you even hear a special song, know it's my brother there, telling you to be brave. He is right there with us."

I crumpled the paper and walked back to my seat, avoiding eye contact with everyone. I took my seat and closed my eyes while Zach took the podium and began to read the poem "The Dash." Dani reached for my hand, and I held it tight.

I needed to be brave, today and the rest of my days.

A

Today, we are going to the apartment Emmett shared with Zach to pack up his things. My mom doesn't feel up to doing this; most days she doesn't feel up to doing anything. Kelly, Dani and Zach's mom, is staying here with her while my dad, me, Dani, and her dad, Adam, go. We can each pick what we want to keep, and the rest will be boxed up and brought back here. One day, I will help my parents go through it.

How can we just pack up his life in boxes? How do I know what to keep and what not to? Something that meant the world to Em, which might under normal circumstances mean nothing to me, now means everything because it's all I have left of him.

I squeeze my eyes shut as the music gets louder to try block out the memory of my last trip to Philly. It's not the thought of the drive there that threatens to crush me, but what came after.

"We did everything we could." Those five words will forever be instilled in my brain. The words that I will always associate with the night I lost my brother. The words I replay in my head over and over again.

That night, I had to say goodbye to my brother. A simple word: goodbye. I've said goodbye to my brother a million times before when I knew I would see him again. How am I to say goodbye this time, knowing I won't?

My bedroom door opens, and my dad peeks his head in. I pull the earbuds out of my ears.

"Sorry, sweetheart. I knocked, but you didn't answer."

My dad is like me, red-rimmed eyes and pale skin. It's as if the day he lost his son, the life was sucked straight out of him. I know that's how I feel.

I sit up on the bed and wipe my eyes. "It's okay. What's up?"

"The Jacobses are on their way. Adam ran to pick up more boxes, so we will be getting on the road as soon as they get here."

"Okay, I'll change and be down in five." I give him a weak smile.

He nods and closes the door behind him.

I shuffle off the bed and place my phone and earbuds on the nightstand next to a photo of Zach, Dani, Emmett and me from this past Thanksgiving, the last time the four of us were all together. I pick up the frame and focus on the smiles on our faces. Will the three of us ever smile like that again? I set the frame down when the tears threaten to break free.

I quickly change my clothes and make my way down the steps the same time the front door opens. I watch as Kelly Jacobs enters the house and walks straight to my mom. She pulls Mom into a tight embrace, holding her up. I am thankful that my mom has a best friend like Kelly to help her through this.

Speaking of best friends, where is mine?

I walk out the front door toward the Jacobs family minivan and see Dani sitting in the back seat staring at our house. She hasn't been here since before the accident. It's too hard for her, she says. Sometimes I wonder if she forgets we're all going through the same tragedy.

"All set?" Dad asks as I approach my door.

I shrug. All set for what? To pack up my brother's things? I'm not really sure that is something I can prepare for. I know we don't have to do this today. Zach said that he didn't plan to get another roommate and that Em's belongings could stay as long as we needed them to, but my dad thought this would be a good part of starting the healing process. We all deal with grief differently; being proactive is his way, I guess.

I take a seat next to Dani and buckle my seat belt.

"Hey."

"Hey," she responds, but doesn't take her eyes off my house as we pull out onto the road.

Small talk fills the ride. Dani doesn't add much to the conversation, just blankly stares out the window. Before I know it, we are pulling into the parking space marked for guests. Dad and Adam take empty boxes out of the trunk. Boxes that soon enough will hold the last of my brother's things. Silence takes over as we make our way to the main entrance.

    I notice Dani stopping in front of the empty parking space next to Zach's Jeep—my brother's parking spot. My chest begins to tighten, and I see her frozen in place with her eyes squeezed shut. I slowly walk over to her, her eyes still closed, and grab her hand. She jumps slightly, but I try to give her a reassuring nod. She returns a smile, but it quickly fades as she looks over her shoulder at the empty spot. I realize I need to take the lead and begin the walk to the entrance. Her hand remains in mine the entire way to the apartment door. With my best friend by my side, I can get through this.

CHAPTER 2
ZACH

Today is the first day of my spring semester. I'm supposed to be excited, most likely oversleeping, and quickly grabbing a shitty student union coffee. But here I am standing in our—no, my—fuck. I keep forgetting it's only my apartment now. So here I am standing in *my* apartment, drinking coffee out of my mug, having been awake for hours. Sleep doesn't come easy these days, because all I do is dream about my best friend. I would much rather block out that night than see it playing over in my mind every night.

I walk from the kitchen to the living room to stand in front of the bedroom doors. Mine, I always keep open, but Emmett's door remains closed. It hasn't been opened since the rest of the furniture was picked up and taken back to his parents' house. The day we packed up his things was a hard day for all of us. It was Dani's first time here since we left for the funeral days after the accident. Emotions ran high, especially when we found a present for her that Emmett never got the chance to give her. The only saving grace that day was seeing my best friend's obsession with orange Gatorade was worse than we thought—we found a total of thirteen bottles in his room.

I should grab my shit and head to class, but instead, I find myself walking toward the door. I reach for the handle and turn it, then lean against the doorframe and look around the empty room.

There is no trace of Emmett anywhere. I close my eyes and can picture the many times I stood in this very spot, giving him shit about my sister or waiting for him to get ready to go to class or a party. Now I stand here, remembering the very last time I did that.

"Hey, man, what's up?"

"Nothing much. My sister coming up this weekend?" I asked, leaning against the doorframe, my arms and ankles crossed.

Emmett continued to grab a few books off his desk and threw them in his backpack. He clearly wasn't planning to come with me to the pre-end of semester bash. Any reason to throw a party—it was close to the end of the semester, so shit, why not call it a pre-end of semester bash since we'd have the big end of semester bash after finals?

"Nah, I have to get a jump start on studying for finals so I can head home to see her next weekend. English Lit is kicking my ass, so I'm heading to the library for a study group."

Well, shit!

"Are you sure? Can't you take tonight off, dude? Come on—we're so close to being done with the first fucking semester of college! We need to celebrate that."

"Ha!" Emmett's laughter overtook the entire room as he finished packing his bag. He slung it over his shoulder and headed in my direction. "Zach, you'd find a reason to celebrate anything. Someone gets laid—let's throw a party! Someone breaks a nail—let's throw a party! Hell, someone farts—let's throw a fucking party." He slapped his hand on my shoulder as he walked past me.

"Why don't you come out for a little bit? Just stop by for a moment, say hello, and then go on to the library." I followed him into the kitchen.

Emmett reached into the fridge and pulled out a bottle of water, opened it, and took a large gulp. He shook his head as he screwed the top back on.

"Not tonight. I gotta get this shit done so I can see my girl next weekend. Why don't you stop thinking with the tiny head between your legs and start thinking with the head between your shoulders, fuckwad?"

"Woah. Woah. Woah. No need to insult my dick—it's anything but tiny. And did you just call me the little dude in Shrek?"

"Beside the point." He shook his head, laughing.

I loved our ridiculous conversations. It'd been like this our whole lives. We were more like brothers than friends, or possibly even an old married couple. We loved to mess with each other. Sometimes I felt bad that my sister had to put up with both of our shenanigans.

"You need to stop dicking around, bro, and find yourself something solid. I know you're just going there tonight for pussy."

"You mean like what you have with my sister?"

He nodded while I snickered and rolled my eyes. That sort of love wasn't in the cards for me.

"Nah, that's a once-in-a-lifetime kind of love. You guys are your own..." I searched my thoughts to come up with the right word but came up empty-handed. "Well, I don't even know what you guys are."

"Easy pussy eventually gets old."

Yeah, like he knew—he'd only ever been with one girl. Gross. I cringed at that thought. This conversation had gone downhill quickly. I walked back to my room to grab my coat and heard him call out to me.

"Zach, one day, man. One day you'll find her, and you'll just know. She's gonna knock you on your ass."

"Yeah, sure, whatever, Em."

Emmett opened the front door. "I'll see ya later, fucker. Don't forget to wrap it up."

I heard the door click shut as my best friend walked out the door—for the last time.

Fuck, if I'd have known that would be the last conversation I would ever have with my best friend, I would've talked about something more meaningful than my sex life. If I had only known, I would have forced him to stay home.

I reach for the doorknob and exhale a deep breath before closing the door with a little too much force. I'm not sure if I've hit the anger stage of grief yet, or if I just don't know how exactly to express my emotions these days, but I know we're most likely not getting the security deposit back as I pass the newly spackled hole in the drywall from where I punched the wall a few weeks back. My hand has healed physically, but the wounds I carry on the inside, I'm pretty sure will never go away.

I look down at my watch and see that I'm going to be late if I don't hurry up and head to campus. I take one last look around, chewing on the inside of my lip, fighting back the emotion. I could easily say fuck it and skip class, but it's the first day of classes, and I don't want to start the semester on the wrong foot or in the professor's bad graces.

Look at me, caring about my education. Maybe a little bit of Emmett has rubbed off on me. I place my cup on the counter before grabbing my backpack off the couch and walking out the door.

I make it to class with about five minutes to spare and grab a seat toward the back in a row that has two empty seats.

Nope, not going to do this now. Nope. Keep your shit together, Zach.

I swallow down the emotion that has been trying to break through since I made my way across campus to class. Our entire lives, if Em and I had a class together where we weren't assigned seats, we would always sit together. I take a seat, needing to push the thoughts of my best friend not being here and all the things he won't ever get to do away, at least for the time being.

I am focused on pulling out my textbook and binder when I hear movement to my left.

"Excuse me, is this seat taken?"

Without even looking up to see who the male voice belongs to, I say, "Nah, it's all yours, man."

"Awesome, thanks." I hear the sound of the chair moving as the person takes a seat next to me. "Hi. I'm Kyler."

I look over at him. He extends his hand. I stare at it for a moment before doing the same.

"Hey. I'm Zach."

CHAPTER 3
ZACH

Two weeks into the semester, and it's already kicking my ass. A night out is just what I need. The party animal from last semester is on vacation, possibly permanently. I guess being at a party reverts my mind back to *that night*. But staying in and getting drunk by myself gets old.

Kyler Lawson, the transfer student who I met on the first day of the semester, is meeting me here at the apartment. It turns out we're both communications majors and have most of the same classes. We hit it off pretty well and decided to meet here before heading out to the party.

I race home after my last class and a long workout in the gym and take a quick shower. After throwing on a pair of jeans and a dark gray Henley, I walk out to the living room and take a seat on the couch. I check the time and see Ky isn't due to arrive for another fifteen minutes. I decide to check in at home by FaceTiming my sister. I dial her number and wait.

The call connects and my sister's face appears. She's in her bedroom, and the light is dim, but there is enough for me to be able to see her face is pale and her eyes are rimmed red, the same look she's had for weeks now.

"Hello."

"Hey. How's it going?" I ask as I lean back on the couch.

"It's all the same, just like the last time you asked yesterday."

Dani's voice is soft and lifeless. It kills me to see my sister in so much pain. I wish she would just talk to me—hell, to anyone. My parents finally convinced her to go to a therapy session, but I don't know if she'll open up to them, a complete stranger, when she doesn't open up to the people who are closest to her.

"It's Friday night. Got any plans?"

"Same thing I do every Friday." Her tone now becomes harsh.

Every time I call to check up on her, it's the same thing. It's like being on a daily merry-go-round of me trying to get her to open up and she cuts me off. I'm not sure why I expected this to be any different. We're all hurting. Doesn't she realize that? I only wish she would open up about it. The thought of my sister always staying home alone instead of enjoying her life makes me hurt to remember the vibrancy that used to live inside her. I don't even recognize the woman she has become. All I want her to do is to snap out of it and make her realize we all lost someone we loved that day.

"You know you can always come to visit if you need to get out of the house, right? We could have some brother-sister bonding time. Maybe Haylee would want to come too."

She tenses at the mention of her best friend, and my heart breaks a little more. She has shut out the one person who needs her most right now.

"No." She holds her hand up and adjusts herself on the bed, making the camera shake. "Zach, stop. I can't be there, and you know that." Her voice breaks, and that was not my intention.

"I'm sorry, I didn't mean to upset you. I want you to know that I'm here."

"Yeah. Sure. I need to go."

Before I can say goodbye, she hangs up. I set my phone down on the table and rest my elbows on my knees.

Running my fingers through my hair, I exhale a breath. "Son of a bitch."

I think about calling her back to apologize, but as I reach for my phone, there's a knock at the door. *Perfect timing.* I'll call her tomorrow. I'll be home next week for Em's birthday, and hopefully I'll get some time with her while I'm there for the weekend.

I open the door and find Kyler standing there looking at his phone. He looks up. "Hey."

"Hey, come on in. I need to grab my phone and wallet." I move to the side and allow Ky to enter the living room.

I leave Kyler in the living room and run back to my room.

"Wow, this is a nice place."

"Thanks, man. We like it. Moved in last August," I reply walking back into the living room.

"We? Oh, you have a roommate."

I freeze, not even realizing I said "we" just moments before. That one little word threatens to crush my chest. I adjust the collar on my shirt, feeling as though the heat just kicked on in here. There is no longer a "we"—that is something I am not sure I'll ever be able to get used to.

"Yeah. No. Shit, it's complicated." I grip the back of my neck, not wanting to get into this now.

"Recent breakup? That sucks." Kyler stands there completely oblivious to the emotions boiling inside me, but I swallow it all down and nod.

"Something like that."

Kyler nods, not pressing the subject, thankfully, as we make our way out of the apartment. Will it ever get easy talking about Emmett?

I need a damn drink.

Later in the night, the party is packed, and Kyler and I just lost after a four-game winning streak at beer pong. My troubles are pushed aside as the alcohol flows through my veins.

"Good game, Em." I slap Kyler's back and walk away from the kitchen.

"Who's Em?" Kyler asks from behind me.

I quickly turn around to face him. The air leaves my lungs as if someone has just punched me in the gut. My throat goes dry, and the beer and shots I've consumed tonight threaten to come back up.

"I'm sorry, what did you just say?" Did I hear him correctly?

"Who's Em? You just said, 'Good game, Em.' Who's Em?"

Fuck.

"Oh shit. Did I? I didn't even realize that." I slam back against the wall.

I close my eyes and try to even out my breathing. The room, all of a sudden, got warmer, and I run my sweaty palms up and down the outside of my thighs. Now is not the time for an anxiety attack.

"You okay, Zach? Your face just went super pale. Please don't tell me you're gonna get sick."

"Nah. I'm okay." That's the biggest lie I have ever told. I'm far from okay.

"So, who's Em? Your ex? Guess it was a super-fresh breakup, huh?" Kyler asks, leaning up against the wall next to me. He slowly sips out of his red Solo cup.

I know he's not asking to be cruel. He's new this semester, so it's not like he would've known Emmett or was friends with him. Well, I figured we would have to have this talk eventually if he and I were going to be friends. I just didn't think it would be like this, and at a party no less. He let the roommate conversation slide earlier, but me calling him Em...yeah, I probably wouldn't give that up either.

I look down at my feet, shuffling them around. To the unknown person, I might seem drunk, but I sobered up pretty quickly when I realized what I called him. I debate telling him the truth or trying to avoid it again and save this for a different time, but in the short amount of time that Kyler and I have known each other, I've realized that we could actually be good friends, and part of me wants to be honest with him. So that's what I do. I take a deep breath and start talking.

"Em's not my ex."

"Fuck buddy? I totally get it."

"He..."

"Oh shit, sorry. Hey, I don't judge." *Wait, what?*

I wave my hands. "What? Nothing like that. I definitely like girls."

"Well then, what is it?"

Why is this so hard? Just spit it out, Zach.

"He's my best friend..." I say out a little louder than anticipated.

Kyler is taken aback by my unexpected volume, sheer confusion written all over his face.

"*Was* my best friend."

I need to remember that simple term—*was*. "Emmett and I were best friends since birth. He attended here last semester and was my roommate. That's who I was talking about earlier when I said the whole roommate situation was complicated."

Just say it. You can do this.

"Oh, did he transfer somewhere else?"

I shake my head. All words seem to have left my body. This conversation is happening now, so I take a sip of my beer, needing the liquid courage.

"He died."

I can see Kyler out of the corner of my eye. His eyes are wide, and shock is written all over his face.

"I-I-I don't know what to say, man. Shit, I'm sorry, man."

Well, that makes two of us.

I grip the back of my neck and continue. "Em was in an accident in December, leaving the library just before finals. My sister came to surprise him with her acceptance letter..."

"Wait," he interrupts, holding his hand up. "Why was she coming to see him and not you?"

"Oh right, I guess I forget there are people in this world who didn't know that my sister and Emmett were together. They had been together since they were kids."

"Gotcha. That has to be crazy, dating your best friend's sister."

I shrug. "Eh, not really. I mean, it just kind of was always Dani and Emmett."

With that, my mind drifts to my sister and the conversation we had earlier.

I chug the rest of my beer. I look over at Kyler, who looks like he's ready to say something, but I cut him off before he has the chance.

I look down at my empty cup. "I need a refill. You good?"

My eyes are burning from the tears fighting to break free, and I push down the emotions currently strangling me. Here I am trying to tell my sister to talk about her feelings, and I can't even handle talking about it. Talk about a hypocrite.

He nods, understanding that I need an escape from this conversation. "I'm good, thanks."

I push off the wall and make my way to the back porch where the keg is located, running away from Ky and the rest of the conversation as if I had a bull on my tail and I was wearing red. As soon as the fresh air hits my face, I exhale a breath. As I refill my cup, I spot Becca, the blonde who sits in front of me in English Lit, and damn, she has an ass that won't quit. Her tits are spilling out of her tank top, and I would bet that if I reached my hand up her skirt, I would find that she wasn't wearing panties either.

The best way to escape the conversation Kyler and I were having and to avoid it coming back up is to get lost in a coed. And the way Becca is seriously eye-fucking me across the room, not to mention how many times I caught her staring at me while Ky and I were on our hot streak, I would say I've found a willing participant.

As I approach, I notice the girls she's standing there with. The redhead next to her looks familiar, and she's looking at me like she knows me, but I can't place her. *Who knows, maybe we had a class together or something.*

"Hey, Becca."

"Hey, Zach."

My eyes wander over her body. When my eyes meet hers, I realize I've been caught. Good thing I wasn't trying to be sneaky about it. She blushes, and I watch as it goes from her cheeks to her chest. I wonder just how far down it reaches.

"And who are these beautiful ladies you're hanging out with?"

The girls surrounding her all burst into giggles except the redhead. Not sure what her deal is. I give them that panty-melting smile.

"This is Amber, Clara, and—"

I Never Expected You

Before she can introduce the redhead, her friend does it for her.

"Whitney," she scoffs.

Damn, what got her panties in a bunch tonight?

"Nice to meet you."

Whitney leans over, whispering something in her friend's ear, and storms off without another word. *Rude much?* Then it hits me where I know her from. She's the one who, last fall, stole my favorite gym shorts and Hopkins lacrosse T-shirt after she woke up and found I had left the apartment. One of the many women Dani and Emmett had to watch doing the walk of shame while I was nowhere to be found. I remember the face, just not the name.

I bring the cup to my lips and take a sip.

"Was it something I said?" I joke.

"Don't mind her." Becca turns to me, crossing her arms and pushing her breasts up a little more.

I settle against the railing, standing so close to Becca that the outside of my thigh brushes against her leg.

I tip my cup against Becca's. "Cheers." After I swallow the amber liquid, I tilt my head toward the ongoing party. "Having fun tonight?"

"Yeah, it's okay. I saw you were hot on the beer pong table." I don't miss her emphasis on the word *hot*. "But to be honest, I'm much better now."

She turns her body to face me, angling her tits so they are even perkier and spilling from her top.

I take a sip of my drink. "Oh yeah? Why's that."

This is too easy. Let me guess: because now she's with me.

"Well, I've been eyeing you up since I first got here and was hoping I would get a chance to talk to you."

"Here I am, babe. I'm all yours."

Getting under her is a definite way to forget my troubles. Our gazes lock as she brings her drink to her glossy pink lips. When she brings the cup back down, I'm still staring at her lips, and I wonder how they would look wrapped around my cock. *Down, boy.*

After a few more minutes of shameless flirting and meaningless conversation with her friends, Becca has settled in front of me so that her back is pressing against my front. I hold my beer with one hand while the other hand rests on her hip. I spread my fingers, grazing the smooth skin where her top has slid up. My pinky dips under the top of her skirt, and what do you know, no panties. I lean in, brushing my nose against her neck, making my way up to her ear. I notice her pulse quicken.

"You wanna get out of here?"

She turns to face me, trailing her finger down my chest down to the bulge forming in my jeans. "I thought you'd never ask."

We say goodbye to her friends, and with my arm around her shoulders, we make our way back inside to search out Kyler. As we pass her redheaded friend—Whitney, was it?—she follows us with a potent stare, causing Becca to flip her off. We finally find Ky chatting with a large group of people. Good, he won't mind if I roll out.

"Hey, we're going to head out."

Ky turns around and looks at Becca and then back at me. "Okay, cool. Was wondering where you went off to—now I see. You good?"

His face visibly shows that he was sorry for bringing up the sensitive subject, even though it wasn't on him; he was just curious.

"Yeah. I'll talk to you tomorrow, man." I hold up my knuckles and bump his fist.

"You two enjoy the rest of the evening."

"Oh, I plan to." I wink at Becca, and she giggles, just like the rest of them.

Man, some days it's just too easy. All I have to do is look at them, flash that sexy smirk, and they are like putty in my hands. Maybe Em had a point—easy pussy will eventually get old, perhaps, but for now, I'll let my dick do the talking. I grab her hand and lead her to the front door.

Once outside, she looks up at me. "Your place or mine?"

Knowing that I no longer have someone there to help me escape and kick these women out of my apartment as Emmett and Dani had so many times, I instantly say, "Yours."

That'll make for a simple getaway afterward while she is asleep.

That is the last thing we say before we are back at her dorm and she is screaming my name.

CHAPTER 4
Haylee

*E*very time I pass my brother's room, I expect him to whip the door open and tell me to get lost and stop eavesdropping. He may have been one of my best friends, but we still fought as siblings do. I would give anything to have him shove the door in my face one more time or pinch my nose as he walked past me, something he did since we were kids. It's the little things like that that you don't think about—that is, until it's gone.

I push those thoughts to the side as I jog down the stairs. I pass the living room on my way to the front door where I see my mom sitting with a photo of my brother in her lap. Most days, this is where I find her. Some days Kelly will come over and just sit with her or try to get her out of the house, anything to remind her that she isn't alone in this. Something I wish my own best friend could do. Dani has been slipping more and more away from me—from all of us actually. She very rarely answers my call or returns my texts.

I grab my keys off the table by the door.

"I'm headed out, Mom. I'll be back later."

I look in her direction, and all she does is nod. It breaks my heart a little more to see her like this. She's still in her pajamas, but I believe she at least showered today. Well, I heard the shower earlier, but I've caught her sitting on the bathroom floor before, crying with the shower running, so I can't say for sure. She used to be so full of light. Her smile always brightened the room. You always knew when she was in the kitchen, her own happy place, because you could hear the music playing throughout with her singing along as she cooked. Now I wonder how she even gets herself out of bed.

I walk out the door and feel the cool March breeze as I make my way to my car. I take a deep breath before starting it, only one destination on my mind. Turning out of the driveway, I pass the Jacobses' house and see Dani's SUV in the driveway, where it always is unless she is at school. We used to spend all of our time together—well, that is, when she wasn't with my brother. Now she tries to avoid me as if being around me brings her pain. I thought it was us against the world.

I think about how our lives might be different had my brother not died, but I can't dwell on things I can't change. I think that might be one thing that separates me from my best friend. If, at the beginning of the school year, you had asked me how I imagined my senior year, I would have told you my plans included Katy Perry dance parties with Dani, visiting my brother in Philly, attending lacrosse games, and hanging out in downtown Annapolis. I wanted to spend as much time with my friends as possible before we all went our separate ways. I did not plan to attend the University of Pennsylvania with Dani, Emmett, and Zach. My dream was to send me to the west coast and attend the University of Southern California to study psychology. I had wanted to be a Trojan since I was young. We visited the campus once while on vacation, and I fell in love.

However, Mother Nature decided to derail all of our plans. Instead of enjoying senior year, I'm getting by each day with the bare minimum while trying to hold myself and my family together. Dealing with the loss of my brother essentially alone, since my best friend is being consumed by her grief more and more each day, has been anything but easy.

I pull through the gates at Glen Ridge Cemetery, a place that seems to be becoming my home away from home. As I turn onto the hill near where my brother is buried, I see a Jeep parked, and my breath catches. Tears fill my eyes. I recognize the Broadneck Bruins Lacrosse and Baltimore Ravens stickers, and while I wish it were my brother's vehicle there, I know that it is none other than his best friend. What is he doing here?

I park behind him and slowly make my way to Emmett's grave. I stop in my tracks and don't know whether I should continue walking or turn around. I see Zach standing there with his back toward me. I suddenly stop my approach. *Oh my God*, I hear him talking to Emmett. I am standing too far away to listen to what he is saying, and I wouldn't want to interrupt this moment with him. I go to turn around and walk back to my car, but I watch Zach drop to his knees, shoulders slumped and head bowed. I don't even hesitate; I rush over to where he is on the ground. His body tenses as I wrap my arms around him.

"Breathe, Zach. It's okay. Let it out."

At the sound of my voice, his body relaxes against mine. His hands grip my arms tighter as he lets it all out. I let him cry in my arms while the tears flow freely down my cheeks.

Zach checks in with me often. Most times, it's just a text; other times he calls. I'm sure he feels as though, with Emmett gone, he has to take over the role of my big brother. I've known Zach my entire life, and he has always been the rock in our lives. Right now, everything is out of his hands. He lost his best friend. He's watching his sister push us all away, all while being away from home. At first, I was jealous of Zach because he got to go back to school and get away from everything that reminded us Emmett was gone, but then reality set in that he and Em shared an apartment while attending the same college. There are as many memories for Zach in Philly with Em as there are here, maybe even more. There is no escaping it.

Seeing him vulnerable like this shows me he is only human. I haven't seen him break down since the funeral, not even when we came here for Em's birthday. I was beginning to wonder what his secret was and if he would share it, but I see that he just hid it better than the rest of us.

His breathing begins to even out.

I speak softly while I continue to rub his back. "Hey. You know it's okay to cry. Doesn't make you any less of a man."

He snickers, brushing off my comment as he adjusts himself so his feet are now in front of him. He pulls his knees up and rests his elbows on them. I take this time to sit down next to him. We both wipe the tears away.

I continue. "You know, I was beginning to wonder what your superpower was in never breaking down. Shit, these days, it seems like all I do is break down, so is it bad to say that for once, I'm glad to see someone else do it?"

"I'm sorry you have to go through this, and I know my sister isn't making this easy on you. You should be able to have the one person you've always leaned on there for you and she's not."

I look down and begin to play with the grass surrounding the headstone.

I shrug. "I know she's hurting."

He grabs my wrist, bringing my attention to his. "No, that's not an excuse. We all are."

I nod as he releases his hand from me.

"I hate that we're all hurting—you, me, our parents, my sister. I hate that there's not a damn thing I can do about it to help anyone. *I hate this.* It's bullshit that he died; he was only eighteen."

The tears begin to fall again.

"I wish I knew when it would get easier, how to act when someone brings him up, or how to keep it all together." He exhales, but in a way that makes him sound relieved for finally saying it aloud.

"No," I say. "There's no rule book. We're all just kind of winging it. If there was a rule book, I'm pretty sure it would tell you not to call his phone over and over just to hear his voice on his voicemail."

His lips form a frown, and I look away.

"Yeah, I guess you didn't need to know how pathetic I am."

"You're not pathetic. You're grieving. As you said, we're all winging it. Plus, if I'm honest, I'd have to admit I've done that when I'm drunk."

We sit in comfortable silence, my head resting on his shoulder, for just a moment longer, letting the events of today and our confessions sink in before Zach stands again.

"Well, I better get going." He reaches out his hand for me to take and pulls me to my feet.

We walk back to the cars in silence.

"Hey, Hails," Zach calls out as he reaches his Jeep.

I turn and face him. "Yeah?"

"You know you can call me anytime if you need to talk, right?"

I nod. "I know. I'll see ya later?"

"Nah, I'm heading back to school. I just needed a moment."

I know exactly what he means. "Yeah, I get those too."

I watch Zach pull off and grab my phone from my purse and dial Dani's number. I hold the phone to my ear and listen to the endless ringing before her voicemail message picks up. I exhale and end the call. No point leaving another message that I know will go unanswered. I start the car and head home to the silence.

CHAPTER 5
ZACH

ME: *Hey, Hails. How was prom?*
HAYLEE: *It was fun. Was nice to dress up and escape my life for a night.*
HAYLEE: *But, it was also weird with Dani not being there.*
ME: *Mom sent me photos. You guys looked great.*
HAYLEE: *Thanks. Not as fun as last year, of course.*
ME: *Well, duh. That's because yours truly wasn't there. I'm the life of the party.*

I wait for a response, and it doesn't come right away. Shit, why did I say that? Of course it was different. Nothing about this year has been the same.

HAYLEE: *How's school?*
ME: *It's good. I have this one teacher, Professor Watts, that's kind of cool. He's not much older than us, which is kind of weird.*
HAYLEE: *Cool.*

I go to type a response when my phone buzzes and I see my sister calling, the last person's name I expected to see. I'm not sure when the last time she called me was. I begin to panic. I hit "answer."

"Dani? Is everything okay?" My breathing is labored, worried of her response.

"Hey. Yeah. Why wouldn't it be?" Her voice is calm as if this is an everyday occurrence.

I bring the phone away from my ear to make sure I was on the phone with *my sister*. "Umm, well, you're calling me, for one."

"Can't a sister call her brother without there being something wrong?"

Who is this girl and what did she do with my sister? The one who has been shutting us all out for months.

"Dani, don't get me wrong. I'm glad you called. I guess I'm just a little confused. You never want to talk to me and when I do call, you can't wait to get me off the phone."

Neither of us say anything and I have to check to make sure she is still there.

Finally Dani speaks up. "Well, that changes now. I was wondering if you wanted to hang out the next time you're home. Like, maybe we could watch a movie or something?"

Baby steps, I tell myself.

The corners of my mouth lift. "I'd love that. I have something going on this weekend, but I can make it home the following weekend. That work for you?"

"Umm, sure." Maybe I should reschedule plans with Ky and his sisters so that my sister doesn't change her mind, but then she speaks up. "I'm really looking forward to it, Zach. I've missed you."

"Yeah, me too, Dani. I'm just getting to the gym. Call you later?"

"Sounds great. Bye."

As I enter the gym doors, a sense of peace comes over me. Maybe, in the long run, we will all be okay. I might just be getting a glimpse of my sister returning to a new normal.

CHAPTER 6
Haylee

Standing on the front porch of the Jacobses' house, I decide to ring the doorbell instead of just walking in. I hear footsteps on the other side before Kelly opens the door. *Perfect. Just who I wanted to talk to.*

"Hi, sweetheart. How come you rang the doorbell? You know you can always just walk in. This is your home too."

I laugh and cringe. "Yeah, that did feel a little weird. I don't know why I did that."

I look down at the ground and shuffle my feet nervously.

"Is everything okay? Dani's not here right now, but why don't you come inside."

Hmm, I wonder where she went. Now is not the time to try to pick the brain of my so-called best friend. I'm not sure I could figure her out these days even if I tried.

"Actually, I was hoping I could talk to you."

"Of course. Is everything okay? Come on in."

"Is it okay to sit out here and talk?"

She nods and closes the door behind her. We walk over to the porch swing. Oh, if this swing could talk...actually I'm not sure I want to hear the stories. This swing has been a place we all have laughed, cried, and pretty sure made out with someone on at some point in our lives. I take a seat next to her.

"What's on your mind, Hails?"

I reach into my bag and grab my two acceptance letters, one to the University of Southern California and the other to the University of Pennsylvania. I hadn't planned to apply there, but my parents had convinced me that it was good to keep my options open. In my mind at the time, I knew I wouldn't need a backup—USC had always been my number one—but I humored them and applied. I guess the joke's on me now that I got accepted to both, and I'm at a fork in the road to decide where to go.

When I saw the acceptance letters waiting in our mailbox, the first thing I wanted to do was call my brother. The joy I knew I would always feel holding that envelope in my hand instantly fell to sadness, and I felt myself gasping for air in a panic. Now that the deadline is finally here, I need to force myself to make the final decision.

"What's this?" Kelly takes the letters out of my hand and briefly reads them both. "Oh my God, Haylee! That is wonderful. Congratulations." She pulls me into her arms in a tight hug, not one full of sorrow or feeling sorry for my loss, but full of love and pride. "Your parents must be so proud."

I pull back from the hug and look down at my joined hands. "Honestly? I haven't told them yet. My mom was having a really rough time the week the acceptance letters arrived, so I've been hiding them in my room."

"What?! Why not? It's great news, sweetie, and we could use all the good news we can get around here." Her smile fades.

I'm sure her mind has drifted to all we have endured lately. I still wish I could wake up from this nightmare.

"I just...I..." I start.

Kelly places a hand on mine, giving me strength and letting me know I can take my time to gather my thoughts.

Taking a deep breath, I continue. "You know that it's always been my dream to go to USC, but after everything that's happened, I don't think I can leave Mom and Dad here alone. I mean, I know you guys are here, but they already lost one child." I fight the tears forming in my eyes.

Kelly pulls me back into an embrace. "You can't base your decision off of that. Your parents will be fine. You need to decide on your own, and know that we all will support you no matter what you choose." She cups both of my cheeks so that I look in her eyes. "You hear me, Haylee? Only you can make your decision, and if you choose to stay or choose to go, we will all be right here with you."

With her hands still on my cheeks, I nod. I finally give in and exhale, knowing that I made the right choice coming here. My phone vibrates, and I look down to see Zach's name. I choose not to answer it.

"Well, I better get back home. I guess I just needed to talk to someone who wasn't my actual parents. They're kind of all over the place these days. I wasn't sure how to bring it up with them without possibly causing another potential meltdown."

I bite my lip to fight back the tears, and Kelly sees the look in my eye and knows that if she pulls me into a hug, I will lose it. Fuck, I would like to be able to go one day without getting upset and missing my brother.

Instead of pulling me into her arms, Kelly leans over and kisses my forehead. "I'm here for you always, Hails. I mean it. We all are. The only way we're going to get through this is by sticking together. I love you, sweetie. Come by anytime." We both stand, and as she heads back toward the door, she stops and turns back to me. "But don't use the doorbell—that was just weird."

We both laugh, and she goes back inside and I walk down the front porch steps back toward my car.

My phone vibrates again with Zach's photo appearing. This time, I answer.

"Were your ears burning or something?"

"Umm, hello to you too. No. Wait, what does that even mean?"

"Well, usually it means that someone was talking about you, but I'm at your parents' house and just got done talking with your mom, so maybe you just sensed me being here, but that's… kinda weird."

He lets out a laugh. "Yeah, that's weird, but all right. No, I'll be heading that way this weekend. Just thought I'd check in."

Oh man, this is starting to get ridiculous. Enough with the checking in. If he wants to call, then he just needs to call. I hate it that when he says he's checking in. It feels forced, as if he's waiting for me to break.

"I'm fine." Simple as that.

"Haylee." His tone is firm. "Don't give me that bullshit. I get that enough from my sister when I know damn well she is anything but fine. I want you to be honest with me. Speaking of which, did you see my sister at all while you were there?"

Honest? Does he want to know how bad I'm struggling to keep it together? No, I refuse to go down that path right now. Finally reaching my car, I sit in the driver's seat for a few moments, leaving the vehicle shut off.

"Honestly, I just want the day to be over. That's how I feel. Honestly, I want to have a day where it doesn't hurt so much to breathe. I want to talk to my best friend—fuck, I want to talk to my brother. But I can't, and I have to wake up tomorrow and start the day all over again. Is that honest enough for you?"

Unsure how to respond or shocked by my honesty, Zach stays silent. Neither of us says anything, so I decide to break the silence first.

"Any plans for while you're home?"

"Dani asked me to hang out a bit, which is weird—I mean, in a good way. Maybe she's coming around. I don't know. I'll take whatever time with my sister I can get. Any plans for you?"

I wince at his comment. Yeah, I would take whatever time I could get with her too. So much for me and her against the world.

"Umm...not really. I was thinking of having a bonfire in the backyard. It's been a while and only so much time I'm at home left, so thought why not."

"Huh. That'd be cool."

"Yeah, I think so too."

"Well, I better finish up and get to class; my break is about over. See you later this weekend?"

"Yeah, sure. Bye, Zach."

"Bye."

We've been through so much that sometimes it just overwhelms us all. I know he means well, but I wish that he would just let me breathe for a bit. Big decisions and emotions are not my besties these days; then again, my own best friend isn't really my bestie either. But Zach had a point—that has to mean something that Dani wanted to hang out with him. Graduation is quickly approaching, and our time is winding down, even though I have no clue what she's planning to do next since deferring college in the fall. Maybe she is finally ready to take a step in the right direction, and I can get my best friend back.

Sitting out by the bonfire in my parents' backyard, I am happy to have seen this week end. Only two more weeks left of school. After talking with Kelly, I finally made my decision. I even had the courage to discuss it with my parents last night. Like Kelly said, they were happy either way; they wanted what was best for me and not them. The golden and orange glow from the fire lights up around my acceptance letter to USC. "Congratulations." I read that line over and over.

My attention diverts to the rustling of the bushes on the side of the house, and I quickly fold up the letter. I jump to my feet when a shadow emerges from the darkness, but my fast-beating heart begins to calm down when I see that it's only Zach.

Clutching my chest, I yell, "Were you trying to give me a heart attack?!"

He throws his hands up innocently before placing them back in his pockets. "Sorry. I guess force of habit, just walking around the side like that."

I settle back in my chair. "What are you doing here?"

"Dani fell asleep early watching a movie, so I just thought I would check in on things."

"You don't have to do that, you know."

He nods, but I have known him my whole life—he is not letting up at all and will continue to be a pain in my ass. He takes a seat in the open chair right next to me.

I turn my attention to the folded-up acceptance letter to USC that's in my hands.

"What's that?" Zach tries to grab it out of my hands, but I pull back.

"It's nothing." I take a deep breath. "I mean, it was something, but it's not anymore."

I crumple it up and toss it into the fire. I know that the decision was my own and that I could have still gone, but honestly, my life is here. I can't just up and leave my parents, and Dani especially, after all we've been through recently. Sticking around will be good for me, I think.

"Well, we've got some celebrating to do." I push to my feet, feeling a little anxious over my decision.

Zach looks over at me, confused. "We do?"

I nod. "Yep. Looks like I'll be joining you in the fall at UPenn."

"What!" Zach jumps to his feet and pulls me into a hug, lifting me off the ground. "That's awesome!" He quickly puts me down, and it finally hits him. "Wait, what about USC?"

I shake my head and bite the corner of my lip to fight back my tears. "Plans changed. It wasn't necessarily what I expected, but this will be good."

I wonder how long it will take me to say that over and over until I believe it. In the comfort of my brother's best friend's arms, a single tear falls down my cheek as I watch my dream burn to ash.

CHAPTER 7
ZACH

"I can't believe you graduated today." I press one hand against my heart while the other dramatically wipes a fake tear away. "Oh, you grow up so fast."

I mean it; watching Haylee and Dani walk across the stage to receive their diplomas, I felt like I was watching a montage of their life. I know it hurt both of them that this was a monumental moment, one of many more to come that Emmett missed. *Would they ever get easier?*

Dani shoves me as we walk out on the back deck at our parents' house. "Whatever, asshole. This was you and Em, *just last year*."

She pokes at my chest, and I laugh. Even in the darkness, I know that she's rolling her eyes.

I've missed this playful side of my sister. It's been over six months since she has been herself. Lately, though, she's made more of an effort, so it's a step in the right direction to having my sister back. She relaxes back on of the lounge chairs overlooking the pool, and I follow suit.

I look up at the night sky. Man, I've missed this too. You can't get this type of view in the city. I turn to my sister.

"So, what's next, sis?" I'm sad that she's chosen to defer college a year and won't be joining Haylee and me in the fall.

Dani lets out a long breath as if she were soaking up this

moment. Her eyes meet mine, and she smiles. It doesn't reach her eyes, but it's still a smile, so I'll take it.

"You know, I don't know. I plan to spend this summer figuring out exactly what's next. I've always had a plan, and well, now..." She looks away.

I quickly rise and join her on her chair, swatting at her leg to scoot over. She laughs, but the light of the moon reflects on her tears.

I wrap my arm around her shoulders and pull her into my chest. "It's okay not to have a plan. I'm more of a fly by the seat of my pants kind of guy."

I feel the vibrations of her laugh against my chest; She buries her head further into my chest.

"I know. I just don't know what I want my life to be now. It's time I've figured it out. Time to start a new chapter in my life." Her grip around me tightens, and I pull her closer.

I press a kiss to the top of her head. "I know it's scary, but we're all here for you to figure it out. I'm always here."

"Can we just sit here and worry about it all tomorrow?"

"Yeah, Dani, we'll worry about it tomorrow." I lie here with my sister in my arms as I listen to her breathing evening out.

I am excited to see what her new plan will bring to her future. If there was one thing we learned from losing Em, it's that life is short. We need to live every chance we get *for him*. I hate that she has spent the last six months not living and enjoying the one life we have.

"You sure you don't want me to wait and ride with you?" I stand in my sister's doorway while she hurries around her bedroom in her robe, her hair wrapped up in a towel.

"No, you ride with Mom and Dad. I'll finish getting ready and meet you there soon."

We're meeting the Hanks at Boatyard, one of our favorite restaurants in downtown Annapolis to celebrate the girls graduating.

My parents stop in the hallway.

"Dani, you're not ready yet?" My mom places her hands on her hips.

My sister grunts. It looks like a party in Dani's room. I chuckle to myself.

"No, Mom, I'm running behind. I just told Zach that I would just meet you guys there."

"Okay, sweetheart." Mom steps up to Dani. "I'm so proud of you, Danielle Kathryn."

Dani wraps her arms tightly around my mother's waist. "If you guys never leave, I can't get ready. So, unless you want to miss out on whatever today's specials are and hang here, that's cool with me."

"The girl has a point." Dad kisses her forehead.

I watch my sister as her gaze lingers on watching our parents leave the room.

"See you soon." I give a quick wave before making my way down the stairs.

"Are we ready to order?" the waiter asks, standing at the end of our table.

"Just a few more minutes please," my mom politely responds, but I see the worry on her face.

"Of course. Let me know once you're ready." The waiter leaves.

We've been waiting for forty-five minutes for Dani to arrive. Now, I know it takes girls a long time to get ready, but not my sister.

"Zach, why don't you text her again? She didn't answer my call," my dad chimes in from across the table.

ME: *Hey, are you on your way?*

Haylee leans over and whispers softly. "Why didn't she just ride with you guys?"

"She said she needed more time to get ready. I offered to stay and ride with her, but she was insistent with just meeting us here."

Fifteen more minutes pass and two more visits from the waiter before my dad says, "She's clearly not planning to show."

I look back at the door. *Come on, Dani. Now would be a great time to walk through those doors. Be the new and improved Danielle Jacobs.*

AN AWKWARD SILENCE SAT OVER THE TABLE AT DINNER, AS Dani never showed. My dad pulls into the driveway, and I don't see her SUV. Maybe she pulled into the garage?

"Dani?" I yell from the foyer up the stairs, while my parents look for signs of her on the main floor. I race up the stairs, taking two at a time. "Dani? Are you here?"

Where could she be? I don't bother knocking once I reach her bedroom door. The door swings open. *What the hell?* Photos are no longer on the wall. The drawers of her dresser are open and empty. I rush to the closet, and the boxes of Emmett's things are missing as well.

"Mom! Dad! Up here!" I spot a small piece of paper lying on her bed.

My palms begin to sweat, and my heart feels like it will beat out of my chest. This isn't happening. My sister left.

Oh, Dani, what did you do?

CHAPTER 8
ZACH

I feel helpless not being able to do anything from the apartment here in Philly. Sitting on the couch with my head in my hands, I hear the key in the front door.

I turn around and come face-to-face with him.

I jump up and run over to where Emmett is putting his keys on the table.

"Please tell me you found her, Em."

Emmett has to be able to hear the desperation in my voice. He looks down at his feet and shakes his head in defeat.

"No, I looked everywhere for her—I thought of all the places she could be, and no such luck. I even thought about boarding a plane to Hawaii since we had talked about honeymooning there one day."

I run my hands through my hair. "Fuck!"

I pace back and forth. I can't believe I'm stuck in this apartment in case she comes here while everyone else is out looking for her.

"I can't believe I didn't pick up on anything with her. I'm her big brother. I should have known something was up—she had been so cut off and distant, and then all of a sudden, she wasn't. I just thought I was finally getting my sister back. Damn it, how did I not realize this? No..."

I stop pacing and turn to Emmett, my fists clenched.

"No, this isn't my fault. This is yours." I catch him off guard, causing him to step back when I poke him hard in the chest, but my anger is only growing stronger. "This is your fault. You left her. You left her all alone. Why did you leave? You fucked everything up!"

I step forward and push him with both hands, ready to throw a punch at my own best friend. Why isn't he fighting back or telling me this isn't his fault?

"Say something, motherfucker!" I grab the collar of his shirt and slam him against the wall, my rage pouring off me like sweat. "You fucking died and left us all to pick up the pieces, and she couldn't handle it, so instead of leaning on us—she fucking ran."

Em's hands touch the top of my shoulders and squeeze. It's written all over his face; he knows it. He looks down, and when his eyes meet mine, they are filled with tears matching my own.

"I'm sorry," is all he can manage to say over and over again.

Fuck, I miss him.

The front door opens, and a familiar male voice says, "Hey, man, I didn't expect you home so soon. I went and grabbed pizza and beer—I was too tired from unpacking to cook. Want a slice?"

"Yeah, sure, sounds good." I stand and follow Ky to the kitchen.

He sets the pizza box on the island, lifting it to reveal a mushroom-and-sausage pizza. Oh, fuck yeah, my favorite. At least my stomach can be happy.

We both take a seat as Kyler cracks open a beer, handing it to me before opening one for himself. The way we are consuming the pizza, you would think we've been starving for days.

"So, how was graduation?"

I'm not ready to come to terms with my sister up and leaving without even saying goodbye, just leaving a note, not to mention the imaginary conversation I just had with my dead best friend. I should keep my answer short.

"Yeah, it was good."

And I mean, it's not a total lie—graduation itself was good, given the circumstances. I was so proud to see my sister walk across the stage, especially with everything she had been through lately.

"How were things here? You get all settled? Sorry I wasn't here to help."

"Oh no worries, I had it handled. My sister's boyfriend and a friend of his helped me. It was pretty easy."

"Good deal. Well, welcome home."

"Thanks."

I finish my second slice of pizza and down the rest of my beer. "Well, I'm fucking beat. I'm gonna head to bed—it's been a long weekend."

I rise from my seat and throw the empty bottle away.

"Yeah, no problem. I'll see ya tomorrow."

I turn and head to my room. Once I close the door, I sit on the edge of my bed and call my parents to check in, and of course, no news yet. I shoot Haylee a quick text, and that's a dead end too. I lie back on the pillow and decide to send a text for what seems to be the millionth time in twenty-four hours.

ME: *Dani, what the fuck were you thinking? Please, just call me. Are you okay?!*

No response, just like the rest. Sleep doesn't come, and my mind is racing. I feel like I've gone back in time and am suffering through a loss all over again. I cover my eyes with my forearm to hide the tears even though there is no one in my room to see. I never expected life to turn out so fucked-up. Where was the damn warning label?

 I sit by the phone all night waiting for a call, text, just something letting me know she's okay, but it never comes.

CHAPTER 9
Haylee

ME: *I miss you.*
ME: *Why won't you call me? Just let me know you're okay.*
ME: *We can get through this together, Dani.*

Summertime used to be my favorite time of the year: no school, beach trips with the family, and spending all hours in Dani and Zach's pool. This summer, it's not my favorite. It's my first summer without both my brother and best friend. My time by myself here before heading off to college in the fall is just a reminder of all I have lost.

Zach decided to stay at the apartment in Philly. He's taking a few classes over the summer and working as well. I talk to him just about every day. It's nice to be close with a Jacobs still, even if he's not the one I would rather turn to. We both have suffered the same loss, a sibling and a best friend. I may have said goodbye to my brother permanently, but Zach has no idea where his sister even is.

Is she even okay? Is she ever coming home?

We have no answers, just that her mom received a vague text that she was alive and not to worry. But telling someone not to worry, especially when they have no information, is like telling someone not to look down while on the edge of a cliff.

Today is the big Fourth of July cookout at the Jacobses' house, although I guess it's not that big anymore—it's just them and us. Mr. Adam decided not to extend the massive invitation to the neighbors and coworkers and their family who were typically invited in hopes of avoiding questions to both of our families.

There's honestly not much else to do here besides work on my tan, so that's what I'm going to do. Zach had texted earlier that he was bringing a friend home with him: his new roommate, Kyler. All I know about him is that they met this past semester and they hit it off great. He was looking for a new place to live, and Zach had an open room. Zach and I had talked about it one night; he was worried about someone else moving in there, but I know he was lonely even if he didn't want to admit it. From what Zach has shared about him, he seems like a cool guy.

I'm sitting in a lounge chair, lost in the memories of playing chicken in the pool with my brother, Dani, and Zach. Oh, if this pool could talk. Between the pool and the front porch swing, I'm not which would have the better stories. I laugh at the thought.

"What's so funny over there?"

I turn to see Zach standing there in board shorts, a black wifebeater tank, and a hat worn backward.

"Yeah, I saw you out of the corner of my eye, and your face alone made me laugh."

I stand, not caring that I'm only in a bikini, and walk toward Zach to hug him.

"You're a bitch. You know that right, Hails?" He lets out a loud laugh.

"Yep, I'd be worried about my personality if you didn't think that. It might mean I've lost my touch." I wink and smile at Zach before noticing the guy standing behind him.

This must be Kyler. Tall, dark-haired, and very handsome.

I push Zach to the side. "Didn't your mother teach you any manners, asshole?" I direct my attention to the stranger. "Hi, I'm Haylee. Maybe you should have your head examined for being friends with this guy." I tilt my head in Zach's direction and extend my hand to Kyler.

"Hey, I'm Kyler. Nice to meet you. I've heard a lot about you."

I frown at his words and give Zach the evil eye.

Zach throws his head back in laughter and puts his arm around my shoulder, pulling me closer to him. "All good things, of course, Hails. All good things."

His laughter continues, and it's almost as if I've channeled my brother from wherever he is because I find the perfect opportunity where Zach isn't paying attention and push him into the pool. Emmett was always notorious for pushing folks into the pool. It was usually Dani, but I think he would only use that as an excuse to touch her. Gross!

Kyler and I are both laughing by the time Zach emerges from the water and starts to chase me around the pool to give me a wet hug or possibly to drag me into the pool with him.

"Really? What are you guys, ten? No running by the pool," my dad yells which make us laugh harder.

I stop in front of Zach and put my hand out. "Okay, okay, how 'bout a truce?"

He looks down at my hand as if contemplating it, and I instantly regret being vulnerable in front of him. With that damn Jacobs smirk, he reaches down, then throws me over his shoulder and sprints to the pool.

I Never Expected You

"Zach! Put me down. Zachary Brian Jacobs, put me down *now*!"

Of course, Zach does not listen and jumps right in with me in tow.

Later that evening, with full bellies, the three of us lounge in the pool chairs, waiting for the fireworks to start over the river. I wonder where Dani is and if she's doing the same thing. I wonder if wherever Emmett is now, he can see fireworks. Is that weird to think?

"Hey, why don't you come to Philly for the weekend and hang out? It'll be good to get away from here, I'm sure. You can stay in my room, and I'll sleep on the couch. Ky and I can even show you around."

"No, I don't want to be anywhere near your bed." I make a face. "I'd rather be in the small percentage of women who *haven't* seen you naked, thank you very much!"

Zach holds up a finger to speak, but I quickly interrupt him.

"And no, taking baths as kids doesn't count."

Kyler lets out a deep belly laugh. "Damn, I like her. She's hilarious. I'm going to look forward to having you around in the fall."

"I'm serious. Think about it, okay?" Zach asks, the playfulness in his voice gone.

I give him a forced smile, knowing he won't drop the subject otherwise, but in all honesty, I'm not sure I can handle being in that apartment. I hope I made the right call going to UPenn in the fall. *How am I supposed to go to school there—the same place Emmett spent the last of his days—if I can't even visit, surrounded by the ghost of my brother?*

CHAPTER 10
Haylee

"Hey, Dani, it's me. Well, I'm all packed up and getting ready to head to college. I don't know where you are, but I wish you were here."

I don't even know why I bothered calling for the millionth time this morning. Dani hasn't returned any of my calls or texts all summer—why start now? I guess a part of me hoped that when I had arrived on campus here at the University of Pennsylvania, I would see her. That she had changed her mind about school and would be joining me. I imagine the surprise on her face when she sees me here and not on the other side of the country.

I am alone in the dorm room unpacking when I hear a knock at the door. I look around the room as if I would find the answer as to who's on the other side. Maybe my parents had forgotten something or my roommate, Cami, left her key when she went to the cafeteria earlier. I'm not prepared though when I open the door to see Zach leaning against the doorframe.

"Hey."

"Hey back. What are you doing here?"

How did he know this was my dorm or that I was here?

"I go to school here; don't you remember?" His face lights up with that wicked Jacobs smirk.

I narrow my eyes at him and let out a loud sigh. "No shit. I meant, what are you doing here in my dorm room?"

"Technically, I'm not in *your* dorm room because you haven't invited me in." He shrugs, still smirking.

Ugh, what is it about the Jacobs kids that scream smart-ass? My best friend's smart-ass comments are one of the many things I miss about her.

He raises his eyebrows at me, making a clicking noise with his mouth while waiting for an invitation to come in.

I step aside and extend my arm. "Please, Zach, do come in."

He tips his imaginary hat. "Why thank you, Hails."

Stepping past me into the room, he looks around.

"Nice place you got here. Can't say I'm sad to have not done the whole dorm life thing though."

I take a seat on my bed, and Zach grabs the chair from my desk, dragging it close to where I sit. He does the typical guy thing, flipping it around before straddling it, and leans his arms on the back. He looks back to where my roommate's stuff is all sprawled out over her bed.

"So, have you met your roommate yet?"

Really? Did he come here to talk about my roommate? It's been a long, emotional day. I'm physically, mentally, and emotionally drained. I think if I weren't so exhausted, his small talk wouldn't bother me.

I tilt my head, trying to figure him out. "Why are you here?"

Avoiding my question, he asks one right back. "Why didn't you call me for help? Your dad called me as they were leaving campus, asking if I would check in on you. I didn't even know you were here already."

Great! My dad called him and asked him to check on me. So

what is this, a pity visit? He doesn't need to step into the role as big brother—I already have... *Fuck!* I feel like the room is beginning to close, and I quickly stand up from the bed and walk toward the window.

Zach must see it written all over my face. He starts to rise quickly from the chair, however his foot gets stuck because as soon as he's standing straight up, ready to take a step, he's tumbling to the ground, taking the chair along with him.

I turn around at the commotion and instantly burst out laughing when my eyes meet his. Quickly, Zach joins in on my laughter, and before I know it, I'm sitting next to him on the floor. He's fine; embarrassed, if anything, that his super-suave personality is flawed. He obviously has his sister's grace. His eyes meet mine, and I stop laughing when I remember why I had gotten up in the first place.

"Is it okay to laugh?" I ask him without taking my eyes away from his.

I bite my lip nervously. I was looking forward to this whole experience, but today has been nothing but a hot mess of emotion. I spent most of the day imagining my brother helping me move into my dorm, thinking how cool it would be if we were at the same school, but then remember that had he still been alive, I would be on the other side of the country.

Zach scoots closer to me on the floor and wraps his arm around my shoulder, pulling me into his chest. "Yeah, Hails, you know I think laughter is a must. If I don't laugh, I get angry. And to be honest, I'm tired of being angry. My anger pretty much cost us the security deposit."

I jerk back, looking at him with furrowed brows. What the fuck is he talking about?

As if he can sense my confusion, he continues. "One night, right after all of Em's shit was taken back to your parents' house,

I got drunk, by myself, and got so mad that he wasn't there drinking with me that I punched a hole in the wall. I messed up my hand a bit, but at least nothing was broken."

"Except for maybe the wall," I add.

"Smart-ass," he mutters under his breath. His grip tightens a little around my body. "He would want us to laugh. Fuck, he loved to laugh."

Silence consumes the room as I wipe the tears away from my cheek.

Zach leans his head against mine. "You wanna go and get a pizza or something? Then we can come back and I can help you unpack. Not because anyone asked me, but because I want to, Hails. We're friends—that's what we do. We look out for each other. You're kind of all I got."

I don't give myself time to overthink things. "You know what? I'd like that. I'm sorry for not letting you know I was here."

Zach stands first and extends his hand to me. "Don't worry about it. You can make it up to me by paying for the pizza."

I take it, and he pulls me up to my feet with a little more force, causing me to fall into his arms. We are standing just a few feet away when the dorm room door swings open, revealing my roommate.

"Oh, I'm sorry! I didn't mean to interrupt anything."

I let out a giggle. "Don't worry, Cami; you weren't. Zach Jacobs, meet Cameron Byram. Cameron, meet Zach Jacobs."

"Nice to meet you."

"You too. You can call me Cami. Only my parents call me Cameron, and it's usually when I've pissed them off." As Cami takes Zach's hand, I see her eyeing him up and down.

Oh boy, here we go again. The last thing I need is him getting involved with my roommate.

Rolling my eyes, I turn to grab my bag. "We're headed to get some pizza. We'll be back later to finish unpacking."

"See ya later. Nice to meet you, Zach."

"You too. I'm sure I'll see you around."

As Zach and I walk out the door and it closes behind us, I turn to him. "Don't even think about it, Jacobs!"

He smirks and lets out a loud laugh.

"I don't even know what you're talking about, Hanks." He emphasizes my last name as he says it.

"I'm serious. Don't try to sleep with Cami, okay? Don't make this situation awkward for me. Just keep it in your pants!"

His face goes serious for a second as he wraps his arm around my shoulders. "I think I can keep it in my pants for you."

He lets out another laugh as I push his arm off my shoulders and mutter "asshole" under my breath. I know he heard me; the sound of his laugh grows louder as we make our way down the hallway.

CHAPTER 11
Haylee

Zach: *Ready for your first college party?*
Me: *You do realize I've been to a college party before, right?*
Zach: *Touché. Yeah but not as a college student. I'm gonna give you the full college experience.*
Me: **eye roll emoji**
Zach: *Whatever. Meet us at the apartment, and we can head over from there.*

I stare at the last text message Zach sent, and my palms begin to sweat and my heart instantly beats harder. *Meet at the apartment.* Those four words flip my stomach. I knew attending college here, it was most likely that I wouldn't be able to avoid *the* apartment the whole time, but I did well for at least the first week of college.

I think about canceling altogether or seeing if I can just meet him and Kyler at the party.

"You know, if you keep frowning like that, you're just going to get premature wrinkles," Cami instructs while browsing her closet for something to wear tonight.

I snicker. "Ha. I'm sure I have enough premature wrinkles without frowning."

Since losing my brother, I feel like I've aged at least ten years if not more. What's a few more wrinkles?

There's a dip in the bed as Cami plops down next to me.

She slaps my thigh. "What's on your mind, girlfriend?"

"It's...it's..." I try to find the words for how I'm feeling. "It's just that this will be the first time I'm at *the* apartment since my brother..." I look down at my hands, unable to finish that sentence.

"Oh, honey, I'm sorry." She wraps her arm around my shoulder and pulls me into her.

I'd told her about Emmett and everything our second night living together over cheap wine and Chinese takeout. Talk about really opening up to someone quickly. She had seen the framed photo of him and me and had asked if he was my boyfriend. Super gag moment—you know, since we look so much alike and all. I guess I'm used to living in a small town and everyone knowing we were related.

"Just tell him to meet you here."

I shake my head. "No, I need to do this. I can do this. I chose to come here, knowing that I couldn't avoid it forever. I guess deep down I had just hoped to avoid it a little longer."

She twists her mouth as if she is planning something. "I know just what you need."

She eyes me up, and why do I instantly feel worried over the look she is giving to my outfit choice? Cami jumps up from the bed and struts back over to the closet where she continues looking for an outfit.

"You sure you don't wanna come out with us? It might be fun." Having Cami there with me would give me an easy escape if I needed one.

"As much as I would love to hang out with Hottie McHotterson and that sex-on-a-stick roommate of his, I have a date." A smile spreads across her face, and I'm not sure if it's because she's excited for her date or if it's at the thought of how attractive she finds Zach and Kyler.

I internally roll my eyes as I remember her drooling over both of them at our door the other day to go to dinner.

"Of course you get a date the very first week of college."

"Don't hate. Don't hate." Cami fusses over a few more hangers. "A-*ha*!" She pulls out a black tube top with a slight dipped V to front.

"Ooh, that will be hot, your date is going to be excited to rip that off."

"Oh, no. This, my dear, isn't for me. I've already got my outfit, and for the record, no, I don't plan on keeping it on long."

Wow, she is the female version of Zach.

"This is for you." She holds the top out in front of me.

"Hell no. I can't wear that."

"You can, and you will. Pair it with that jean skirt I saw in your dresser. You need to bust out of your comfort zone. Escape reality a little bit."

Little does she realize if I met the boys at the apartment, I would definitely be out of my comfort zone.

Before I know it, I'm dressed in the outfit Cami had picked out and am standing outside Zach and Kyler's apartment. *My brother's apartment.* My phone vibrates.

Zach: *Running late. Just got out of the shower. Door's open.*

I stand in front of the door and tell myself over and over that I can do it. I reach for the doorknob, take a deep breath, and turn it. Standing in the front hallway, I look around the apartment. The last time I was here, I was with Dani, my dad, Adam, and Zach, cleaning out my brother's room. The wall that used to hold my brother's Baltimore Ravens flag is now empty. I look to the end table that used to house the photo of me and him that currently resides on my dresser in my dorm room.

My heart catches in my throat. *Breathe, Haylee. Just breathe.* There is no sign that he ever lived here.

No one has noticed that I was here, so I can easily make my escape. I turn and place my hand on the doorknob to run when I hear a door opening behind me. *Shit.*

"Hey, Hails," I hear the deep voice call out behind me, and I close my eyes.

What I wouldn't give to turn around and see my brother standing there in the doorway in jeans and one of his many classic T-shirts—the T-shirts that were all packed up the last time I was here, most of those with Dani, wherever she may be now.

I feel a hand brush my shoulder, pulling me out of my thoughts, but it catches me off-guard and I jump back, my back slamming into the door.

"Oh shit, are you okay?"

I step away from the door, rubbing my back where the knob hit me. "Yeah, sorry. I was..."

I look up and my eyes meet Kyler's. I can see why Cami finds him attractive; he just doesn't do it for me. But it's not Kyler's good looks that distracted me. I see past him at the open door behind him. My brother's room. I shake that thought from my head. It's not my brother's room anymore; it's Kyler's. He lives here. Kyler notices that something has grabbed my attention and follows my eyes to behind him.

"Shit," he mutters under his breath. Turning back around, he looks at me with sorrow in his eyes. Without having to say anything, he understands why I'm uncomfortable. "Are you okay?"

I nod. I'm afraid that if I open my mouth to say anything, the wrong thing will come out. It's not that I'm mad that he lives with Zach—really, I'm not. He's a great guy, and I'm happy Zach has him. It's just that I miss my brother. Will that pain ever go away? Can I ever be in this apartment and not think of the last time I was here, packing up my brother's life?

I'm quickly pulled into Kyler's arms into a big hug. See? How can I not like this guy? He never knew my brother. He barely knows me, but here he is comforting me. I can't help but allow a stray tear to fall down my cheek. Oh, Cami would be so mad if I messed up the makeup she did.

A throat clearing tears us both apart, and we turn to face Zach standing there, his hair still damp from the shower.

"Now Hails, if I'm not allowed to sleep with your roommate, then you can't sleep with mine."

I choke out a laugh as I wipe the tears away.

"Oh shit, are you crying? Ky, what the fuck did you do?"

"Hey, don't look at me." Kyler backs up and throws his hands up innocently, then heads to the kitchen while I make my way to the bathroom to clean myself up.

Zach grabs my arm. "Hey, are you okay? What's going on?"

The color has left his face, and his eyes are full of concern.

"I'm fine, really." Seeing his jaw tense at my choice of words, I continue. "It's just that it's the first time I've been here since we..."

I look down at my feet. Just admitting that to him, I'm ready to lose it again.

Zach looks up straight toward Ky's room. He grips the back of his neck nervously, and his face goes pale. "Shit, I don't know what to say. I'm sorry, Hails. I'm an asshole."

I touch his arm. "No. I mean, yes, you are." I can't hold back my laughter, and I look up to him with playful eyes while he is still serious-looking. "But I should have told you that it was weird. You always ask me to be honest, and I should have been."

Silence overtakes the apartment as I stare at Zach and wait for an answer.

He pulls me into a hug, wrapping his arms around my shoulders. "I just don't want you to ever keep anything from me, okay? I let my sister do that, and well, look at how it..."

Kyler cuts him off before he can finish that sentence, joining us in the living room. "You know, we can totally cancel tonight, order some food and stay in. Whatever you guys want to do."

I'm really starting to like Kyler. He came into our lives in the middle of chaos and is a genuinely caring guy.

Zach and I break apart. "No, I want to go out. Zach promised me the full college experience of a party where I'm finally a student." I wink at him, and he lets out a deep laugh. "Let me just freshen up a little, and I'll be ready to go."

Zach nods as I make my way to the bathroom, and he heads toward the kitchen.

After wiping the smeared makeup and fixing my hair a little, I make my way to the kitchen where I find Zach and Kyler waiting with three shot glasses full of a clear liquid in front of them.

Kyler hands me one before picking up his own.

Zach holds his in the air. "To a new year, new lays, and new friendships."

"Seriously? You're so disgusting." I roll my eyes before downing my shot of tequila.

After Ky slams his empty glass on the countertop, he places his hand on my shoulder. "Oh Hails, you have no idea."

CHAPTER 12
ZACH

Three months later...

It's been three hundred and sixty-five days since I lost my best friend. I miss his laugh, his goofy smile... fuck, I even miss the way he looked at my sister. When I lost him, I lost her—it just took six months to lose her physically.

It's been months of texting and calling with no response. How can you just cut the people you love the most out of your life without looking back? I know she's hurting, and maybe I don't get it because I may not have lost the love of my life, but I did lose my best friend, and that doesn't feel too good either.

I tossed and turned all night last night, debating whether to reach out today. I mean, she won't pick up on a typical day; why would she today, of all days? I could have called, but with texting I'm able to get more out without being cut off by the stupid voicemail.

ME: *I told myself I wasn't going to do this today, but here I am reaching out knowing that you will ignore this. Dani, I know you are hurting today and every day for the past year, but come the fuck home.*

Me: *Whatever you are facing and battling, we can do it together. We are headed to the cemetery around 10, and then Mom is having lunch at the house. I don't know where you are, but please come home. If not for you, then for me, for Haylee, for the Hankses. We all need you for fuck's sake. I miss him too you know.*

Me: *Please just answer me. I'm going out of my mind that you are out there somewhere by yourself and you won't let me help you. I'm your big brother and I'm supposed to protect you from all things big and bad and I couldn't protect you from this, so I feel as though I've failed you. D, I didn't want to do all of this over text, but I know that you wouldn't answer if I called you, and I would be limited on what I could say via voicemail.*

Me: *I have to have faith that you are actually reading these texts and not just ignoring them. I need you today and every day, Danielle. Please, I'm begging you. I love you, sis.*

I wait and wait, but responses never come. Then again, I guess I shouldn't be too surprised. I had told Haylee that I would drive home today. Haylee and I have spent a lot of time together the past few months—going to parties, studying, and leaning on each other whenever we have a hard day. I guess you could say it's a perk of having her here; she's someone who knows what it's like to go through what's playing in my mind. Some days I don't think I would be able to get through without her.

Looking at my phone, I see that I need to head over to the dorms to pick her up so we are on time. I finish my coffee and place the mug in the sink before grabbing my keys and walking out the door.

We don't talk much the entire ride there; both of us aren't

ready for the emotions that today will bring up. Haylee stares out the window while I grip the steering wheel so tight, I think I might break it. *Why did he have to die?*

Pulling into the cemetery, I have flashbacks of doing this last year, taking my best friend to his final resting spot. I pull in behind the Hankses' SUV.

"You ready?" I look over at Haylee, and for the first time since I picked her up, her eyes meet mine, and it breaks me in half.

"If I say no, can we just forget about all of this?"

I give her a weak smile because honestly, I'm right there with her. I would like to forget what today is and why we're here, forget that he died, not because I want to forget him, but because I want him to be alive.

Before I can reach out and grab her hand to give her a reassuring squeeze, she exits the Jeep and walks toward where our parents stand. I take a deep breath and get out to follow her. A part of me hopes that I'll see my sister standing there waiting for us, but as I approach the gravestone and see only my parents and Haylee's, I know she isn't coming.

I hug both my parents, along with Natalie and Brian. Haylee stands back away from the crowd while her parents say some words and a prayer. Finally, Haylee walks up to the grave and places the flowers down that we had stopped for along the way. I watch her shoulders fall, and her head drops as tears rip through her body. I can't take this anymore. I take the few steps to close the distance and wrap her in my arms, pulling her body against mine. She cries into my chest, and I go back in time to the many times Dani cried in my arms. Knowing my sister is alone today breaks the remaining pieces of my heart.

We all stand there in silence. I run my fingers down her hair as if it is the natural thing to do. Once she has calmed down, Haylee slowly backs out of my arms, and a weird feeling overwhelms me—I instantly miss her touch. I try to shake off the feeling as Haylee stands next to me. Our fingers accidentally brush with our close standing, and instead of pulling back as I would typically do, I do the last thing I expect and take her hand in mine, wrapping my fingers around hers. I don't even think twice about holding Haylee's hand. As our parents talk, I don't even realize that I'm brushing my thumb over her knuckles in a soothing way. Today is the third-worst day of my life, and just her touch alone is somehow easing the pain. I don't know what this feeling is, but part of me doesn't want it to leave.

We share memories of Emmett, some causing us to laugh while others bring on more tears from missing him more. After a while, we decide it's time head back to the cars. I acknowledge to my parents that we will see them back at the house for lunch. Haylee and I stand toe to toe at my Jeep as both sets of parents climb into the SUV parked in front of us and drive off.

I look down at my feet and am startled by the fact I haven't let go of her hand yet, but then again, she hasn't let go of mine either. Is it strange that I like her hand in mine? Yes, it is bizarre. I mean, this is Haylee Hanks.

I try to shake off the feeling. Our eyes meet, and I notice that her eyes are as blue as the ocean. The way the sun is shining down on us, she looks like an angel. I become completely consumed by my thoughts.

"Why are you looking at me like that?"

Oh shit, how was I looking at her?

"Sorry, it's just been a long day."

That was the stupidest response ever. Of course she knows that. What the hell is wrong with me?

She takes her hand out of mine, and I mourn the loss, but then she wraps her arms around my waist and tucks her face into my chest. My heart begins to beat faster, and the sadness I felt all day is eased by her closeness. I rest my cheek against the top of her head and find myself smelling her shampoo. Okay, seriously, what the fuck? I am way in over my head here.

CHAPTER 13
Haylee

ME: *Happy New Year Dani. I hope this year brings you whatever peace you are looking for. I miss you.*

"So, what's up with you and Hottie McHotterson?" Cami asks as I fold the clothes from my bag and put them back in my dresser.

She sits on her bed, facing me with her legs crossed under her and a bowl of taco dip in her lap. Her platinum-blonde and purple hair is up on top of her head in a messy bun.

Zach just dropped me off after our winter break. It was a nice change to be away from the dorms, but being home wasn't easy either. It was the second Christmas without Emmett and our first without Dani. There was a giant elephant in the room that no one wanted to talk about. Kelly and Adam had tried to get ahold of Dani with no such luck.

I wish I knew where she was, but she hasn't been returning any of my calls or texts either. Doesn't mean I haven't continued to try. Somehow, I know that when she is ready, she will answer...I hope. I would give anything for a movie night, Katy Perry jam session, or hell, just a damn hug from my best friend.

"I wish you would stop calling him that. He has a name, you know."

"Yeah. Whatever. What's up with you two? I always see you together, and he is one fine piece of ass. Like seriously, I'd climb that like a tree." She takes a chip and scoops it into the dip before shoving the entire thing in her mouth.

This girl could live off taco dip and ramen. I let out a laugh at how crass she is. This girl is one hundred percent insane, but I have to say I love her. She has made the whole college experience pretty interesting, that's for sure. I thought Dani and I didn't have a filter, and then I met this one right here. I shake my head because, well, she's insane if she thinks something is going on between us.

"Oh my God! Do you have to be so...so..."

"Truthful? I mean, seriously, how have you not sucked, fucked, and rode him off into the sunset?"

If I had had a drink in my mouth, I would have spit it all over her.

"Yeah, I think you've been smoking a little too much, Cami. I've known him my whole life; we're just friends. He's kind of taken on the role of pseudo big brother, watching out for me since—" I close my eyes and exhale a harsh breath. "—Em died. Sometimes it's annoying, but others, it's nice to know that there's someone who cares. There is definitely *nothing more* going on there. That's just gross. He's probably slept with half the girls on campus."

I finish putting my clothes away and sit on the edge of my bed, facing her. I fold my hands together, starting to fidget at the mention of my brother. I hope one day it will get easier when he comes into the conversation. I still have to fight back the tears. Sometimes the feeling gets to be so much that I don't even fight to hold my tears back and just let them fall. This is one of those moments. I take a deep breath, count to three, and blow it out.

"So, then you won't mind if I ask him out?"

"*What?*" I sit up straight, and my body tenses. "No, no way! I already gave him the warning to keep his hands to himself."

It's her turn to be surprised. "What! Why would you do that?"

"Cami, once he sleeps with a girl, he doesn't call her again. I'm pretty sure if you looked up manwhore in a dictionary, there would be a picture of Zachary Brian Jacobs. I'm just saying. If he sleeps with you, do you know how awkward that would make things here? We could never hang out here, and it would be awkward with him trying to avoid you. I've already lost one Jacobs out of my life. I refuse to lose another one because you both can't keep it in your pants."

She holds her hands up innocently. "Okay. Okay. You have a point. Doesn't mean I can't ogle him every time he's here."

I roll my eyes at her.

"Hey, at least admit he's hot!"

"I mean, yeah, he's good-looking, but he's Zach. That's just... that's just..."

What word am I looking for here exactly? I'm not sure. Zach is very attractive, but all you have to do is ask him, and he'll agree. Modesty is definitely not one of Zach's traits.

"Exactly. It's just the truth. *Zach Jacobs is hot.*"

"Whatever. You're insane."

"This is probably true, *but...*" She elongates her but, and oh Lord, here we go. "If you're not banging him, are you at least banging that good-looking friend of his?"

"Oh my God, I can't with you! Go get laid!"

We both burst into a fit of laughter as she responds, "I'm trying to, but you're over here clam jamming me."

"I'm sorry—I'm what?"

"Clam jamming…you know, the female equivalent of cock-blocking."

"Who are you and where the fuck did you come from?" I can tell that even with her craziness, Cami and I will be friends for a long time, and I could use all the friends I can get these days.

CHAPTER 14
ZACH

"Dani, for fuck's sake, you need to cut this shit out and come home. You're being a bitch making Mom worry about you. We're all worried about you. Just let someone know you're fucking alive."

I slowly walk toward the bathroom to take a shower after an intense workout. I definitely overdid it, and my body will probably hate me tomorrow, but it needed to work out all those holiday and birthday treats. I turn the water on and strip off my sweaty clothes, dumping them in a pile on the floor. I step into the shower and let the warm water wash away the dirt, sweat, and insanity.

The mintiness of the tea tree shampoo wakes me up as I massage it through my hair. I close my eyes and press my palms to the cold tile wall and hang my head so that the water can rinse the soap from my head and body. While the water feels great, I know what will feel even better. My body needs a release. That's exactly what I need. With one hand still against the wall, I grip my cock and begin to stroke it, closing my eyes and letting the fantasy take over.

Walking up behind her, pressing my body against hers, I trace my hands up her arms slowly, leaving goose bumps in their tracks. Her left arm reaches back, gripping my neck as my fingers slowly trail down her breasts, the water dripping down her hard nipples. The soft moans coming from her mouth go straight to my dick. My erection presses up against her ass. As she slowly turns around, her hand grazes down my abs, her nails pressing into my skin as her hand lowers to my dick the same time she falls to her knees.

My breath quickens, matching the pace of my hand. "Oh shit," I quietly say, trying to keep my voice down.

Even though her hands are petite, her fingers wrap around my erection. My head falls back with my eyes closed, enjoying the feeling as her hand strokes my hard cock back and forth. Her thumb brushes the tip, ever so slightly teasing me before she replaces her thumb with her tongue, causing my body to jolt. As I look down, I meet the most beautiful blue eyes I have ever seen, lashes wet with water from the shower, but they don't belong to a faceless stranger. Nope, they belong to Haylee.

Fuck. In reality, I am alone in my shower with my hand wrapped around my cock. What is wrong with me? My heart is racing at the thought of Haylee in front of me on her knees. This girl has been taking over my mind since the day in the cemetery. There is no way I can go without finishing; my cock craves its release.

I wrap her ponytail around my fist and push her head down farther as she takes more of my cock into her mouth. Her lips press against my pelvis, causing her to gag a little, but holy shit if the tightening of her throat around it doesn't go straight to my balls. I have to fight off the feeling of coming right now. Shit, I don't want this to end.

Her mouth moves back and forth; her hand follows the same motion as her tongue massages and teases me.

"Shit, baby, I'm gonna come."

I don't even freak out over calling her "baby." Even if this is just a fantasy, the thought of my cock deep in her is driving me insane. My grip tightens as I stroke faster. I can't hold off my orgasm. Before my thoughts can go back to pulling her up from her knees and fucking her senseless against the tile, my legs begin to give out as hot cum releases all over my hand and down the drain.

Now I am completely confused as to what just happened. Not only did I just come harder than I ever had before, but it was to the thought of my little sister's best friend. I finish up getting clean before turning the water off and stepping out. Wrapped in a towel, I head back to my room and check my phone. There's a text from Haylee. Shit, could she somehow know what just happened? No, that's stupid. If people knew when others jerked off to the thought of them, then Mila Kunis's head would be spinning.

HAYLEE: *Hey, my afternoon class was canceled. Want to grab a coffee?*

Okay, good, she has no clue. I could use an afternoon pick-me-up.

ME: *Yeah, sure. I just got out of the shower so give me like 30 minutes or so.*
HAYLEE: *Okay. See ya soon.*

I drop the towel and lean against the edge of the bed as I put on my boxers. My mind instantly wanders back to Haylee and what she might look like naked and bent over this bed with my cock going in and out of her. Fuck, how am I supposed to meet her for coffee now? This is Haylee Hanks, for fuck's sake!

I quickly throw some clothes on and head over to her dorm. I only have to knock once before she opens the door. A smile lights up her face. I swallow hard, trying not to picture her naked and moaning my name.

"Hey."

"Hey, come on in. I only need a few more minutes, and then we can go."

I follow her into her dorm room and close the door. Haylee is sitting at her desk chair, putting on her shoes. Her hair hangs in her face. I turn around and take a few deep breaths. I need to control myself. I can do this. Friends jerk off to the thought of friends, right?

I decide to look around and focus my attention on anything else but her. I notice the photo of her, Ky, and me from the Halloween party last fall when Ky and I dressed up as Sonny and Cher. I'm pretty sure Ky is still mad at me over making him be Cher.

"Hey, you okay?"

I turn around to tell her that I'm fine and am rendered speechless as I see her pulling the strands of her long hair into a ponytail. I want to wrap those stands around my hand, pull her toward me, and taste her all over. Fuck! Fuck! Fuck!

"Zach?" She steps closer.

Under normal circumstances, I wouldn't have an issue with her invading my personal space, except now the closer she gets, the harder the time I'm having controlling my dick. It's already throbbing, begging for another release just being in the same room as her.

Quick. Come up with something.

I need to get out of here before she notices the bulge in my jeans. I'm forever grateful to at least be wearing a longer hoodie right now, but the more I stand here with her, or hell, even just being in the same vicinity as her, I might poke someone's eye out with this thing. Talk about a weapon of mass destruction.

I shake my head, going over scenario after scenario I can come up with quickly.

I look down at my phone. "Shit, I totally forgot I told Ky I would meet up with him. So sorry, Hails."

I don't even give her time to respond before I am spinning on my heels and running out of the dorm room. Well, looks like another shower when I get home because I need to get as far away from here as quickly as I can, so I take off in a sprint. I need to get this under control; otherwise, I am completely fucked...and not in a good way.

Hell, who am I kidding? I'm already fucked.

CHAPTER 15
ZACH

When I feel my phone vibrate and see her name appear with a text, my heart starts to beat faster. This is Haylee Hanks, the same nerdy girl growing up with pigtails and braces. She and my sister were inseparable and followed me and Emmett around like a lost puppy. When did she become this beautiful woman, and how did I not even notice till now? I seriously think about her more than I'd care to admit. I don't do that—I don't think about the same girl over and over unless it's Mila Kunis or Scarlett Johansson.

HAYLEE: *Hey, stranger! What's up?*
ME: *Hey back! Not much just handing out watching some Netflix.*
ME: *hanging**
ME: *You?*
HAYLEE: *Not much. Was just doing some studying.*
ME: *Cool*

Cool? What is this, the '90s? Who responds with just "cool"? At least she can't tell that I've been avoiding her lately.

HAYLEE: *So I don't know how to say this, so I'll just spit it out. It kind of feels like you've been avoiding me.*

Well, fuck! So much for that. What the hell do I say to that? *Yes, I've been avoiding you because you're all I think about, even when my hand is on my dick?* Ever since that day in the shower when her face popped in my head, I haven't thought of anyone else.

ME: *No, I've just been super busy. This semester is kicking my ass. So much for "easy" classes.*

Phew, hopefully she bought that. I mean, it's not a total lie; the semester is partially kicking my ass.

HAYLEE: *Oh, ok. I was beginning to forget what your ugly face looked like.*

I turn the camera on and snap a quick selfie and send it.

ME: *See, still looks the same!*

My phone vibrates again. This time though, her face appears on the screen from the Halloween party last year where she was dressed up as Supergirl, and she is trying to FaceTime me. Shit, she already knows I'm home doing nothing. If I ignore the call, she'll know something is up, so I take a deep breath and hit "answer." The sight of her on the other side of the phone makes me instantly hard. Thank God she can't see my lower half.

"Hey. You didn't believe I still looked the same, so you had to call me to make sure the pic wasn't a fake?"

"Ha. Ha. Ha. You're so funny." She rolls her eyes at me, followed by a huge smile.

That smile does a number on me. I would give anything to keep that smile on her face.

"So, what's going on?"

"Nothing. I was wondering if you wanted to go out tomorrow night to Steele Toby's? I haven't seen you in forever, and I thought it could be fun."

Steele Toby's is a local college bar. We made friends with Amanda, one of the bartenders, and as long as we don't make a scene, she is cool with our fake IDs. She's always super flirty, but that phrase "don't shit where you eat" doesn't apply to just coworkers, but also to bartenders at the only bar you can drink at underage. I'd hate for her to cut us off after I fuck her and never call her again, so I had to suck it up, taking one for the team, and enjoy the casual flirting.

Haylee bats her eyelashes and gives a pouty expression, and it's at that moment I know that not only can I not tell her no, but I don't want to. I want to make her happy and be the reason behind that smile.

"Okay. Fine," I groan, pretending I don't want to.

"Yay!" The phone picture shakes as she jumps up and down in excitement.

Seeing her face light up like that is totally worth the torture of being around her.

THE NEXT NIGHT, I DRAG KYLER WITH ME TO STEELE Toby's. I look around as we walk in and don't see Haylee there yet. Ky and I walk over and take a seat at the bar. I nod my head in Amanda's direction, and she holds up one finger, letting me know she'll be with us in a moment.

"Well, hey there, cutie. It sure has been a while since I've seen you in here. I've missed you. Always nice having some eye candy while I'm working. What can I get you, boys?"

Amanda leans over with a straight view of her round tits. Usually, I would find the view spank bank–worthy, but shit, that's how I know I've got it bad. Not even Amanda's tits on display are doing anything for me. All I can think of is how I wish Haylee was the one leaning over for a view of her perfect tits.

I blink away the thoughts before my dick gets word of them. "Just two Yuenglings. Bottle is fine."

"You got it, cutie."

I exhale a rather loud breath, trying to keep my composure, knowing I'm going to see Haylee in just a matter of minutes. Maybe she decided to back out for some reason.

Just as I'm coming up with ideas as to why she might not show, small hands cover my eyes from behind and a voice I would know anywhere—the one I always hear in my dreams—says, "Guess who?"

Instead of pulling them off, I savor the moment and the way her skin feels against mine, committing her scent to memory and at the same time telling my dick to get the fuck back to sleep.

"Mila Kunis? Is that you?"

Instantly I regret that answer when I feel pain on my upper arm where Haylee punches me.

I turn to face her rubbing my arm. "Easy, killer. I was just kidding, but shit, who taught you to punch? I would hate to be anyone on the receiving end of one of your punches—once was enough."

I hop off the barstool and extend my hand for her to sit, while I pull out the stool to the right of where I was sitting. Haylee takes a seat between Kyler and me. It's perfect—this way no creeps can walk up to her and buy her a drink. They would need to have a death wish to walk up to a girl sitting between two guys.

Back off, motherfuckers, this is my girl.

I mean, she's not, but I want her to be, right? Fuck, I'm so messed up in the head.

Amanda brings our beers over and asks Haylee what she can get her. The look she gives her...is that jealousy? I don't know what it is, but it makes me want to put my arm around Haylee and pull her close. No one is touching my girl—*fuck, Zach, get a grip!*

Haylee orders a Yeungling too. My girl has good taste even on a college budget. Once Amanda brings her beer back, all three of us settle into conversation, catching up and even discussing the latest episode of *How I Met Your Mother*. That is something Haylee and Kyler have in common.

All three of us are on our second beer when Haylee spins her chair around to browse the room. What or who she's looking for I'm not sure.

"Okay, Jacobs, take your pick. You have a whole room of hot women, most of whom I'm assuming you haven't already put your dick in."

Damn, does she think that little of me? I mean, she wouldn't be wrong; I have been with plenty of women, but right now, she is the only one I want, and not just sexually.

"What are you talking about?"

"I'm talking about I'm going to play your wingman...or wingwoman since Lawson over here is slacking on the job of getting you laid."

Ky nearly chokes on his beer and laughs at her statement.

"First of all, what's with just the last names? Is that what you think guys do? Sorry, Hails, but that's not the case. And second of all, why are you trying to be my wingwoman?" I use the quotes around wingwoman, as she put it, because I've never heard of that.

There is no way in hell I'm having her try to set me up. That is not happening. Before I even have the chance to protest even further, Haylee has stopped a girl with long black hair.

"Hi. Excuse me. I'm sorry, I just had to tell you I love your top. Where did you get it?"

The dark-haired stranger replies, "Oh, thanks. It's just from Kohl's, nothing special."

Haylee smiles as if she's just won the lottery. Little does she know, I have no intention of doing anything with this girl, let alone take her home.

"Well, it's super cute. I love Kohl's. I'm Haylee, by the way." She extends her hand to the stranger.

"Hi. I'm Hannah." She takes Haylee's hand in her own.

Of course her name begins with an *H*. Fuck my life.

"This is my friend Zach."

Kyler fake coughs next to us.

"Oh, and that's Kyler."

It makes me laugh a little that Haylee shows no interest in introducing her new friend to Ky.

Hannah turns toward me. "It's nice to meet you, Zach."

She places her hand on my arm in a similar way that Haylee did, only this has the opposite effect than Haylee's touch. I want to push her hand off me, but I don't want to be rude.

"Nice to meet you too." I stand there awkwardly, grabbing my beer and taking a swig.

"Would you like another drink?" our new friend asks while eying me up and down, trying to picture me naked, I'm sure.

"Thanks, but I'm okay with this one. It was nice to meet you." I turn back to my chair, hoping that she got the point that I'm not interested.

I look between Haylee and Kyler, and both are shocked. When have I ever turned someone down?

"Well, that sucks for you—she totally looked interested. I'll be back. I gotta pee." Haylee hops off her stool and heads toward the restroom.

If she were anyone else, I would follow her and take her right there in the bathroom. Fuck, what is wrong with me?

"Dude, what's up with you?" Kyler asks, pulling my attention back from the direction Haylee walked in back to him.

I turn and see him giving me a look, as if he's trying to figure out what's going on in my head.

"You just turned down a sure thing."

I shrug, pulling the bottle to my lips. "I just wasn't feeling it."

Out of the corner of my eye, I see Kyler has not stopped staring at me. His brows furrow and his eyes narrow. *Did he read right through that bullshit excuse I fed him?*

After a few moments, he turns back to his beer and takes a sip. I can only hope that he'll drop it.

"So, boys, what are we drinking next?" Haylee returns from the restroom and places both hands on our shoulders, pulling us closer to her. "How about a shot? Amanda! A round of shots, please."

This is going to be a long fucking night.

CHAPTER 16
ZACH

Me: Hey, I'm stealing you away today. I'll pick you up in twenty minutes.

Haylee: I can't, I have plans.

Me: No, you don't. I already checked with Cam.

Haylee: What? Remind me to have the dorm room locks changed.

Me: As I said, be ready in twenty minutes.

Haylee: Where are we going?

Me: If I told you, it wouldn't be a surprise now, would it?

Haylee: How am I supposed to know what to wear?

Me: Stop trying to find a reason to get out of it and just accept it.

Haylee: *Eye roll*

Me: Dress comfortably.

Haylee: Ugh, fine. Why are we doing this?

Me: I'll see you in twenty minutes.

Haylee: Who's avoiding now?

Me: See ya later Hails.

Haylee: Whatever! I need like an hour.

Me: You've got twenty minutes. Chop! Chop!

Haylee: *Middle finger emoji*

"Hey, you were up and gone early this morning." I'm sitting at the island eating a bowl of Fruity Pebbles when I hear Kyler's voice behind me.

"Yeah, wanted to get an early run in before heading out."

"You headed home today?" Kyler walks over to the coffee pot and pours himself a cup, then turns to face me, leaning back on the counter and crossing his ankles.

I take the last bite of my cereal before standing and carrying my bowl to the sink to rinse it out. "Nah, I'm surprising Haylee with a trip to the carnival."

Kyler brings his coffee down after taking a sip and narrows his eyes at me, as if he's trying to figure me out.

He opens and closes his mouth a few times before asking, "The carnival?"

"Yeah, I saw a flyer in the quad the other day. There's a carnival in Wilmington; it's a fund-raiser for a charity. I don't remember which one. When we were kids, Haylee and Dani loved going to the local firehouse carnival—like it was a *big* deal to them. Em and I didn't get it—I mean, the rides were cool, and our parents always let us go off by ourselves, but I never really got the hype."

He nods as he takes another sip of his coffee.

"Well, two weeks ago, Emmett would have been twenty, and Haylee's been struggling a little bit, so I thought it would be fun to take her to get her mind off things."

"Uh-huh." I can't tell if there's understanding in his voice or he just wants to be a dick this morning.

"What?" I check the time on my phone to make sure I won't run out of time before I need to pick her up.

"Nothing, man." Ky holds up his hands in innocence.

I Never Expected You

"If you have something to say, then just say it, Ky."

His expression gives nothing away, and it's starting to piss me off. Reaching over to the coffeepot, he refills his mug before walking to the island across from me.

"What's up with the two of you?"

"Who? Me and Haylee?"

"No, you and Erin."

Who the fuck is Erin?

"*Yes*, you and Haylee, dumbass."

Do I tell him the truth? Knowing that the truth will take longer, I choose to go with a lie. "Nothing. We're just friends."

Kyler shakes his head. "Yeah, no, I don't buy that."

He doesn't take his eyes off me, knowing that I just lied my ass off. Shit, guess my cover is blown. I let out a loud breath.

"I don't know what to say."

"Why don't you start from the beginning?"

I throw my head back in a sad excuse for a laugh. "Yeah, that would probably take all day, and I need to head over and pick up Haylee soon, so how about the short version?"

He nods.

"I...I...I can't explain it. I've known her since she was born. I don't know how to explain it, but something happened back in December when we were at the cemetery, and since then I can't get her out of my fucking head." I stand up in frustration, not at him but myself, at the situation. "I don't know what I'm doing. No matter how much I've tried not to think about her, I just can't."

"Is that why you were avoiding her after the break?"

I nod. "Was it that obvious?"

He shrugs and places his coffee cup in the sink. "I mean, a little, but it was more the weird way you blew off that Hannah chick at the bar. I've known you a year and have never seen you turn down pussy, minus that bartender."

I run my hands down my face and grunt. "I know. Ever since I started seeing her differently, I haven't had sex with anyone but myself."

Kyler chokes on air and bursts out laughing. In between his laughter, he manages to get out, "Well, that's good to know...I guess. Actually, no, I feel like maybe there should be some things we as friends and roommates maybe, ya know, keep to ourselves. Like maybe our sex lives—or, well, in your case, lack of."

He chuckles. What an asshole. I knew I shouldn't have told him the truth. I'm never going to hear the end of it, I'm sure.

I roll my eyes at him and get up to leave, but he stops me. "Okay, in all seriousness, though, have you talked to her about it?"

I look down at my feet, knowing that nothing is ever going to come of this if I don't talk to her about it. I wish I had the slightest clue as to what to say. This area is not my specialty.

"I'm going to take your silence as that's a big no. You want my advice?"

"Even if I say no, I'm pretty sure you're going to give it anyway."

He flips me the middle finger. "Just for that, never mind."

He goes to leave, and I grab his arm. "I'm sorry. What's your advice? At this point, I'll take anything. I'm in way over my head here. I'm not this guy, but she...she makes me want to be."

Kyler steps back as if he can't believe what he's hearing. Fuck, I can't believe that I'm even saying this. Who am I and what did I do with Zach Jacobs?

"Wow, you're kinda desperate, aren't you?"

He has no fucking clue.

"Just talk to her. For all you know she could be feeling the same thing and is just as weirded out that it's, well, you."

"I don't know. Maybe. But thanks." I look at my phone. "Shit, I gotta go. Thanks for the chat."

As I walk toward the door to grab my keys, I hear Kyler mumble, "Sure sounds like she's knocked you on your ass," as he walks back into his room.

Woah. In a bit of a déjà vu moment, I remember back to the talk Emmett and I had. No, that couldn't be it. There's no way. I remember his words as clear as day: *"You'll find her, and you'll just know. She's gonna knock you on your ass."*

Could I have already met her?

Pushing the thoughts from my head, I head over to the dorms, thoughts of our last talk still swirling around in my head, and I am almost knocked on my ass—literally—when Haylee opens the door. Not only is she absolutely breathtaking, but at some point since I last saw her, she changed her hair color. I am taken aback by this gorgeous blonde bombshell staring at me and am rendered speechless for the first time in my life.

CHAPTER 17
Haylee

"Holy shit."

Well, that's one way to greet someone. Concerned that I have something on me, I frantically pat my clothing, checking for something, anything that causes a reaction like that. When I threw this outfit together because he said "comfortable," I didn't think it looked that bad. Maybe I was wrong. Perhaps he should give a little more heads-up next time.

Looking around, I say, "Do I have something on me?"

My eyes meet his, and his blank stare fills with confusion. "No, why?"

I stop feeling around. "Then why did you say 'holy shit' as soon as I answered the door?"

"Oh no." He steps closer, and his fingers glide over my new hair.

Oh right, I forgot he hadn't seen me since I went to the salon the other day. I had just needed a change. At Cami's suggestion, I made an appointment with her stylist and here we are. It has for sure taken some getting used to. Every time I look in the mirror, it's as if I don't recognize the person looking back at me.

"You just..." I can tell he's searching for the right words.

I instantly worry that he is going to say he doesn't like it, which is a weird feeling because why do I care what he thinks?

But he catches me off guard with the word he chooses to describe it.

"You look...I mean—damn, you're beautiful."

I can feel my cheeks warm at his compliment. He's never called me beautiful before. I've also never known him to stumble with his words like that. Am I just imagining all of this? He hasn't backed up yet, and my heart begins to race with his closeness. I take in his scent of cedarwood and pear. Our eyes meet for a moment before he backs up, letting go of my hair, as if something scared him. That was weird.

He clears his throat. "Ready to go?"

"Yep. You told me to be ready in an hour, so here I am, ready for you." I dramatically pose for him before breaking into a fit of giggles.

He snickers before turning his face away from me, but not before I notice his eyes darken. Was it something I said?

I reach for the door and close it. "You're really not going to tell me where we're going, are you."

"Nope. Not at all." His smile is as wide as it can be, and it gives me the weirdest feeling in my stomach. Sure hope it wasn't something I ate.

I loop my arm through his as we walk toward his Jeep. At first, it was hard to ride in the vehicle, knowing that my brother had the same one, but I honestly couldn't see Zach driving anything else. It suits him.

We drive for almost an hour. I have no clue where he's taking me, and after the third time he denies my asking, I give up. I focus out the window, listening to the music playing, and see signs for Wilmington, Delaware. Are we headed to the ocean? That seems kind of random. I know it's a beautiful day, but a little too chilly for being at the beach, and we definitely didn't bring any swimsuits. Here's hoping he at least knows where he's going since I have no idea.

Zach parks into a random parking lot and turns the Jeep off. He hops out while I'm still trying to gather my bearings. The passenger door opens, and I am completely shocked to see him offering to take my hand to help me out. Although his hands are rough and calloused from working out, his touch is soft and comforting. He closes the door upon my exit, and I once again link my arm through his.

"So, are you going to tell me *now*?"

"You'll see."

"Zachary Brian Jacobs, just tell..." But I finally see where we are. The words I wanted to shout at him have flown completely out of my mouth. He has rendered me speechless.

"Oh my God! Is this a carnival? You brought me to a carnival?" I launch myself into his arms, thankful that he is quick on his feet and doesn't fall back as he catches my weight.

My arms wrap around his neck, and I feel his body stiffen at first. Oh great, he's uncomfortable being this close to me. I slowly start to back away and slide down off him, but his hands lightly touch my hips to keep me in place against him. Our bodies are so close I can smell the mint on his breath. I'm not sure how long we stare at each other, lost in each other's eyes.

I'm overcome with emotion. I can't believe he did this for me. I'm the first to break our staring contest. There are those feelings again in my stomach—if this were anyone else besides Zach, I would say they were butterflies, but that would be insane for me to get those around him. Right?

I look around us and take it all in. Turning back to face him, I can feel tears fighting to breach the surface. Every summer, the four of us would go with our parents to the local firehouse carnival. It was a tradition. There was one year where I was sick, so our parents had decided to skip it. However, Dani and I were so upset that the following week after I was better, our parents drove two towns over to go to the next one. That's one thing I miss about small-town living—the family fun-filled carnivals and mostly the funnel cake. Oh my, I hope they have it here. Lost in my memories, I don't even realize that the tears have spilled over.

"Hails, you're crying. Shit, I fucked this up, didn't I?" He cups my face, brushing his thumb along my cheek and wiping the fallen tears away in such a soothing manner. It is the same soothing touch that comforted me at the cemetery.

I shake my head. "No, this is amazing. Seriously, I can't believe you did this. I don't know why you went through all this trouble."

He grips the back of his neck and chews on his bottom lip, and his eyes meet mine again. They are full of innocence and vulnerability, a look I am not used to seeing on him.

"It's been hard lately on both of us, especially you. Don't think I haven't noticed, Hails."

I feel as though my heart actually skips a beat.

"I notice everything about you."

Why does that admission make me want more with him? This is Zach we're talking about. I think I've been letting Cami get in my head too much—Zach and I are friends. All I have to do is keep telling myself that and I'll eventually believe it.

He continues. "I just thought getting us out of the city and having a little fun would be good for both of us. I know how much carnivals mean to you."

I reach up on my toes and kiss his cheek. He leans into my touch, and the feel of my lips against his skin, it's almost electrifying. It's not like I haven't ever kissed his cheek before, but this time, it feels different. *This is insane.*

Shaking this feeling off in the hopes I can forget about it and have a great time after he went through all this trouble, I extend my arm toward the entrance. "Shall we?"

He smiles, and my knees go a little weak and the sensation of falling takes over.

"Woah, you okay?"

"Yeah, umm, I must have tripped over my foot or something. You know I'm so clumsy."

Fuck, what was that? God, he must think I'm such a fucking idiot. Now that I have my bearings, we walk toward the entrance, and of course when I pull my wallet out, Zach swats my hand away.

"No, this was my idea, so my treat. Put your money away."

"You're crazy; I can pay for myself, you know."

"I know, but I just told you I've got this. Buy us a funnel cake inside, okay?"

My eyes light up, my mouth waters, and my stomach growls just at the mention of a funnel cake, the best food invented, like ever.

"You got it."

As we walk through the entrance, I am transported back to being a kid and blink the memories away. Today is not a day to mourn the losses we have faced over the last fourteen months. Zach went through all this trouble; the least I can do is enjoy myself and not make a complete fool out of myself, yet again.

"What do you wanna do first?" The sound of his voice brings me back to the present.

"All of it!" I jump up and down because I can't believe we're actually here. The excitement I feel overpowers the sadness.

He throws his head back in laughter at my response.

"Okay, how about funnel cakes because I don't even

remember the last time I ate one, and if I don't get one in me soon, I'm gonna go savage on your ass."

He sarcastically places his hand on his chest. "Well now, we can't have that, can we?"

I nod, and Zach leads me over to the concession stand. His hand gently presses against my lower back, sending a shiver up my spine. I quickly catch my breath and hope he doesn't notice.

The funnel cake tastes even better than I remember. I'm pretty sure I made noises that one shouldn't make when eating food and definitely shouldn't make in public. Of course, when it was our time to order, Zach went back on his word and wouldn't let me pay for them either.

With stomachs full of funnel cakes and fresh-squeezed lemonade, we head over to play games. My mind is seriously playing tricks on me today. While playing the ring toss, I watch how defined Zach's jaw is while he concentrates. Defined jaws are so sexy—how have I never noticed that before? Of course, I miss every shot.

During the baseball throwing game, my gaze lowers as I watch his muscles flex against his black Henley. The way his sleeves cling to him is sending all sorts of feelings to places they have never been before, at least not in the presence of Zach. I completely zone out most of the game, imagining what it would be like to run my hands up and down his strong muscles.

"Oh look, they have the water gun horse race game. Isn't that your favorite?"

The sound of his voice brings me back to the present. That game was more Emmett's favorite, but he always let me win, so I said that it was my favorite. I'm sure if either of them had ever played to full potential, I would not have won as much as I did.

"Aww, those are so cute." I notice the teddy bears hanging.

"Well, let's get you one." He smiles, and my insides are liquid.

Am I the only one feeling this?

A younger kid joins us. We take our positions, and the bell rings. I focus everything I have in aiming the gun at the target.

DING. Son of a bitch. The little motherfucker. The kid who came up last minute to join won and won't stop talking shit. This kid is seriously killing my mood. I get up to walk away and feel Zach's hand grip my arm, stopping me in my tracks.

"One more try," Zach tells the carnival attendant, handing him another dollar. "You're going down, punk."

He directs his attention to the little kid that won't stop running his mouth that he won. What the hell, where are his parents? I sit back down.

All the saliva in my mouth instantly dries, forcing me to feel parched at just the feel of his arms wrapped around me. What is happening right now? Zach takes my hands and wraps his fingers around mine, ready to aim the water gun at the target. Zach leans in. His head is directly against mine. I can smell the mint on his breath from his gum.

"You ready, Hails?"

I can feel his breath against my ear. His body is pressed up against mine so that our hearts beat the same rhythm. I try to control myself so I can focus, but him being this close is doing all sorts of things to me right now. I can't even explain it. The starting bell rings again, and Zach's hands tighten around mine as he focuses.

"We won!"

"Of course we did. Did you doubt me? We make the perfect team." Zach hands me the black teddy bear with the red heart on his left paw that the guy behind the counter gave him.

"You know, Jacobs, if I didn't know any better, I would say

this was a date." I let out an awkward laugh. Let's get real—me on a date with Zach Jacobs? Ha!

There is something I see in his eyes...I can't describe what it is, but at that moment, I start to realize that maybe all of this—the feelings, the moments, the lost looks—all of it is not just me. Perhaps there is a possibility that he feels this too.

"Go on the Ferris wheel with me."

"Umm...I'm sorry, are you nuts?" I look at him as if he has lost his mind.

He says he notices everything about me, but does the fact that I don't do well with heights entirely skip his mind?

"I promise to protect you."

I expect him to laugh, but he doesn't. I see that seriousness in his eyes again. Something that I've never noticed before tonight. Damn it, Cami, for getting into my head. Something about the tone and seriousness of his voice makes me believe his statement.

I swallow as a new flash of nerves comes over me. As I try to get my anxiety under control, my body betrays me, and I nod in agreement. How is it that he can get me to agree to him about this as if I can't say no to him? We walk the short distance to where the Ferris wheel is, and with each step, I try to come up with a reason not to do this. It isn't until his hand finds its way back to my lower back, applying the slightest pressure as if reassuring me that it will be okay, that my nerves start to dissipate.

Once situated in the bucket seats, the bear between us, the ride begins to move backward and my heart just about stops. My grip on the bar tightens to the point where my knuckles are turning white.

"Hey, come here." Zach extends his arm and nods his head in his direction for me to scoot in closer to him. I slowly do so in hopes I don't move the seat. The Ferris wheel comes to a quick stop, of course, when we are at the very top. Fuck my life. I bury my face in Zach's chest and tighten my grip around his waist. I breathe in his masculine scent, and it instantly calms my nerves. Shit, he smells good.

"Hey, it's okay. I've got you, babe."

He just called me babe, and I'm not freaking out. It is actually an opposite feeling—as if it was natural and he had been doing it for years. His thumb rubs my shoulder as he pulls me closer into his chest. His voice calms me in a way that I would have never imagined. Is this what it was like for Dani and Emmett? This is ridiculous to think that Zach and I could have that.

I look up and find him already staring at me. His blue eyes are looking deep within me, and it ignites something in me. It's in that very moment that I am willing to finally admit the truth that I don't want him to let me go. These arms are the arms I want to be wrapped up in; I want to be lost looking in his eyes and for his smile to make me weak in the knees. I can't be the only one feeling this. What *this* is I'm feeling, I don't know, just that something has changed between us.

Still in his embrace, I whisper in a shaky voice, "What is happening between us?"

He exhales a breath in a way that makes me feel like he has been holding it in for a while. Is it possible he has been feeling this too?

"I don't know, Hails. I can't explain it. All I know is that I can't get you out of my head. Let me take you out."

I push up off his chest, our faces just a breath away from each other. I no longer notice that we're stuck at the top of the Ferris wheel overlooking the city. It's just Zach I see and feel. If a light breeze came through, our lips would be touching.

"Okay," I whisper against his lips.

Holy shit, is this happening? Before I can press my lips against his, the cart starts to move, and instead of the excitement pushing me forward, I fall backward, but Zach's hand stops me from getting too far away from him. His fingers lace in mine, and I notice how perfectly my hand fits into his.

We are doing this—his smile is as genuine as mine. I just agreed to go on a date with Zach. You would think that would scare me, and I would be nervous, but it's quite the opposite. I'm no longer scared of the heights, or should I say, the drop.

Zach was right when he said he had me. I just have to hope that he won't let me fall without being there to catch me.

CHAPTER 18
ZACH

This night could not have been more of a disaster. Fuck, I just wanted to show her the perfect date. First, my Jeep wouldn't start earlier, requiring Kyler to give me a jump start. I stopped to pick up a bouquet of daisies, her favorite flower, and of course, they were out, so I had to get her red roses. How cliché? She had loved them anyway, but I wanted to prove to her that I knew the little things like her favorite flower. Now, the restaurant has lost my damn reservations. I'm not sure this night can be salvaged. Maybe we were just doomed from the beginning.

Standing outside of the fancy restaurant, I continue to look down at my shuffling feet, feeling extremely fidgety. Right now, I'm lost in my thoughts, trying to come up with a plan B. Of course, I don't have a plan B—who has a plan B for a date?

Haylee approaches me, drawing me out of my thoughts as I feel her body heat against mine.

"I'm sorry tonight is a complete disaster. I...I..."

"Are you okay?" Haylee asks as she steps in closer to me, placing her hand over my cheek.

I lean into her touch, closing my eyes to remember this feeling, knowing that after tonight, all hope for a second date is probably lost.

"I'm sorry, I'm nervous. I just wanted tonight to be perfect."

I Never Expected You

I know she is used to seeing me as Mr. Cool, with my shit all together. Right now, I feel anything but.

"What? Why are you nervous? It's just me." She removes her hand from my cheek, and I already miss her touch, but then she reaches down and grabs my hand.

Her touch brings me ease. How is that even possible?

I look down at my feet once more before I lift my eyes to meet hers. "That's exactly why I'm nervous, Hails." I interlock our fingers in our already joined hands. They fit perfectly together. "You're you, and I'm me. I know that you had trouble saying walrus until you were twelve, calling it a 'walwus,' or that you know that I wet the bed till I was seven. Shit, how about the fact that we all used to take baths together?"

"Well, I didn't know that fact about you, but I do now."

Fuck, I did it again. I have never felt more vulnerable than I do right now, but I see a smile come across her face before she breaks out in a fit of giggles.

"Do you still have that blanket in the back of the Jeep?"

"Of course. Why?" What does a blanket have anything to do with salvaging our date?

"As you said, we've known each other our whole lives, so you know that I am super easy to please with a cheeseburger, fries, and a chocolate shake. So, what do you say..." Haylee looks behind her to the burger joint a few doors down. "...we get ourselves some food to go and go back to the Jeep, get that blanket, and head to the park for a late-night picnic by the fountain? I know you went through all this effort to make tonight perfect, but I didn't need a fancy dinner for that. I just need you."

If I don't kiss her now, I am definitely going to regret it, so for the first time tonight, I act instead of thinking. I place one hand on her hip and pull her close to me. This is her chance to tell me to stop if this isn't what she wants. She has to feel this connection, though; it can't just be me, right? I step in closer to her so that our bodies are almost touching. The other hand I use to cup her cheek. I lean down, our lips barely touching, a ghost of a kiss. I breathe her in. She smells of lavender and honey. Before I can fully plant my lips on hers, the reality of our surroundings comes to life as a taxi blasts his horn, causing us both to jump back. Well, so much for that—the moment is gone.

I reach down and grab her hand.

"Come on, baby girl, let's go get you that shake," I say followed by a wink.

Her reaction to my nickname isn't lost on me either. Her eyes gets brighter, and her smile goes wider.

By the time we reach the park, the street lights are starting to come on, but luckily there are some events at the park, so it is still open. I grab the blanket out of the back of my Jeep and hand it off to Hails before reaching and grabbing our bag of food and two milkshakes. It takes us a few minutes to find the perfect spot. I set the food bags down and spread out the blanket before we both take a seat. In the Jeep, I took off my jacket and tie and rolled up my sleeves. I noticed the way Haylee was looking at my arms as I rolled my sleeves up, and clearly, she liked what she saw. I wonder if seeing my arms like this turns her on and makes her wet. *Fuck, keep it PG, Jacobs!*

The conversation comes so easy with Haylee. What is it about this girl? I can't exactly figure it out, but with all other girls, I was never interested in talking, just getting in their pants if I'm really honest. But with Haylee, at least once I pushed the nerves aside, we haven't been able to shut up. This is nice, like really nice. I take Haylee all in as she takes a large bite of her cheeseburger in her fancy dress. She has never looked more beautiful than she does now.

"Here."

I look up from my burger to see Haylee has dipped one of her fries into her shake and is ready to feed me. I lean in and take it from her, my lips grazing her skin. Holy shit, fast food has never been sexier than it is at this moment.

"See, I don't know what they taught you in *your* house, but in my house, you dip your french fries *in* the milkshake. They go together like peanut butter and jelly."

"Now you're speaking my language, sweetheart."

She lets out a belly laugh. "Please don't tell me that at twenty years old, peanut butter and jelly sandwiches are still your favorite food."

"Hell yeah, they are!"

Her laughter continues. "Now, that's just the cutest thing ever."

"Do you think I'm cute, Miss Hanks?"

She shakes her head with a big smile. "Nope! I said the fact that you still love PB and Js is cute. Not you."

I scowl at her in a devious way. "No, that's not it. You think I'm cute." This is the perfect moment to try that first kiss again. "Yep, you definitely think I'm cute. Otherwise, you wouldn't have gone through the trouble of getting all pretty to go out with me."

She tilts her head to the side, probably trying to avoid getting smothered with the sexual tension surrounding us. "Did you just call me pretty?"

"Yes, but I didn't mean it."

Her smile fades. Mine doesn't.

I lean in and cup her cheek, running my thumb along her cheekbone. "You're absolutely beautiful."

I go to move forward to meet her lips with my own and *splat*!

What the fuck is that, and why is my hand all wet?

Haylee snorts. She actually snorts with laughter. So consumed by Haylee, I hadn't noticed the wrapper full of ketchup that we had been using between us, and I placed my hand right in the middle of it, getting ketchup everywhere. *Real smooth, Zach! Real smooth!*

She presses her lips together, trying to hold back more laughter, but I can see it in her eyes, how much trouble she is having concealing it. Am I ever going to be able to kiss this girl? Is this some weird way of the universe telling me not to?

After I clean the exploding ketchup off my hand, the conversation continues as we finish our meals. I rise to my feet first, gathering up the trash and running it over to the can before jogging back to help Haylee up. I reach out and take her hand. That instant spark is there again—the same one I felt in the cemetery.

"Well, Cinderella, I better get you back to the dorms before you turn into a pumpkin."

She smiles and takes my hand as we head back to the Jeep.

The ride back to the dorm is quiet but not awkward. I reach over to Haylee's hand and link our fingers. *This feels right.* I don't know if she doesn't want this date to end as much as I don't. If Haylee were any other girl, I would be asking to come back to her room, make her come so hard, and then leave, never calling her again.

But Haylee isn't any other girl; she's my Haylee. Yep, I just called her *mine*. And right now, while walking her back to her dorm room, hand-in-hand, I keep stealing glances at her and see the smile written all over her face.

When we reach the door, Haylee stands there, unsure of what to do next. We've had many moments tonight already where I went to kiss her, and somehow the universe has prevented it. Makes me wonder if maybe it was Emmett's way from wherever he is, trying to be funny. I'm not wasting another moment. She goes to speak, perhaps to say good night, but I cut her off. I step forward and grip both cheeks, pulling her toward me. My lips crash onto hers.

She hesitates for just a moment; I assume, like me, she can't believe this is happening. She reaches up to the side of my neck before gripping the back of it. I kiss her with everything I have—everything I had been fighting the past few months. I wrap my hands around her waist, pulling her closer as I back her up against the door, ending in a slight thump as her back hits the door. When I lick her lips, seeking entrance, her lips part for me. The feel of her tongue against my own is incredible. Her mouth is warm and inviting, and by the tiny moans escaping her mouth, she is enjoying this just as much as I am. When I pull her lower lip between my teeth, her knees go weak, and she grips my shirt to stay balanced. Fuck, that is such a turn-on, knowing that I make her this way. I grind my hips against hers; there's no way she can't feel what she does to me.

I regrettably break the kiss first, but I don't think she wants me to take her right here against her dorm room door. I don't even know if her roommate is home. I run my thumb against her bottom lip and lean in for one last kiss.

"I'll call you later?"

"Uh-huh."

I'm not even sure if Haylee is on this planet at the moment. Her eyes are hooded, her cheeks flushed, and she's panting.

"Thank you."

She tilts her head, finally out of her daze, as if I've just said the wrong thing. "For what?"

I step toward her and place her arms above her head with another thump against the door. I start with a kiss to her collarbone and then move my way up north.

When I get to just below her ear, I whisper, "For showing me all that I've been missing."

I line our mouths up one last time and kiss her with enough passion that, even if this is our one and only date, she will remember this kiss the rest of her life.

"Good night, baby girl."

Turning around with keys in hand, she glances back at me over her shoulder, and I am tempted just to fuck her senseless right here, but this is different with Haylee. Of course I want to be inside her, desperately—then maybe I can stop jerking off to the thought of her—but with Hails, I actually want to be with her and spend time with her outside of the bedroom. This girl very well may be the death of me.

I turn and walk away with a quick wave as she enters her room.

CHAPTER 19
Haylee

I am still floating on cloud nine from *that kiss*. I finally close the door to my dorm. Leaning my back against the door, I close my eyes and bring my fingers to my lips that just moments ago were against Zach's. Oh my God, what a kiss it was. My thoughts take me back to the way his lips gently brushed mine, parting them with his tongue as they sought entrance, and I gladly gave it to him. I had heard the rumors back in high school of how good a kisser he was, but wow. Nothing had prepared me for that—the most perfect kiss of all time.

I am entirely in my own world that I don't even notice Cami standing right in front of me, eyebrows raised and arms crossed as if I were caught by my dad sneaking in past curfew.

"Well...?"

I try to hide my flushed cheeks and bruised lips, but I'm not sure how long she was standing by the door, and those doors are anything but thick.

I walk over to my bed and take a seat so I can take off my shoes.

"Come on, Hails, don't be such a wankpuffin! Spill the details of you and Hottie McHotterson!"

"First of all, where the hell do you come up with these words?"

She shrugs. "I once slept with a British guy. He used all sorts of crazy words. I like that one the best. Well, that and titty-bollocks."

I laugh and roll my eyes at her. Only she would use words like that. I decide now is as good as ever to cut her off before she shares even more of her sexual past.

"And second of all, I don't *kiss* and tell." I emphasize the word kiss followed by a wink.

BAM! A pillow is thrown in my direction and smacks me right in the face.

"Ha! I knew it! You and Hottie McHotterson are so cute together."

"I don't know what we are, together or not, but I had a really nice time tonight. Nothing seemed to go right," I laugh, but it was sweet that he tried to make such an effort. "But it really was perfect. Also, can you stop calling him Hottie McHotterson? He has a name."

"Oh, I know he does. Zach. Zach." Instead of saying it, she moans his name. "I'm sure I'll be hearing a lot more of his name if that was any indication. Oh, and Hails, I won't say it..."

"Say what?" I continue to laugh because I know what she would say, that she was right all along. We don't need anything else increasing her ego.

Cami grabs her shower basket and heads to the door. She stops abruptly and turns back to me, smiling.

"Just kidding. I told you so!"

She quickly closes the door behind her as I throw the pillow in her direction and miss. I plop back on my bed and realize everything is so different now. For the first time in a long time, I am honestly happy, and that is all thanks to Zach.

ZACH: *Thinking of you.*

Me: *Thank you for tonight.*
Zach: *The pleasure was all mine.*
Zach: *I'm off to dream of your lips on mine again.*
Me: *Me too.*
Zach: *I know tonight didn't go as planned, but can I take you out again?*
Me: *It was perfect, and yes, I'd like that.*
Zach: *Goodnight, babe. Sweet Dreams*
Me: *Goodnight.* <3

ZACH IS CURRENTLY WALKING ME ACROSS CAMPUS TO MY next class after stopping in the campus coffee shop for an afternoon pick-me-up. It feels easy being with Zach, although it's still fresh and new. We haven't even had sex yet, which has to be a record for him. Even though I've known Zach my entire life, this side of him is totally new for me. I don't even remember seeing this side of him with girls he "dated" in high school.

As we cross the grassy path toward the English building, Zach freezes. His grip on my hand tightens, and as I look over to him, I see that his jaw is tense. My eyes follow to what has his attention to see that there is a busty blonde walking straight for us. She stops directly in front of us. *Seriously? Put some clothes on, skank.*

"Hi, Zach."

"Hey, Becca."

"Haven't seen you around in a while. I've missed you."

"I've been around."

Okay, this is getting awkward. Time to cut in before she

orgasms from eye-fucking him. Does she not see us holding hands right now?

"Hi, I'm Haylee." I extend my free hand to shake hers, but she looks down, staring at it before turning her attention back to Zach.

Is this bitch serious?

"Is there something you wanted?" My cat claws are beginning to come out.

"Oh, please, sweetheart. You're just the flavor of the week. He's going to do the same thing to you as he did with all of us, so don't get too attached."

I feel the tears threatening to spill out, but I refuse to let either of them see me cry. What if she's right? I know he has a past. I don't wait for him to agree with her, so I release Zach's hand and walk on toward the building.

"Buh-bye," I hear the bitch say as I pass her.

"Fuck, Becca, why are you such a bitch?" Zach raises his voice behind me. "Hails, wait up!"

I choose to keep walking.

"Haylee, stop."

I feel a tug on my arm and am pulled back to face Zach.

"It's cool. I need to get to class."

"Hey, don't listen to her—to any of them. Those hookups were *nothing*. I slept with them because well—" He pauses. "—I was stupid and didn't think I would ever find something like this." He laces his fingers through mine and brings our conjoined hands to his mouth, pressing a soft kiss over my knuckles. "This. Is. Different. You. Are. Different."

"I know you have a past..."

"No." Zach presses a finger against my lips to keep me from continuing. "That's what they all are—the past. They aren't and could never be you. Do you *hear* me?"

I whisper just loud enough for him to hear, "Yes."

His hand releases mine and grips the back of my neck, pulling me to his lips. I open willingly and welcome the warmth of his mouth. I fist my hands in his shirt as we pull away and press my forehead against his chest.

Zach wraps an arm around my shoulders. "Come on, let's get you to class. Then tonight I was thinking maybe we could hang out at the apartment, do homework, and maybe order some takeout."

"Yeah, I'd like that. But you think we could add in some making out too?" I pinch his side.

"Oh, hell yes, we can totally pencil that in."

CHAPTER 20
ZACH

I have my elbow propped up on the bar, leaning against it. Kyler is talking to me about something, but I'm not paying attention. My attention is solely on her: the most beautiful girl—no, woman—in the room. It's almost as if there is a glow of light around her.

How have I never noticed how beautiful Haylee is in all the years I've known her? I've been missing out on something special all these years. The past few weeks have been amazing. From the study sessions where we sit and do homework, dinner or coffee dates that we fit in our busy schedule, or just hanging out at the apartment. Tonight, we all came out to Steele Toby's to relax after a stressful week of midterms. I like that our groups of friends all mesh well together.

Since our first date, I can't get Em's last conversation out of my head. Is it possible that she could be *the one*? I'm totally crazy to be thinking those thoughts now, right? I mean, we haven't even been together that long. We haven't even done more than kissing—lots and lots of kissing. I've wanted to prove that Haylee is different than all the other girls by taking it slow. Although, my balls are bluer than blue.

Was this what it was like for my sister? Fuck, I wish she were here to talk to about all of this. Would she be okay with me dating her best friend? Fuck it—she dated my best friend, so anything less than her approval would make her quite the hypocrite.

Why am I standing here thinking about that when I could be with my girl?

"I'll be right back."

Kyler moves his attention to see what I'm looking at as I leave my spot at the bar.

He chuckles. "Yep, sure. I'll see you at home."

At least that's what I think he said. I'm not too sure; my sole focus is closing the distance between Haylee and me.

I walk up behind her and wrap one arm around her waist. I brush her blonde curls off her shoulder and lightly nip the skin between her neck and shoulder. Her arm rests on top of mine, keeping herself wrapped in my embrace. It is her way of acknowledging that I'm there. She is trying to have a conversation still, but I can hear her breath catch before the speed of her breathing changes altogether every time my mouth comes in contact with her skin. I can feel her pulse racing from my other hand on her wrist.

I whisper in her ear, "What do you say we get out of here?"

She turns to face me and looks up with desire.

"Take me home, Mr. Jacobs," she says with a wink.

Her voice is full of want, and I haven't even touched her. On the short Uber ride back to the apartment, her thigh never loses contact with mine and her hand lightly but with just slight pressure rubs my leg. The higher it gets, the harder I get. This car needs to get home like *now*!

I don't touch her the entire elevator ride up. I know if I touch her even in the slightest, I won't be able to hold back. I step up to the front door, and as I slide the key in to unlock, I feel her hands, palms spread, rise up my sides around to the front of my abs and slowly back down over the hard bulge in my pants, exerting a groan from my mouth. Either she is ready for us to go all the way, or she just really feels like being savage and torturing me. Tonight is going to end with my cock releasing in her though—whether it's her mouth or her pussy is up to her. I plan to worship every inch of her either way.

I compose myself long enough to open the door and let us into the apartment. I am thankful that Kyler is still at the bar. I spin around, catching her off guard, and claim her mouth with mine. I suck on her lower lip, pulling it into my mouth. She lets out a soft whimper, and if my dick wasn't hard enough already, he just wanted to prove a point that he could get even harder.

I reach up under her ass and lift her, and she wraps her legs instinctively around my waist. I don't break the kiss once walking back to my bedroom. I shut the door with my foot. I slowly set her down to her feet in front of the bed, and the closeness of her body against mine causes me to shiver. Her body feels so good pressed against mine.

Her hands slide under my shirt, and the tips of her fingers apply pressure against my abs as her nails scrape their way over them. As her hands make their way back down, her fingers trail the top of my jeans. I reach for the hem of her shirt and look into her eyes for permission. Once we go there, there's no going back.

She nods, and I lift the shirt over her head, exposing her purple bra. She reaches for the buttons of my shirt and slowly undoes each one. Haylee runs her hands along my shoulders and pushes the shirt off. When I reach around to unhook her bra, I pull her flush against my skin so that I can feel her soft flesh against mine. I trail kisses along her jaw and neck down her chest, finally finding her hard nipple. I trace my tongue around one before pulling the hard bud between my teeth, causing my girl to begin to pant heavily. Her hands grip the back of my head, and she threads my hair between her fingers tightly to keep my head in place and feasting on her gorgeous tits.

I push her back on the bed, then unsnap the button on my jeans before discarding them and my boxers on the floor. I join her on the bed and see that she has already taken off her leggings and panties. My girl is lying naked on my bed, ready and waiting for me.

Haylee Hanks is naked and in my bed.

I watch as her eyes peruse my naked body, narrowing in on my cock. When her eyes meet mine again, she has pulled her bottom lip between her teeth.

Is she as nervous as I am?

"Fuck, you're so beautiful."

I crawl up toward her, placing kisses along her thighs, her hips, her belly button and up until I find her juicy, plump lips. There is no going back at this point.

"Zach." Haylee breathes my name as she arches her back, pushing her body against mine as I gently suck on the skin between her neck and shoulder.

My hand reaches down and strokes her clit in a circular motion, applying the slightest amount of pressure. Two of my fingers slide inside her wet folds as my tongue slips into her mouth. I know I need to be inside her before I blow my load right here. I reach for a condom from the nightstand and unwrap it, placing it over my dick. My eyes seek hers, and I can see she is nervous. She's biting her bottom lip, an action I know we both do. I've never done it more than I have the past few months. This girl makes me lose my mind in both the good and bad way. Now I finally get to have her.

"Baby, we don't have to do this."

"No, no, I want you. I want you so bad it hurts. Please, Zach. I need you inside me." She cups my cheek, and her touch feels as though it's leaving a permanent mark on my skin.

I know that once we go down this road, things will never be the same. I don't think I want them to ever change after this.

I kiss her harder and with more passion than I ever have as I line my cock up with her entrance. I lace our fingers together and place them over her head. She is already so soaking wet that it's easy for me to enter her, but I choose to take my time, savoring every moment. Our eyes meet and don't leave each other as I slowly slide inside her. I'm not even sure if either of us blinks.

Holy shit, this feels amazing. There is no awkward adjusting to my size once I am fully inside her; it's as if we're made for each other.

Sliding in and out of her, I'm overcome with emotion. I've been with plenty of women before but never like this. I should say, I've fucked plenty of women, but this, with Haylee right now…no, this isn't fucking. This is making love.

"Fuck, Hails, you feel so good."

Her back arches up as I press deeper inside her.

"Zach, just like that," she cries out as her head falls back against the pillow.

In and out.

In and out.

In and out. Her pussy begins to contract around my cock. Haylee's nails dig into the skin of my bicep as she screams my name. The feeling of her orgasm, along with all the feelings inside me, makes me follow her right over the edge. The only sound in the room is the sound of our heavy breathing. There is a thin layer of sweat over both of us. That was the most incredible experience of my life.

I lean my forehead against hers.

"Hi."

"Wow, that was..."

I don't let her finish that statement before I place a tender kiss on her forehead. My lips linger, not wanting to separate from her. If I could keep her here forever, I would. I slide out of her, already missing her touch, and get up to dispose of the condom in the trash can. Returning to the bed, I get under the covers and pull Haylee against me, wrapping her in my arms. She doesn't say much. Was that as intense for her as it was for me? For the first time in a long time, I feel like things are going to be okay.

I run my fingers up and down her arm, and she settles further against my body. I lean down and kiss the top of her head.

"Good night, baby."

"Mmmmmm."

I tired my girl out tonight. I can only imagine how long she would sleep if I fucked her hard. Shit—down, boy. I want to let her sleep. We can go for round two and maybe three tomorrow.

I let sleep take over as I drift off, dreaming of a future with this girl lying next to me, who I never expected to want to spend my life with as anything other than my best friend's little sister.

CHAPTER 21
Haylee

I wake up wondering if last night had been a dream. After weeks of seeing each other, Zach and I had finally taken the relationship even further. Last night could not have been more perfect. It was like something out of a romance movie. I roll over and reach for Zach, and I am met with an empty space on the bed.

Oh no.

"Zach?" I sit up and look around, but I don't see any sign of him.

I get up and walk toward the dresser and grab one of his T-shirts. I throw it on over my head and walk to the bedroom door. I slowly open it, in hopes I see him on the other side. I don't see him anywhere in sight, but I do awkwardly see Kyler sitting on the couch. I grip the bottom of the T-shirt and yank it down, making sure to cover all my lady bits.

"Hey."

"Well, good morning." He emphasizes the good part, and I know damn well he is aware of what happened between Zach and me last night.

Oh my God, did he brag about it to him?

"Have you seen Zach?"

"No, he left a little bit ago."

I Never Expected You

Right. Of course he left. This is exactly what he does. He fucks a girl and then never talks to her again. I remember Dani and Emmett both telling me of many mornings they had to kick his conquest out of the apartment after he miraculously had disappeared. Great, I had stooped to that level and had become one. What is wrong with me to think that he could actually have feelings for me, that last night was real. I'm such a fool—the conversation with the girl in the quad replays in my head over and over.

Don't cry. Don't cry. I gather up my clothes and throw my leggings back on. I take one last look around and realize the only person I can be mad at is me. I knew his reputation, and yet I still took a chance hoping he had meant all that he said, but clearly that was just all part of his plan to get into my pants.

Fuck, I wish I had Dani or Em here. The one person I have left is the one person who made me feel this way. I'm so stupid. Why didn't I take my own advice that I gave Cami at the beginning of the year?

I open the bedroom door.

"Bye, Ky." I rush past Kyler, praying that the tears hold back before I'm out of the apartment.

I grab my purse from the table

Standing in line at the coffee shop, I can't help but be sad. I feel like Zach and I could've been something great. It's crazy, I know, but I never felt like that about someone before—in and out of the bedroom. I guess I was just another notch on his bedpost. I try not to think how disappointed in me Emmett would be for falling for it. Reliving the past few weeks is just torture on myself. Last night was too good to be true. I wonder how many women he has pulled those lines with.

"Hey, Haylee," I hear the deep voice behind me say.

That voice does nothing to me as Zach's did. Is that how it's going to be from now on? Will I compare every man from now on to him? Lord help me if that's the case. I turn around and see Chad Davis, the quarterback for the football team, standing there smiling at me.

"Hey, Chad. How's it going?"

"Good. I need caffeine. Have to start every day with it."

Yeah, no shit. Why the hell else would you be in a coffee shop? Wow, nothing gets past this guy.

I nod in acknowledgment because what the hell am I supposed to say to that. Usually, I would have a witty response, but I'm too exhausted from getting my heart broken to think. I just want some caffeine and to make it back to the dorm and forget all about Zach Jacobs. The sad part is, even if we didn't work out, I still have to see him—a perk of our parents being best friends.

"Where's Jacobs? Aren't you two joined at the hip?"

I swallow down the sadness as I respond. "Yeah, that didn't exactly work out."

I face forward, hoping he gets the hint that I don't want to talk about it, or really in general.

I place my order with the barista, and Chad quickly chimes in. "Put your money away, I've got this."

"No, that's okay, I've got it."

Chad puts his hand on mine, and I don't like the way his hand feels on my skin. It doesn't make me feel the same way Zach's did. Fuck, I am so screwed. Will I compare every guy from now on to Zach Jacobs?

"Okay, well, how about instead of letting me buy you coffee, you let me take me to the big party tonight."

My phone vibrates in my pocket, and I reach for it, only to

see Zach is calling. I hit the Ignore button and put it back in my pocket.

Being out partying is the last thing I want to do right now, but I remember Zach had mentioned it, so it's safe to assume he'll be there. I can't let him see that he broke me, so I do the last thing I ever expected to do.

"Pick me up at eight."

CHAPTER 22
ZACH

Kyler and I stand over by the keg. For once I didn't feel like coming out to a party. That's how I know I have it bad. Maybe everything Emmett said that last conversation was true—when I'd know, I'd just know. And I know.

"Oh shit," Kyler mutters into his plastic cup full of cheap beer.

I look up in the direction he is looking, and I see her. *My Haylee.* She is stunning. Her blonde hair is down and curly just how I like it. I itch to glide my fingers through her locks, grip it between my fingers so I can pull her close and taste her. My thoughts of all the ways I want her are interrupted when I see she's not alone. Fucking Chad Davis—quarterback for the Quakers, the all-American boy next door, and *total douchebag*! I don't know what girls see in him, and why is my girl with him? I didn't realize I actually growled as I saw him wrap his arm around her shoulders.

"You okay, man?"

"What is she doing with that tool? I don't get it. We were happy. I don't understand what happened. When we had sex last night, I don't even know how to say it, Ky. It was the best of my life. She just gets me. Then all day she avoided my call.

When I went to the dorm room, Cami made up some excuse that she wasn't there. But I'm pretty sure she was."

Kyler turns to me, lowering his beer. "Zach, I'd hate to break it to you, but before Haylee, you were a bit of manwhore."

"Yeah. So? But Haylee…" I steal a glance over at her. She still hasn't noticed me looking at her. "She's different. She is something special. She's not like the rest of them."

He nods, taking a sip of his drink. "But does she know that?" He points his cup in her direction. "I mean, does she really know that? And not just think you did all that to get in her pants? You were gone when she got up this morning."

"I ran out to get us breakfast."

"Yeah, but she didn't know that."

"I left a…"

Shit, I totally didn't leave a note. I shake the thought from my mind, but fuck, is he right? Had I treated her as I would have every other girl, or at least in her mind, did she see it that way? Did she think I would say anything to get pussy? I mean, she wouldn't have been wrong. Last year, all I had to do was call a girl beautiful and she was handing me her panties before spreading her legs.

I look over at her and realize I never told her what she means to me. I want it all with her. I want what Em and Dani had, and the only girl I want it with is Haylee Hanks. Her blue eyes meet mine for a brief moment before she quickly looks away. It's at that moment that I realize she owns me. It was so quick that I can't even be sure she had seen me, but the way it made me feel told me she had. My chest tightens as my heart beats faster.

"*Fuck!*" I set my beer down and run my hands through my hair before dragging them over the stubble on my face. "I messed up, Ky. I need to fix this. I've never felt like this about a girl. I need her. Shit! I'm gonna go talk to her."

Before I can even move, I feel Kyler's hand on my arm holding me in place. "Zach, you can't just go up to her and talk to her, especially when she's here with another guy. I know it sucks, but you need to prove to her that she is different. You can't just walk up to her and say, 'Hey, baby, you're different. I want you.' If I were her, I'd probably throw my beer in your face and go home and bang that douchebag Chad."

I turn to look at him. "What the fuck, man? Whose side are you on here?"

Is he for real suggesting she go home with that guy? Who knows what the fuck kind of diseases he's got, and I bet he has a microdick!

"I'm on yours. Seriously, I am. I'm just saying you need to do something *big*. Chicks dig that shit."

"And what do you suggest I do, almighty love guru?"

He takes a sip of his beer and shakes his head. "Oh, no, you don't. Love is not my area—never has been, never will be."

"Love? Who said anything about love?" I pause.

Is this what it feels like to be in love? I shake my head at the thought. I care about Haylee a lot—I mean *a lot*—but is this love? Maybe. I never really have been in love, if, after all, that is what I'm feeling. I don't want anyone's arms around hers. I don't want anyone to have her in the way she gave herself to me last night. I want her pressed up against my body, her hands intertwined with mine, her lips on mine, kissing me and only me.

Something big. Something big. I look around the room knowing that If I don't do it now, there is a chance that she might go home with that dumbass. Not that I think she's a slut—she's far from it—but I don't want his hands anywhere near my girl. This shit needs to happen and *now*. *Think. Think.* What

I Never Expected You

the fuck would Emmett do right now? He would definitely know what to do. I close my eyes and take a deep breath, listening to the music play.

BAM, that's it! I look around. I quickly chug the last bit of my beer and hand Kyler my cup before I turn to walk away.

I hear Kyler yelling in the background, "What the fuck? I didn't mean right this second. Oh shit."

But I choose to keep walking. I walk up to Aaron, who is in charge of music, and lean in and ask him for a favor. He looks at me like I have two heads, and I nod so he understands that he did hear me correctly. He shrugs, but nods and moves to the music to find my selection.

It's now or never. Fuck! I wipe my sweaty palms on my jeans and walk toward the beer pong table—that seems like a good enough stage to do this. If only Emmett and Dani were here to see me now. Dani would definitely laugh; I think Em would too, but I think he would also remember the time he pulled this shit at Dani's sweet sixteen. A moment I will forever wonder what the hell I was smoking for agreeing to dance to that, but here I am about to do it for my girl. Well, hopefully, she is my girl after this.

I climb up on the beer pong table during the middle of the game as everyone yells.

"Zach, what the fuck, man?"

"Are you serious?"

"What the fuck are you doing!"

I ignore them and look around the room till my eyes find her. The music switches over from some Calvin Harris song to an '80s slow jam. Not only does the change in music grab everyone's attention, but seeing me stand on the beer pong table has all eyes on me. Her eyes lock on mine as I begin to sing the words of Foreigner's "I Want to Know What Love Is."

I couldn't think of a better song to profess my feelings to her. It's true, I've found heartache and pain lately, but there is something about *her* that makes me want to be a better man, and *she* has helped heal those wounds.

I am not the best of singers, but I enjoy getting down on karaoke. I give this song all I have, channeling my sister and Haylee's moves from their typical Katy Perry dance-off. I can only imagine what everyone is thinking, but honestly, I don't fucking care. My eyes never leave hers in hopes she realizes this is for her. It's all for her. I want to know what love is, and she is the girl I want it with. I'm not fucking around.

As the song gets closer to the end, I jump down off the table, and the crowd separates as if in the middle of a damn John Hughes film when they realize I'm not just some drunk asshole doing this for fun, but I'm headed to get *the girl*.

I don't see anyone else around, just Haylee. I walk up to Haylee, who is frozen in place. I take that as a good sign; she didn't run off. I reach up and cup her cheeks, my thumb rubbing against her porcelain skin. She closes her eyes and leans into my touch, another good sign.

"I'm fucking crazy about you, Hails."

Before I can say any more of the quick little speech I thought of to say in the fourteen steps it took to get to her from the table, her lips are crashing against mine. I pull her tight against my body, knowing well she can feel my hard cock pressed against her, but I don't care. She is in my arms, and that's all that matters. My tongue plunges into her mouth as I realize it feels as though it has been forever since I have tasted her even though in reality it hasn't even been more than a day. As our kiss deepens, I run my fingers through her hair, working my way down her back and over her ass, my fingers kneading deep enough in her skin to leave a mark.

I end up lifting her, and she instinctively wraps her legs around my waist. Fuck, that's hot. I need to get Haylee out of here and fast. I'm ready to bust right through my jeans. I don't want to lose the feeling of her lips against mine until I feel her bite my lower lip hard, forcing a deep growl from my throat. It is at that moment I pull back from her. Her cheeks are flushed, and we are both out of breath. I place a quick kiss against her forehead before I reluctantly release her back to the ground, but she still keeps her hands clutching to my shirt.

"Hi." I brush the hair that had fallen in her face from our make-out session.

"Hi." Her raspy voice is even sexier.

It's time to take my girl home. So I do what any man would do in this situation: I lean down, reach behind her legs, and lift her as if she were a new bride.

Am I thinking about marriage right now? I shouldn't be, but for some crazy reason it doesn't freak me out like I feel it should.

I kiss her one last time before I focus on getting her out of here. I look around as I move forward, making sure I don't knock into anyone—I am carrying precious cargo, of course. People cheer and slap my back as we make our way to the front door. When I look to the left, I see Chad playing tonsil hockey with some sorority girl. *Real classy, asshat!* And to think he thought he was good enough for Haylee. Fucking Chad!

I quicken my pace as I feel Haylee's lips meet my neck as she begins to nip at my skin and ease the sting with her tongue.

"Baby, you know I love when you do that, but I need you to stop if we have any chance of hell of making it back to the apartment, let alone getting out of this house."

CHAPTER 23
Haylee

*O*h my God. Is this really happening? I must be dreaming. Zachary Jacobs is carrying me through the streets of Philadelphia. He got up in front of a college party and belted out "I Want to Know What Love Is," and not just for anyone but *for me*. I am thankful that the apartment isn't too far from campus.

"You know you don't need to carry me, right?"

He makes no move to put me down and laughs, and I feel the rumble in his chest.

"Seriously, put me down, Zach."

"Not gonna happen, sweetheart. You better get used to it." He looks down, smiling at me.

Shit, I could get lost in those blue eyes. They're eyes I never thought I would see looking at me the way he does. I nearly collapsed during his performance, and when he walked up to me, *holy shit*, it was like a scene from a movie.

When he says I better get used to it, he can't mean what I think he means, can he? How is this my life right now? We finally reach his building. I am thankful that Kyler is still at that party, and hopefully he doesn't come back anytime soon. As we wait for the elevator, I look up at Zach and find his eyes locked on mine.

"Come here."

I let out a little giggle. "You're holding me right now. I'm not sure I can get any closer to you."

"You have such a smart mouth. The things I want to do to that mouth..." He doesn't finish that sentence, no matter how bad I wish he would. I can feel the blush and heat creep against the skin of my chest and face. It all of a sudden got much hotter in here. Instead, he leans down, pressing a soft kiss against my lips. I tighten my arms around his neck, and before the kiss can go any further, we are interrupted by the ding of the elevator's arrival.

Zach doesn't even set me down as he fishes his keys out of his pocket and opens the front door of the apartment. Once inside, he heads straight for his room, kicking the door shut behind us with a loud boom. He walks us over to the bed, placing me down gently before pulling his shirt off to expose his hard body. Thoughts of exploring it the other night come to mind, and I feel as though I might combust if he doesn't touch me soon. I quickly back up against the pillows as he climbs on the bed after me, settling between my legs.

"Haylee." I love the way he breathes my name.

Zach reaches for the bottom of my shirt, and I lift to allow him to pull it off and throw it behind him, not caring where it lands. His eyes are filled with desire and something I didn't see the other night. Whatever it is sets me on fire, and I know I'm going to like it.

Gripping the back of my neck, he pulls me to him, claiming my mouth with his. This kiss is full of passion, desperation, and frenzy. Will I ever get enough of him? I feel this kiss all the way between my legs. My tongue sweeps out, brushing against his. I dig my nails into his back as I thrust my hips against his, seeking friction, forcing a deep groan out of his chest. He moves back to his knees, and that devilish Jacobs smirk is on his handsome face. How did I get to be so lucky to be here with this man? Slowly, like painfully slowly, Zach places kisses along, my neck, chest, and stomach on the way down to my jeans.

I need more. I crave more. Finally, he snaps the button on my jeans and slides them down. There is a deep noise coming from him as he takes my body in. He looks as if he is a lion about to pounce on its prey, and to be honest, I wouldn't mind that. He slides my jeans off, tossing them in the same direction as my shirt.

I'm lying in just my bra and panties, and Zach hovers over me, taking my wrists in his hands and pinning them above my head. My body begins to writhe underneath him in anticipation. His grip on my wrists tighten, not in a hurtful way but more in a sexy, domineering way.

His hot breath burns my skin with passion as he whispers in my ear, his raspy tone sending shivers down my spine. "Tell me, Haylee, did you think it was funny to show up with another guy?"

"Ummm..." All words leave my head as Zach bites my earlobe.

He flips me over, and I gasp in surprise. He grabs onto my hips and brings me up to my hands and knees.

"Did you like that it made me jealous? It drove me insane to see his hands on you, on what's mine." His fingers trace down my spine, causing me to shiver when I am anything but cold. His hands leave my skin, and I instantly miss the contact.

SMACK!

His palm comes in contact with my ass. It causes me to jolt forward in surprise. "This. Is. Mine." Zach's other hand has a firm grip on my hip, keeping me in place he leans down to whisper in my ear. "You. Are. Mine."

I Never Expected You

He rubs the sting away in circular motions before spanking me again.

SMACK!

This time I let out a sound I don't even recognize. Zach leans down, pressing the front of his body to my back.

"Mmmmm," he moans, "I bet you like it when I spank you, don't you, Hails."

I don't even know who I am as I nod in response. Zach makes me feel like a different woman.

"I bet if I slide my fingers into your pussy right now, I will find you soaking wet."

His fingers glide up my thighs, and he pushes my soaked panties to the side before sliding two fingers inside, coating himself with my wetness. He doesn't go slow.

"Zach." It comes as more of a whimper as I tried to catch my breath. His fingers plunge in and out of me at a ravaging pace.

SMACK!

"Oh fuck, baby, you definitely like it when I do that because your pussy just tightened around my fingers."

"Don't stop. I'm so close."

Who am I becoming? I've always been the shy one in bed, but with Zach, *fuck*! I feel my body start to tense, an orgasm not far away.

SMACK!

Right after his skin comes in contact with the swell of my ass, he moves his hand around to put pressure on my clit.

"Oh, shit!"

"That's it, baby. Let me feel you lose control."

And that's what I do. My body shakes as the orgasm rips through me. I'm pretty sure I black out at one point. I am still coming down from my high that I don't even realize Zach has stripped out of his pants and retrieved a condom from the nightstand until I feel him thrust deep inside me.

"Fuck, Hails, you feel so good. I love being deep inside you."

And is he ever. Oh my God! Only a few strong thrusts and I feel another orgasm coming on. Oh shit!

"Harder, baby, harder."

My wish is his command. The grip he has on my hips is almost painful as he plunges deeper and harder into me.

"Mine," he growls over and over, and he's right—at this moment, I am his.

I would have agreed to anything he wanted to do with me. The second orgasm rips more violently through me, and I am sure we will get a complaint by the neighbors tomorrow of a noise violation, but I don't care. I don't want him to stop...ever. I grip the sheets as my pussy contracts around his cock, bringing on his own orgasm.

"*Fuckkkkkk!*" he yells as he unloads into the condom.

Holy shit! I collapse on the bed, and Zach collapses on top of me, still inside me. I try to calm my breathing, but I feel as though I just ran a fucking marathon, maybe even two.

Zach gets up to dispose of the condom and comes back before I even move from the same position. He slides into bed next to me, pulling me to him.

We're both exhausted and sweaty, overtaken by emotion—at least the latter for me as I replay tonight's events over in my head. What a night—from accepting Chad's invitation to showing up to the party and seeing *him* but wanting not to make eye contact. I knew that if I looked at him, I would cave. But the thought of his proclamation and what happened here in the apartment causes my heart to beat faster.

My head rises up and down to the same rhythm as Zach's chest. I run my fingers up and down his light dusting of chest hair. Shit, I never thought chest hair would turn me on, but on Zach, hell yes it does. His fingers strum up and down my back, in a relaxed state. This may be the most relaxed he has been in over a year. Did I bring him the same sense of calmness that he brought me?

As if he knew my mind was racing, he speaks first. "I meant what I said earlier, Hails. I'm fucking crazy about you. I want you. I want to be with you. I want it all with you. I know it sounds crazy, but it's the truth."

I rotate on his chest to face him.

"This is crazy, right? I mean, what you did tonight, singing in front of a crowded college party, that was..." I search for the words to say.

"Big? Bold? Romantic?"

"Asinine?"

His smile quickly fades. Shit, that was supposed to be a joke. I adjust myself quickly, climbing up to straddle his lap. I cup his cheeks as he takes in the view in front of him, my naked body pressed up against his. I'm not even sure when my bra came off. I guess it was like magic.

"Eyes up here, Jacobs." I laugh as his eyes go from my naked breasts to my eyes. "Okay, asinine is not the word I would use to describe your little performance—*unexpected*. Definitely romantic, but unexpected. It was perfect."

His hands roam my sides as I feel his cock start to harden underneath me. I see my man consumed by vulnerability, and at that moment, I realize that this man consumes me in every way.

Do I love Zachary Jacobs? I always have, but now I am questioning, *am I in love with Zachary Jacobs?* I... I... I am.

He reaches for a condom and puts it on. I lock my eyes with his as he lines himself up with my already wet entrance, and I bite my lip, ready to say what I want to say.

"Zach, I... I..."

But he cuts me off with his mouth on mine. This kiss though is not messy; it is sweet and full of love. When he pulls back, our eyes both open and meet.

"I think I'm in love with you, Haylee Hanks."

Holy. Fucking. Shit.

"I think I love you too. And I want to be with you."

I barely get "you" out before he is sliding into me. This time there is no spanking; it is not rough, or frantic. This is slow, just like the first time. I love this man. We spend the rest of the night making love to each other before falling asleep in each other's arms.

*

"Hey, wait a sec!" I shout to Zach as I hear him heading for the front door.

He hurries into the kitchen, and I can tell he's already running late.

He stops and admires my outfit—his T-shirt, and only his T-shirt. He swallows boldly as if he is contemplating skipping class altogether. I'm grateful Kyler left for class early this morning, because I might not say no if he were to lift me on the island right now and have his way with me. I'm sure the cold countertop would feel good against my skin since he got a little carried away with his spanking last night. There is definitely the outline of Zachary Jacobs's hand on my ass. He's left his mark on my heart *and* my body.

Breaking him out of his daze, I grab the bag from the counter and strut over to him, swinging my hips in a sexy way knowing that it'll tease him and have his mind elsewhere during the day. I rise on my toes so that his T-shirt lifts just above my ass. I lean in and kiss him on the cheek, my lips lingering just a second too long on his skin.

"My morning class isn't until later, so I made you lunch—your favorite."

"You made me a PB and J? Did you—"

I cut him off. "Yes, babe. I cut the crust off."

He smiles when he realizes I remembered, and I laugh that he still eats PB and Js, for one, but without the crust.

"Have a good day."

I go to walk away when Zach grips my wrist and pulls me back to him, crashing his lips on mine, staking his claim, and giving me a preview of what's to come later.

I break the kiss reluctantly, but I know he will be fired up when he gets home.

"You're going to be late, and I need to shower."

I walk toward the bathroom, swaying my hips a little more than I need to, and I hear him yell, "Thanks, Hails—definitely going to need to walk this off!"

CHAPTER 24
Haylee

"Are you sure you wanna do this now?" Zach and I are walking from the parking lot to the restaurant where we are meeting our parents for my dad's birthday dinner. Today is his birthday, so Zach and I came down to Annapolis to meet them at his favorite waterfront restaurant.

Zach pauses and turns to me, his hand still linked with mine. "Why wouldn't we want to do this now?"

I bite my lip nervously. "I don't know. I just don't want to upset them."

Zach tucks a strand of hair behind my ear, and I lean into his touch. "Baby, what's going on? You're not making any sense."

It's been two weeks since Zach and I officially got together. We haven't told our parents yet, but Zach thought this was the perfect opportunity to.

"I just don't want to bring up any bad memories since Emmett and Dani were together and all. I know it's stupid. I don't want to upset my dad on his birthday. This—us—is all so new."

He tips my chin up between his forefinger and thumb and places a sweet kiss on my lips. "This is one of the many reasons why I love you, but it's going to be fine. I promise. We're not them. We're Zaylee."

I pull back, flattening my lips and trying to hold my laughter in, but that is the funniest thing I have ever heard.

"I'm sorry—Zaylee?"

He has a massive smile on his face, and I can't help but let the laughter escape.

"Yeah, you know, Zaylee... Zach and Haylee, me and you..." He motions his hands between us.

My boyfriend is adorable—oh my God, that is so weird. Saying "my boyfriend" in reference to Zach.

"Like Brangelina or Amandom."

I tilt my head to the side. "Amandom?"

"Yeah, Amanda the bartender has herself a new man. He's always sitting at the corner of the bar while she works, and I guess all the regulars gave them that nickname. You've never noticed him?" Zach asks, as if I see him every day. I'm not even sure I've met him before.

"Oh, no, I guess I've never really noticed him, but I think if you have, then maybe you're spending a little too much time in the bar and not enough time—"

But he cuts me off before I can finish. "In your pussy."

I smack his chest and throw my head back in laughter. "You are crazy; you know that, right?"

I start walking ahead. Zach reaches out for my hand and pulls me back to him with enough force that I knock into his chest. He leans in closer, our lips just a breath apart.

"I am crazy...crazy in love with you."

His lips then meet mine, and we spend a few moments lost in each other, possibly a little too friendly for the streets of downtown Annapolis.

We are brought back to reality when people start whistling around us, and one guy yells, "Get a room." I tuck my head into his chest in embarrassment, and he kisses the top of my head.

"Come on, let's go get this over with and give your dad cardiac arrest for his birthday."

I throw my hands up in the air and shake my head at him. "There's the asshole I know and love. I knew you couldn't always be such a sweetheart."

"Hey, for the record, you always knew I was an asshole." He winks, and his voice grows serious as he leans down to whisper in my ear. "And you know very well that I'm not always a sweetheart."

The tone of his voice alone causes my heart to beat faster and my core to tighten.

He extends his arm in the direction we were walking. "Shall we?"

I nod, knowing damn well if we continue this conversation, we may end up being late to dinner.

We walk hand in hand till we reach the restaurant. Zach opens the door for me, and as I walk through the door first, he places his hand on my lower back. The hostess lets us know that the rest of the party has already arrived, and she leaves to walk us to the table.

Zach places his forehead against mine. "You're my girl. I love you."

I place a quick kiss to his lips. "I love you too."

My grip on his hand tightens as we approach the table where our parents are seated. My mom is the first to notice us.

"Oh, look who's finally..." She pauses as she sees us standing hand-in-hand. "...here."

Oh shit, this isn't good. All four adults make faces back and forth. I can't tell if it's that they're mad or confused. Why isn't anyone saying anything?

I Never Expected You

Zach clears his throat, and I look up at him and mirror his smile back at him.

"Well, shit," I hear Mr. Adam say as he reaches into his pocket and retrieves his wallet.

What the hell is happening?

I watch both my mom and Ms. Kelly break out into a fit of laughter while Zach and I exchange confused looks.

We watch his dad hand over a fifty-dollar bill to my dad.

My dad kisses the money. "Happy birthday to me!"

Zach chimes in. "Umm, does someone want to fill us in with what's going on here?"

My mom stands and walks over to us, hugging us both. "Well, you see, we had a feeling something was going on with you guys—call it parents' intuition. And your fathers decided to bet on how long it took for you two to admit your feelings."

"What!" Zach and I both exclaim at the same time.

My mother goes back to her seat, and Zach holds out my chair for me before he sits next to me.

"I thought it wouldn't happen until after the school year was over, but your dad thought otherwise."

"Maybe next time you'll listen to me, Jacobs. Have I ever been wrong with my intuition? No, that's right." My dad sits back in his chair, arms crossed, looking like he is feeling pretty proud of himself.

I'm so glad our parents find this amusing and our dads bet on us. How could they see this coming before us? Was it that obvious? Well, this dinner sure is turning out to be interesting.

Kelly props her elbows on the table after the waitress came around for our drink orders. "So tell us how this all went down?"

Zach and I both share a loving look, and he continues to caress my hand under the table while we explain the details of it all, of course leaving out the sexual parts and the spanking. I squirm in the seat a few times at the mere thought of that and feel my panties dampen. This is nice, though; our smiles never leave our faces as we steal glances at each other throughout dinner, and I watch similar smiles on our families' faces too. This is something good that both our families needed.

We say goodbye to our parents outside of the restaurant. With his arm around my shoulder and me tightly tucked into him, Zach and I head toward the parking garage where his Jeep is parked.

"See, that wasn't so bad." I feel the vibration of his laughter against my body.

"I can't believe they bet on us." I feel mortified that they did that, but knowing our dads, I shouldn't have expected anything less.

He lets out a loud laugh. "I know. That was fucking epic."

I punch him lightly in the gut. "It's not funny."

He looks down at me with a raised eyebrow.

"Okay, okay. It's hilarious and mortifying all at the same time."

"I told you it would all be okay, Hails. Maybe you should start listening to me from now on. Huh?"

"Yeah, okay, probably not gonna happen." I look up at him and see his eyes darken. "But how about I suck your cock on the ride back to school instead?"

Zach takes off running toward the garage, nearly pulling my arm out in the process. I think I'll take that as a yes.

CHAPTER 25
Zach

Seven months later...

One year ago today something changed between Haylee and me, only she didn't know it at the time. For the past eight months, we have been inseparable. If you had asked me one year ago where I pictured my life, I would never believe myself saying "standing at my best friend's grave placing flowers with my girlfriend whom I love very much in my arms." I'm still trying to figure out how it is that we've managed two years in this world without *him* though.

"You doing okay, Hails?"

Her arms tighten around my waist, but she lets out a relaxing breath, letting me know she's doing okay. I know this is hard, and at times, she puts on a brave face, but I know her well enough to know when she is just pretending to be strong.

She nuzzles her face in a little more to my chest. "Yeah, I'm fine."

"Don't bullshit me, Hanks."

Her beautiful blue eyes meet mine. "I'm fine, seriously, *Jacobs*."

It always makes me laugh a little when she tries to act like one of the guys and call me by my last name. She pushes up on her toes and presses her lips quickly against mine.

She breaks the kiss and giggles and turns so her back is to my front.

"What's so funny?"

"I was thinking of something ridiculous my brother would probably say just then to break up our kissing. Like 'get a room—no, wait, that's gross, don't do that.' Or 'get your filthy paws off my sister.'"

"Ha! Remember that time I caught him and Dani making out on the back deck?" I ask, resting my cheek against the top of her head.

"Which time?" Haylee breaks out into more laughter, knowing that there was more than one occasion that any of us had caught them making out on the back deck, let alone anywhere else.

Those two could never keep their hands to themselves, but for the first time in my life, I get it. Every minute I'm with Haylee, I just need to touch her to remind myself that she's mine.

I tickle her side, which causes her to flinch. "Gross! These are our siblings we're talking about, Hails. I meant the time where I threatened to spray them with the hose if he didn't remove his hands from her."

"How do I not remember this story?" She settles back against my chest.

"I grabbed the hose. I don't think he realized I was serious, or maybe he didn't want to take his hands off her. I don't know. Sometimes I don't even know what was going through his head at times. What a goof. Anyways, he picks up Dani, and she's kicking and screaming and just runs straight for the pool, jumping in. She still had all of her clothes on and everything."

Haylee bends over in laughter. "Oh my God, that was such an Emmett thing to do. Did he say why?"

"Oh yeah. He was so proud of himself. Dani was splashing him, asking him why he did that. He pulled her into his arms, then looked over at me and said, 'What you gonna do now, Zach? We're already all wet, so I guess I get to keep my hands on her now.'"

Haylee's laughter stops abruptly, and I wrap my arms tighter around her and kiss the top of her hair before leaning my cheek against her head.

"I'm sorry, baby. I didn't mean to upset you."

"No, you didn't. I love hearing stories like that, especially ones that I hadn't heard of before. It's just…I can't believe it's been two whole years. I wish Dani were here. I miss her so much too."

I know exactly what she means. I can't believe this is another anniversary that my sister has been gone. No one has heard from her. I'm really worried about her, but there is only so much I can do if she refuses to answer my calls or texts. She clearly needs time. I miss her so much. I hate that Haylee can never see her brother because he died, but I can't see my sister because she chooses to stay away. It just makes no sense. I wish she were here so that she could see how happy I…*we* are. I know it hurts Haylee for that too.

I'm not sure how long we stay there for. I always lose track of time when we visit; time stops here. It's as close to Em that we can actually get. Haylee's breathing evens out against my chest, and she steps forward toward the grave. She bends down and presses her hand over *Emmett Adam Hanks*.

"Fuck! I miss you so much. I'm sorry she's not here. I'll see you later, big bro. I love you."

Haylee presses her hand to her lips before placing it back on the stone. She pauses for a moment and then rises to her feet. Her hand finds mine and laces our fingers. I brush my thumb over her knuckles as I always do.

"You were right, man. She knocked me on my ass, and I wouldn't have had it any other way. I just wish you were here to see it. Love you, man." I place my hand to the corner of the stone, wishing it were Em's shoulder I was squeezing.

Haylee turns to me. "What was that about? Who knocked you on your ass?"

A smile tugs at the corner of my lips. I brush a stray hair out of her face, cup her cheek, and claim her lips in a less-than-appropriate kiss in a cemetery.

"That, Hails, is a story for another time."

Still in a daze from that kiss, all she can do is nod.

I nod toward her car. "Come on. I told my mom we would meet them at your parents' house to help them decorate their tree."

We walk back to the car. "I can't believe they got a real Christmas tree this year. We always had a fake one."

I open the passenger door for her. "Things change. I love it."

"You know what I love?" She has a twinkle in her eye that I know what she is thinking.

"Me naked?"

A blush creeps up her cheeks, and she bites her lip. Emmett is for sure rolling over in his grave at the moment. *Sorry, buddy.*

"Well, yes—which *will* be happening later. But I was going to say, I love you."

"You better." I close the door once she is seated and walk around to the driver's side.

I lean over before putting my seat belt on and pinch her chin with my thumb and forefinger. "I love you, Haylee Hanks. More than you know."

And I truly mean that with all my heart. I release her chin and wink. My girl knows what that means. I start the car and head to her parents' house so we can get the family shenanigans over with before I can get my girl in bed and show her just how much I love her over and over again.

I meant what I said: this girl seriously has knocked me on my ass. I figured I would fall in love *one* day, but I never expected it to be with my best friend's sister. Haylee makes me want to be a better man. She believes in me, and I want to give her the world.

CHAPTER 26
Haylee

Me: *Remember to NOT come home tonight.*
Kyler: *What? I'm just outside the front door. You're kicking me out of my own place?*
Me: *Damn it, Ky! We talked about this! You said you wouldn't be home tonight.*
Kyler: *LMFAO. I wish I could've seen your face just then.*
Kyler: *I'm just kidding Hails. I just pulled up at my sister's house. Plan on sleeping on the luxurious sleeper couch, so you owe me one. The whole place is yours.*
Me: *Not cool. That was a major dick move, but you're the best.*
Kyler: *You two kids have fun.*

Kyler out of the apartment for the evening. *Check.* Romantic mood set with candles, music, and sexy lingerie. *Check.*

A home-cooked meal. *Ch—wait, what's that smell?*

"Oh no, dinner!" I race over to the oven and pull the door open, revealing a cloud of smoke.

Well, so much for a home-cooked meal. The kitchen is now filled with smoke. Reaching for the oven mitts, I take the pan of charred pot roast and place it on the stovetop. Now, when I say charred, I mean it went through hell and back. It was definitely dead.

"Well, it can't get any worse." As soon as I exhale, the smoke detector begins to beep.

Fuck! I throw my head back in frustration.

I look around and find the detector, but I can't reach it. Tonight is turning out to be awful. I just wanted to do something special for Zach. I sit on the floor against the island with my knees to my chest and listen to the chirping of the smoke detector.

"Haylee! Babe? Where are you?" I hear the front door slam shut and Zach's voice fill the apartment.

Zach crouches in front of me, cupping my face so that I look at him. My eyes fill with tears. "Baby, are you okay?"

I nod. Physically I am; mentally, I'm not so sure. I just wanted it to be perfect.

"First things first, let me turn the beeping off and open a window to air out the smoke. I'll be right back."

"I'm not going anywhere." I exhale and rest my head back on my knees and hug them tighter.

"What happened?" Zach sits down next to me, pulling me into his lap.

"I wanted to make tonight special. I worked it out with Ky so that we had the whole place to ourselves and had dinner all planned out, and it's all ruined."

He brushes a stray hair out of my face. "You tried to cook for me?"

I wipe the tears away and nod. His palm caresses the back of my head, bringing me closer to his chest. "I called your mom and she gave me her pot roast recipe that I know you love. I figured it would be easy since it all goes in one pan. Nope—I figured out how to fuck it up, and well, I guess I shouldn't be too surprised."

"It's the thought that counts?" he more so asks than says.

That forces me to laugh. He rises to his feet and helps me up.

He claps his hands together. "Now let's see if we can salvage any of your... Woah!"

Zach spots the burnt-to-a-crisp pan. If his eyes were any wider, they would be in the apartment above us. It would probably be better to just replace the pan instead of trying to clean it.

He bends over in laughter.

"Why are you laughing?" I shove his arm, but he continues to laugh.

He wipes the tears from his eyes. "I'm sorry, baby, but you're a terrible cook. I was also remembering when you tried to bake my sister's cupcake recipe for your mom's birthday, and you used salt instead of sugar in both the batter and frosting."

I cover my face with my hands in embarrassment. Again, I had just wanted to do something nice, that time for my mom. Dani had always made her birthday cake, and with Dani still missing, I wanted to try to give my mom something special.

"Aww, babe, come on, it's not *that* bad." Zach yanks my hands down and backs me up against the island before wrapping my arms around the back of his neck. His hands settle on my hips.

He closes the distance between us, and I allow myself to forget about the disaster that is this evening as his lips crash onto mine. When he sucks my lower lip into his mouth, I let out a soft whimper.

"How about you go take a nice relaxing bath, and I'll clean this?" He motions his hands to the mess behind us. "And order some takeout."

I Never Expected You

I rise up on my toes and press a brief kiss to his lips. "I'd like that."

"Now, go relax, baby." Zach smacks my ass gently.

Fifty minutes later, I emerge from the bedroom, changed into one of Zach's oversized T-shirts. My breath catches at the view in front of me. The coffee table is pushed to the side and decorated with the candles I had out for tonight. A blanket is laid out in front of the couch, just like on our first date.

An assortment of Chinese takeout is spread across the blanket. Zach sits there waiting for me with his back against the couch and one leg propped up. He looks just as delicious as the Chinese food. His eyes meet mine.

"Wow, you have no idea how sexy you look in my clothes."

I give a little twirl, and he smirks as I join him on the blanket.

"I mean you look sexy in *and* out of everything, but I love you best in my clothes. You look like mine."

I adjust onto my knees in front of him. "I *am* yours."

"And I'm yours. Now I say we eat this food and then..." He waggles his eyebrows. "I plan to take full advantage of having the place to ourselves and make you mine on every surface of this apartment."

I bite my lip in anticipation and clutch my thighs together, hoping I can make it through dinner before I take him up on his promise.

CHAPTER 27
ZACH

One year later...

Haylee smiles at me. "I am so proud of you, college graduate!"

I wrap my arm around the back of Haylee's chair and pull her close to me. She places her palm on my thigh and leans into my body.

"Thanks, baby girl. This will be you next year. We'll throw you a big party."

I can't believe I did it. I graduated college. I think back to the moment I got my acceptance letter to the University of Pennsylvania; I couldn't believe that I had even gotten in. Emmett and I were supposed to do this together. This morning I couldn't fight back the tears as I broke down in front of Haylee while getting ready for graduation. Em should have walked across that stage with me, my sister there to celebrate as well. But both weren't there. I didn't even know where to send a graduation announcement to Dani, and there was no surprise that she didn't return my calls or texts asking for her address so that I could send her something.

The past four years in college have been intense, some of the best and worst days of my life. While figuring out the worst ones out was easy, it was narrowing down the best days that was harder. There were too many to count, from falling in love with the most amazing girl sitting next to me and seeing not only our relationship grow, but I've got to watch her turn into this strong, caring, and badass woman. I think my love grew for her even more while she, Ky, and I were vacationing in New Orleans. Some guy came up to her in the bar and told her that he would guess her weight if she sat on his face. Before I could step in, she spun around and and threw a mean right hook. We got to talking to him, and surprisingly, Bennett and his buddy, Hunter, both became close friends. But it reminded me to never get on my girl's bad side again.

Our families are celebrating at a restaurant near campus. Kyler's mom and sisters have joined us as well. I look behind me and see Haylee's dad and mine standing over at the bar. Now is my chance.

"I'll be right back." Haylee looks up at me and puckers her full lips.

I lean down and press mine against hers. She turns and resumes her conversation with Kyler's sister Lauren.

"There he is! Our big college graduate." My dad's hand slaps my shoulder playfully.

"Thanks." I direct my attention to Brian standing next to him. "I was hoping I could talk to you." Not wanting to leave my dad out, I say, "You can stay too."

"What's going on?"

I wipe my sweaty palms on my dress pants. *Deep breaths, Zach.* Why am I so nervous about having this conversation?

"You seem nervous? You want a drink first?"

"Yes. No. I don't know. I mean, sure."

My dad gives me a strange look, trying to figure out what's

wrong while Brian orders three shots of Jameson. The bartender brings them over.

"To Zach."

We all clink our glasses together, and I quickly down the shot. Okay, with a little liquid courage I can do this. I clear my throat.

"Brian, you've known me my whole life. You've watched me grow up and know that sometimes I do things without thinking."

That earns a laugh out of both my dad and Brian. Okay, maybe I do things without thinking more than just sometimes.

"But this time, I have given this a lot of thought. Your daughter means more to me than anything in the world. I didn't think I could love someone as much as I love her. Wow, I sound as sappy as Emmett did." I let out a nervous laugh. "You know, he once told me that when I met *the girl*, she was gonna knock me on my ass, and shit, if he wasn't right. She is the other half of me; she makes me be a better man. With your permission, of course, I want to ask Haylee to marry me."

Everything about his girl makes me want to be a better man.

I look back and forth between my dad and Brian, almost expecting one of them to hand the other money just like they had when we had announced we were dating, but neither do. Both are sporting a happy smile.

My eyes meet Brian's. I see compassion, the same I see in his daughter. Shit, I could stare into them forever—Haylee's, not Brian's, of course. And that's exactly what I plan to do.

Brian places his hand on my shoulder, giving it a fatherly squeeze, his eyes now filled with unshed tears.

"Zach, you put a smile back on my baby girl's face. You make her happy."

We both turn and look back in the direction of the table,

where we see Haylee laughing, not seeing us, or at least she doesn't acknowledge us.

"You have always been a son to me, and I would be honored to make that official."

"What are you saying?"

"Maybe we should give that diploma back." My dad is full of jokes; all these years later, they're still not funny.

"Ha. Ha. Ha. I just want to make sure I understand. This is kind of a big deal."

"Zach, of course you have my blessing to ask her. I just ask one thing…"

Before he can finish, I feel arms wrap around me from behind, and I know those arms. Our conversation halts as to not give away what we were talking about.

"Mom says we can't order till you guys are back, and I'm starving."

With our hands interlocked, I run my ring finger over hers where one day soon she will wear my ring, I hope, letting the whole world know she is mine.

"Sorry, sweetheart, we were having a celebratory drink with Zach. We won't keep you waiting anymore."

"What was that all about?" Haylee leans on my arm as we follow dad and Brian back toward the table.

"Oh, you know." *Quick, think of something.* "They were asking me about the house."

Kyler and I are packing up the apartment this weekend and heading to the suburbs just outside of the city, where we found a three-bedroom rancher. The house is a middle ground between Kyler's and my jobs. I was offered a full-time job at the sports marketing firm I interned at last year, while Kyler will be working as a marketing manager at the mayor's office.

Haylee still has one year left of school, but somehow, I was able to convince her to say yes to moving in with us. Let's hope that I can get her to say yes on one other question. The third bedroom, we are going to convert into an office/guest room. It will be nice to have space for overnight guests in case any of our parents visit and want to stay over.

"I can't believe I'm moving in with you crazy assholes!"

"Oh, please. You pretty much live with us anyway. This will just be official. And all of your stuff will be kept in one spot instead of hauling it back it and forth between there and your dorm."

"Yeah, yeah, yeah." She rolls her eyes at me.

Once back at the table, I pull out her chair, but before she can sit down, I lean down and whisper in her ear so only she can hear, "You better watch it, baby girl, with the eye rolling. You may get a spanking for that later."

She turns her head. "Maybe I'm counting on it."

She takes her seat and looks up at me while she scoots the chair back in. She bites her lip and rolls her eyes yet again. She giggles to herself, and I have to tell my dick to knock it off at the mere thought of spanking her later. Hell, just the thought of touching her gets me hard.

After dinner, we are all enjoying the company and conversation discussing the house and summer plans when my phone vibrates. Luckily Haylee is in the bathroom because I look down and see it's her dad. I quickly open the text.

BRIAN: *We can finish our conversation back at my house. Let me know when works.*
ME: *Haylee is going out with Cami this weekend, so I can come down without her knowing.*
BRIAN: *Sounds good. See you then.*

I put my phone back in my pocket just as Haylee returns to her seat. Phew, that was close.

⸺

Two days later, Haylee is spending the day at the spa with Cami while I find myself pulling into her parents' driveway. I walk up and don't even get a chance to ring the doorbell before it opens, and I see Brian standing there.

"Sorry, I saw the Jeep pull up. Still is weird…" He trails off without continuing.

Fuck, maybe I should just sell that thing. He saw the same Jeep his son drove pull into his driveway.

"Come on inside." Brian moves out of the way, and I walk into the foyer. "How about we chat in my office?"

I follow behind him to the back of the house where his home office is.

"Here, have a seat." He extends his hand to one of the chairs in front of his desk while he walks around and opens a drawer.

He walks back around and takes a seat in the chair opposite mine.

"I told you that I would give you permission on one condition."

"Of course. We didn't get a chance for you to say what that is. I want you to know, sir, that no matter what it is, I'll do it. I want to spend the rest of my life with her; she means the world to me. I mean it."

Brian holds his hand up. "I know you do, and it's nothing crazy, so put those thoughts away."

He takes a deep breath and looks down at the small box in his hand that he had grabbed from his desk. "A long time ago, I had a talk with Emmett. I told him that when he was ready to put a ring on Dani's finger, he would get this ring. Not that we wanted them to rush anything, but come on, we all knew it would happen. This ring was my grandmother's ring."

He opens the box and turns it around to show a simple white-gold band with a diamond in the center with two purple stones on the sides of it. I don't know much about rings. I figured I would need to enlist Cami, Kate, or Lauren's help when I went to go pick out the ring.

"So back when...when...when I realized I would never get the chance to give this to my son to propose with, I knew that it would go to Haylee. I had hoped that one day, the man who wanted to spend his life with her would come to me, just like you are, and ask me for permission, and I could ask that you give her this ring. I had taken it to our jeweler downtown and had Emmett's birthstone added to the ring so that it would have a part of him for her."

Wow. I'm trying to hold back my feelings, but that is just deep.

"I...I don't know what to say." I choke out the words; I am utterly speechless.

"I understand. I know it's a lot. If you choose to not give this to her, then I will give it to her as her something old when she gets married."

"Oh no, I don't mean that. Of course I would be honored to give her this ring. I don't know what to say because this is... She is going to love this, Brian. It's going to mean so much. Did...did my sister know about this?"

He shakes his head. "Not that I know of."

Brian closes the ring box and hands it to me. As soon as my fingers graze the smooth velvet, I feel my best friend as if he were here with us.

This is real. This is really happening. I am going to ask Haylee Hanks to marry me.

Brian leans back in his chair. "So, tell me, any idea how you're going to pop the question?"

I laugh, settling back in my chair, and shake my head. "Not a damn clue."

CHAPTER 28
ZACH

Ten months later...

"He...hello?" I'm still half-asleep, and I don't even look to see who is calling. I hear silence on the other end. I clear my throat and speak again. "Hello?"

"Zach?" My breath gets caught in my throat. I'd know that voice anywhere. Now fully awake, I quickly sit to the upright position, not even concerned with waking a sleeping Haylee next to me.

"Dani?"

My voice is full of desperation. Is this real? I'm not sure why I'm asking—I know it's her. I only need confirmation that I'm not currently dreaming. I have had this dream over and over again and wake up missing her more.

"Dani, are you there?" *Fuck, please don't have hung up.*

Her voice is shaky, but she responds. "Yeah, I'm here."

I hear her begin to cry, and I wish I could hold her and tell her how happy I am to hear her voice. I don't know what this means, but if this is all that I get with my sister, then I'll take it. I need to keep her on the phone as long as possible.

I look over to Haylee and see that she is still sound asleep. Of course the one night we fall asleep early I get this call.

Thank God I didn't sleep through this. Who knows if she would have answered if I called back. I can't think like that.

I get up from the bed and quietly exit my bedroom. I walk down the hall to the living room and settle on the couch.

Dani still hasn't said anything else, but I know she hasn't hung up because I can hear her breathing. We sit there in silence, and you know what, I don't mind it.

"I didn't think you would answer."

"What?" I try not to raise my voice too loudly. "Why wouldn't I answer? Dani, you're my sister. Of course I would fucking answer." Pinching the bridge of my nose, I fight back my tears as I hear hers on the other end of the line.

"Where are you? Are you okay? Shit, I have had this conversation in my head over and over again for years, and now that I finally have you on the phone, I don't even know what to say."

She laughs. My sister *actually* laughs. Damn, I've missed that sound. "Well, that's funny because I've been sitting here for hours rehearsing what to say, and a few times I almost backed out from calling you altogether. But just hearing your voice, I know I made the right choice."

"I'm so happy you called."

"Me too. Zach?"

"Yeah, sis."

"I want to come home."

I let out a breath I didn't even realize I was keeping inside, or it is possibly the same breath I have been holding since we arrived back at my parents' house to discover she had packed up and left us.

"I want that too. I waited to so long to hear you say those words. Have you called Mom and Dad?"

"No, not yet." She hesitates, and I picture her either biting her lip or twirling her hair. "I was hoping I could come stay with you for a little bit and then take it from there maybe. Is that okay?"

"Of course. Dani, anything you need, I'll help with. Do you need me to get you? Where are you?"

"I'm up in a small town in New Hampshire."

"New Hampshire? Wow." I let out a light laugh.

Damn, I never would have figured my sister to move to the north and forever be cold. Winters in Maryland can be brutal, but damn.

"It'll take me a day or so to settle things up here and pack up. I can be there in a few days?"

"That's perfect. I'll set up space for you. Let me text you my new address. I live just outside Philly now."

"Oh shit, right, you would have graduated by now. Wow, I guess I missed a lot, huh."

"It's okay. You're coming home."

I am again met with her silence. Fuck. I need to make sure she doesn't back out of this.

"Dani?"

"Yeah, I'm coming home. I'll see you in a few days."

"Okay. And Dani?"

"Yeah?"

"If you need anything, you call, okay? I'll drop everything and come help."

"Okay."

"I love you, sis."

"Love you too."

Click. Haylee says those three words all the time, but to hear them from my sister, I can't even describe the feeling.

I open a text message to her and send her the address. Once it's sent, I decide to torture myself and scroll through all the hundreds of text messages left unanswered. I push that to the

I Never Expected You

back of my mind; all that matters is that she wants to come home. She *is* coming home.

I wipe the tears I finally had allowed to fall. I'm grateful Kyler isn't home to see me crying, although it wouldn't be the first time he had witnessed it. I slowly walk back to the bedroom and sit on the bed. I see that Haylee changed positions but no sign of her having woken up. Shit, Haylee. I never said anything about her to Dani. I guess I was just so overwhelmed by her calling.

I stand back up and walk over to the closet and pull out the box of ties. Inside I find the small black velvet box where the engagement ring I still have yet to give her sits. I've now tried four times to propose, and something always happens. It's like I'm reliving our first date all over again. The first time, it was just a coincidence, but multiple times, I know my best friend is fucking with me from the grave.

I open the ring box, making sure to block it from Haylee's view if she were to wake up. I look down at the diamond-and-amethyst ring that has been burning a hole in my pocket for months now. I can't wait for my girl to wear this proudly on her finger to show the our friends and family, the *world*, that she's mine.

My mind drifts back to my sister. She actually called—I can't get over it. How the hell am I going to tell her that while she was God knows where, I fell in love, and with her best friend at that? We'll be open and honest and say that we fell in love. Yeah, should be as simple as that.

I walk back to the bed and lie back down in hopes that I will be able to calm my thoughts and sleep will overtake my mind. I close my eyes and wait. I wait for hours, tossing and turning, but rest never comes. I lie on my side and watch Haylee sleep peacefully. A few times throughout the night, she makes almost a purring sound, and I'm half-tempted to wake her up and ask her what she is dreaming about, but I choose to let her sleep. At least one of us will be well-rested for tomorrow.

I look over at my phone and see it's already 5:00 a.m. Wow, how did that happen? I get up and decide to go for a run. I throw on my running clothes and shoes and grab the earbuds from my gym bag. When I walk outside, I feel the brisk morning air before sunrise. I pull up my running playlist on my phone and head out.

I run for as long as I can before I feel my legs start to give out. I don't want to have to call Haylee or Ky this early in the morning to come to pick me up because I overdid it. By the time I get back, I've run ten miles. I walk into the bedroom on the way to the shower and see Haylee hasn't moved. Good. I had hoped that my run would help me clear my head and figure out a way to not only tell Haylee that Dani called since I'm not sure how she'll react but to fill Dani in on all that she's missed. I also need to figure out what I'm supposed to tell my parents. Do I tell them she called? That she's going to be staying here? I can't break her trust and have them show up and bombard her.

I step out of the bathroom wrapped in only a towel as Haylee starts to stir.

"You're up early this morning."

"Yeah, I went for a run. Ended up running ten miles."

"Ten miles?" She reaches for her phone to see the time. "It's not even seven in the morning. How long have you been awake?"

I shrug. "A while."

I walk over to my dresser and grab a pair of boxers out of the drawer and sit back on the bed to put them on. Haylee crawls over and puts her arms around my shoulders, my back to her front.

I Never Expected You

"Are you okay, babe? You seem off. You didn't sleep well and then just ran ten miles. What's wrong?"

I shake my head. Her arms tighten, and she adjusts herself, wrapping her legs around my waist, almost as if I were giving her a piggyback ride. My mind reverts to the memory of carrying her around Baltimore last summer after we splurged on Maryland steamed crabs. The thought brings a smile to my face, and I run my hand up and down her leg in a soothing motion.

"What is it, then?"

I take a deep breath. "Dani called."

CHAPTER 29
Haylee

*D*ani called? Did I hear that correctly? No, maybe I'm still half-asleep and heard what I *wanted* to hear.

"I'm sorry, can you repeat that? I thought you said Dani called."

"I did."

Based on how tense he is and the serious look he's giving me over his shoulder, he isn't kidding. My hands drop from his body, and I stare at him. I begin to back up away from him.

"What? When? Is she okay? Wait, when did she call? Again, it's not even seven in the morning."

"Last night."

Why is he acting all calm about this? Dani called for the first time after all these years, and he's acting as if it isn't a big deal.

"Last night? And you're now just telling me?"

"You were asleep."

"And? Why didn't you wake me?"

"I'm sorry. I was...I don't know, processing it. I'm still trying to figure out if I dreamed it or if it really happened. I've looked at my phone close to ten times to make sure her name was on my call list. We had fallen asleep early, and I woke up when I heard my phone ring. I just answered it, and the moment I heard her voice, I just felt so relieved. I finally heard her voice,

Hails. I've been waiting for years to hear her voice again, and I finally did."

Is he for real right now? I am very happy for him and happy that something or someone knocked some fucking sense into my best friend, but at the same time all of the emotions I've felt and kept inside when she left are rising to the surface, ready to explode.

I soften my voice in hopes of preventing an argument before morning coffee. My mom always said nothing good ever happens before morning coffee.

"So, what did she want?" I decide now is as good a time as ever to get up out of bed. I make the bed while Zach searches for a shirt in the drawer.

"She wants to come home."

Completely perplexed, I ask, "Did she say why?"

"No, just that she wants to come home."

Home. This must be a joke. Home? Who is she and what has she done with my best friend? The same friend who left *home* without even looking. She abandoned us—abandoned *me*. When I needed her most, she up and left.

"Home? As in she's moving back to Annapolis?"

I walk over to my dresser and pull out a pair of jeans and a top. Zach doesn't answer.

"Zach?"

His eyes finally meet mine.

"No, she's actually going to stay here for a little bit. I told her I would set up the guest room for her."

As I pull up my jeans, I freeze before buttoning them. "What?! Are you kidding me right now? What does Kyler say about all this? She calls, and all is forgiven? What, are the four of us just going to play house?"

"Well, I don't know. We didn't talk much about her plans,

and I didn't say anything about having a roommate. I haven't seen Ky yet to talk to him about it, but, I mean, I'm sure he's cool with it."

I completely avoid the part where he made this decision without consulting the other people who live in this house.

"You didn't say anything about having a roommate, meaning Kyler? Or a roommate, meaning me?"

He steps up to me, running his thumb against my cheek. "I'm sorry. I was just so shocked when she called that I didn't think of what to say to catch her up on my life and all she missed out on. And then once she said she wanted to come home, I didn't ask why. I didn't even care. It was just the fact that she's coming back that I was focused on."

Do I mean that little that he wouldn't tell her? I feel the room beginning to cave in. I step back from him.

"Has she even called your parents? Do they know she's moving back?"

He looks down at the floor, pretending to push something around with his foot. I know that means no, and I sure as hell don't have any sort of call or text from her either.

"Okay, let me make sure I understand this. You're just going to let her waltz right back into your life as if she hadn't just left us all?"

"She's my sister, Hails. I would do anything to have her back."

It kills me to see him upset.

"Oh, and what, I don't understand that? Do you think I wouldn't give anything to see my brother or have anything but a one-sided conversation with him? Wow, you're just as selfish as she is."

He reaches out for me, but I yank my arm from his grasp.

"*No!*" I walk out of our room and head down the hallway.

I Never Expected You

"That's not what I meant, Hails, and you know it. It's just…"

I stop and turn to face him. "It's just what, Zach? Please enlighten me! Tell me how our situation is different." My voice catches in my throat as I fail to push the tears down. "You have wished every day that your sister, who fucking walked out on us all because her life was hard, would contact you or come home. Well, guess what, she lost her boyfriend, but I—I fucking lost my brother." I point toward the front door. "And he can't walk through that door or call one day out of the blue—he's gone *forever*. He can't come back. Don't you think I wanted to just escape from life at times? I love you so much, but damn it, my brother died, and my best friend just walked away when I needed her most. Who does that? And you're just going to stand there and defend her and welcome her with open arms? No. I can't."

I turn and head for my purse, which is hanging by the front door.

"Where are you going? We're supposed to head back to Annapolis."

"I know. I'll meet you there. I need space right now." I throw his own words back in his face. "You know, like you got last night after she called. Here is my *processing* it."

"Hails." He steps toward me, but I put my hand up in protest.

"Please don't follow me. I'll see you at your parents' house."

I drive to the one place I need to be, with the one person I need to be with. I hate that I blew up at Zach like that, but some days I hate that he doesn't understand. Yeah, we both lost our siblings, but case in point, his can call and come back home whenever she wants. Mine? Not so much.

I sit on the grass in front of my brother's grave and cross my legs under me.

"Hey, big bro. I guess you know who *finally* called, huh?" I snicker. "Of course you do. You know everything."

I pick at the grass around the stone.

"Why now? Why after all this time? I'm happy for Zach, I am. I want to see him happy, but is he seriously just going to let her waltz back in as if no time has passed? She left—she just up and left without a word. She's missed everything.

"She lost her boyfriend of four years, but fuck, I lost my brother from my entire life. I can't...I—" The tears flow freely down my cheeks, and I don't even bother wiping them. "You died, Em, and I needed her. I needed my best friend, and she fucking left, as if I didn't matter. I knew she would abandon me for you one day, but when you died, she chose your ghost over me.

"And she didn't just leave—she's refused every single text or call for three and a half years! How can I forgive her that? How do I forgive and forget? God, I hate this!"

I pull my legs from under me and drag them in front, wrapping my arms around my knees. I run my hands through my hair. There's no calming my voice.

"It's been four years without hearing your voice, and I want to hear it in real life, not a damn video. I want you to be the one calling me telling me that you're coming home. Why does Zach get to hear his sibling's voice after all this time and I don't? It's not fair! Am I being selfish? Maybe, but I want you to be here. Is that too much to ask?"

The cemetery seems to be a popular place today. I half expect one of the passing cars to be Zach's Jeep, but he got the message that I needed space—I needed this. Maryland spring is in full force early this year, which explains a passing car with its windows all rolled down. A familiar tune blares from their radio. I close my eyes remembering the last time I heard that song and allow the memory to take over. It was Thanksgiving 2011, the last time the four of us were together, at least in the living.

We had already finished dinner and gone our separate ways: Dad and Adam were in the living room watching football, Mom and Kelly were in the kitchen cleaning the last of the dishes and planning their Black Friday shopping itinerary I'm sure. Zach, Dani, Emmett, and I were on the Jacobses' front porch—Em and Dani on the swing, me in the rocking chair, and Zach perched on the railing. Conversation always came easy with us.

"Oh my God, have I told you about the new Bruno Mars song I heard on the radio the other day?" I adjusted myself on the rocking chair, pulling my legs under me.

"Woah!" Zach clutched his chest. "You're tellin' me that you girls listen to something besides Katy Perry?"

Dani and I both glared at him. Ugh, he could be such a jerk.

"Yes, asshole, we listen to other music. Maybe if you weren't too focused on getting in everyone's pants, you would notice."

"I don't want to get into your pants, there, Hanks," he spat back.

I narrowed my eyes at him. Ah! He was so infuriating.

Dani played the referee, holding her hands up. "Okay, you two, that's enough." She turned to me. "No, I haven't heard it yet. Do you have it?"

I pulled out my phone and loaded my iTunes.

"Yep, I just downloaded it the other day. I can't believe you haven't heard it."

"Sorry, I've been..." She looked up at Emmett with this look in her eye—gross!

Whatever she was about to say, I felt the vomit in my mouth.

He leaned in and hovered over her mouth before saying, "She's been preoccupied."

He then slammed his mouth on hers, and yep, I definitely tasted the vomit in my mouth. They were so overly cute; I couldn't stand it. I don't know, maybe I was just jealous of what they had. Yeah, I'd dated, sure, but I'd never had that "this is forever love" like they did.

"So anyway, about that song." I interrupted the make-out session happening before us.

I pressed Play and let the sound of Bruno Mars's "Count on Me" take over the front porch.

By the time the second verse began, Dani had jumped up from where she sat and yanked me to my feet. She danced with me jokingly just like we used to as kids when we watched our parents dance together.

Emmett stood, and I assumed that Dani would turn to dance with him, but she did the opposite.

She pressed her hand to his chest. "Uh-uh, you sit back down; I'm dancing with my bestie."

She turned back to me, and we continued to spin around the front porch. By the end of the song, we were both singing the lyrics, and Dani dipped me back for our grand finale. We both laughed uncontrollably.

"You two are ridiculous. I hope you know that." Zach laughed from where he joined Emmett on the front swing.

With one arm still wrapped around each other and the other on our hips, Dani and I looked at each other with big smiles.

"Silly brother, don't you know that it's always going to be me and Haylee against the world?" She turned and placed her forehead against mine. "No matter what. It's always going to be me and you. You're my best friend."

By the end of the weekend when the boys had to head back to

I Never Expected You

Pennsylvania, we were all singing the lyrics to "Count on Me." What could I say? It was a pretty catchy song, and I loved that it felt like it was written for me and Dani. Our friendship could face anything that was thrown our way.

I stood by Zach's Jeep and wrapped my arms around my brother as he kissed the top of my head.

"You coming with Dani next time she visits?"

"And be forced to hear you love fools getting it on or hang with that assclown?"

Zach heard me, which I meant for him to, and waved to me with his middle finger. I blew him a kiss in return.

I turned my focus back to my brother. "No, seriously, though. I'll see you in a few weeks when you get back. Big number five..." I said in reference to his and Dani's fifth anniversary next month. "...coming up."

He smiled, one that that the mere mention of his girlfriend put on his face, teeth showing, eyes shining. Ugh, and Zach had the nerve to call us ridiculous? Maybe he should have looked at those two instead.

"Yup, got it all planned out."

"Care to share with your favorite sister?"

His laughter vibrated his entire body, and he shook his head.

"Nope. Nice try though. You and Dani are thick as thieves; there are no secrets with you two. I seriously think Bruno Mars wrote that song for you guys."

He looked up and saw Dani walking toward us.

"Hey, sis, do me a favor and keep an eye on her for me, will ya?"

"I always do. I've got her for you. I promise."

With one last hug, I walked back toward the house and yelled over my shoulder, "Love you, big bro."

"Love you too, Hails. I'll see you soon."

Unfortunately, he wouldn't. The accident happened twelve days later, and then he was gone. I turn back to the headstone and laugh. Through my tears, I actually laugh.

"Really, Em? Is that one of your crazy signs?" There are little things throughout the years that have happened that I have convinced myself are a sign from Emmett from wherever he is.

"I hear you loud and clear, big bro. It's me and her against the world. I promised you I would keep an eye on her for you. I guess I haven't been doing the best job, but hey, that's not my fault." I look down at my phone and see eight texts from Zach.

Zach: *Hey, just checking in on you.*
Zach: *Are you okay?*
Zach: *I'm heading to my parents'. Please let me know you're fine.*
Zach: *Baby, I'm so sorry. I'm just all messed up that she called. I didn't mean how it came out.*
Zach: *I love you so much.*
Zach: *Please be careful. I hate that you left so upset...that I am the reason you're upset.*
Zach: *I just got to my parents'. I need to see you.*
Zach: *I was stupid. I should've told her right away. I wasn't thinking. We will tell her when she gets here.*

"It's funny; you'd never believe this Zach was the same guy we grew up with. He makes me happy, you know."

I picture my brother having a smart-ass retort to that, but of course, it doesn't come.

"I am happy for him—I truly am. I just need to figure this all out. I in no way want to hide us, but I worry that if she comes back and we throw this all at her, she may be overwhelmed and just up and leave again. We need to be smart about this." I shift in the grass where I'm sitting. "If you have any ideas, now would be the time for you to start sending those signs."

Buzz. Buzz.

I look down expecting to see Zach's name, but instead, I see Cami. She is supposed to be preparing to head out of the country. Why on earth is she texting me?

CAMI: *Hey, wankpuffin! Any chance you can keep an eye on things at my apartment while I'm gone? I was supposed to have a friend of Ryan's stay there, but they bailed last minute.*
ME: *Not a problem! Hey, would it be cool if instead of just checking on things, I just stayed there for a little while?*
CAMI: *What's going on? Trouble in paradise for you and Hottie McHotterson?*

Ugh. I wish she would stop calling him that. All these years later, I had hoped that she would start calling him Zach, but nope!

ME: *No, things are great. I'll explain it all later. You're the best.*
CAMI: *Let's meet up before we leave, and I'll give you the key.*
ME: *Sounds great.*
CAMI: *Kisses! Talk to you soon. Xo*

"Well, looks like you came through again, big bro. I have to go and tell Zach about my plan. I promise to look after her." I push off the ground and stand, brushing off the grass that stuck to me. I lean down and kiss the headstone. "Love you, big bro. I'll see you soon."

CHAPTER 30
ZACH

The drive from Philly to Annapolis was not a pleasant one. It was spent in silence as I relived the last twelve hours over and over in my head. My mind has been a mess ever since Dani called last night. Add the little sleep and my fight with Haylee, and I'd say I'm a recipe for disaster today. I hate seeing Haylee upset; it kills me inside. Especially to know I am the reason behind it. She asked for space, and I knew I had to give it to her, no matter how much it killed me. I did this, so I needed to give her what she wanted.

I should have never said what I said; I didn't mean it. My head was reeling from the newfound information that my sister wanted to come home. I mean, of course, I have spent the last few years begging to hear my sister's voice, but I didn't mean for it to come out the way it did. I know Haylee has been asking for the same thing. I could never forget our situations.

As I park in the driveway of my childhood home, I contemplate waiting here in the Jeep for Haylee to arrive so we can walk in together, but what if she doesn't show up? She said she would be here, but I don't even know where she's gone. I put on my best brave face as I approach the front steps, wishing and praying that the expression on my face won't give everything away.

I Never Expected You

I enter the colonial-style home and am greeted by my mother coming down the stairs.

"Hi, honey."

"Hi, Mom."

I lean in and kiss her cheek.

"Where's Haylee?"

I clear my throat. "She had some things to take care of. She should be here shortly." *I hope.*

"Oh, okay. I'm sure she'll be here soon. That girl is always on the move." She continues down the hall.

Good, she bought it; now I just have to hope that Haylee does keep her word and show up.

I pull my phone out of my pocket and check it for what seems to be the millionth time since she stormed out this morning. Why hasn't she responded to any of my texts? An unnerving feeling settles in my chest as I think of all the unanswered texts from my sister over the years.

No, stop thinking like that, Zach. She is nothing like Dani in that regard. Get your head out of your ass.

As I go to pull up her contact and call her, my dad and Brian come around the corner from the kitchen.

"Zach! Come join us. Your mother and Natalie are bringing in some appetizers and lemonades. Sit."

My dad motions to the couch, so I join them in the living room and take a seat. I stare out the front window in hopes of seeing her blue Honda Civic pull into the driveway. My leg won't stop bouncing on the ground.

"Son, you okay?" I jump at the sound of my father's voice. "You look like you have a lot on your mind."

"Is it finally the moment? Are you going to pop the question? That ring must be burning a hole in your pocket. I can't believe you haven't asked her yet. You need to get down on one knee and do it." Brian light-heartedly jokes, but I know that he is as anxious as I am for me to ask her.

I scoff. "Trust me, it's not for lack of trying. Something always seems to come up. But no, that's not it."

If only it were as simple as asking my girl to spend the rest of our lives together—that is a cakewalk compared to this. How am I going to explain to my parents that after three and a half years, my sister has *finally* called out of the blue? How do I explain that she's coming to stay with us? I have no clue whether she would or had called them yet.

Just then, Mom and Natalie walk in with a tray of lemonade and a plate of assorted finger foods. They are always going above and beyond for these get-togethers. I think they like to keep busy.

My mom hands me a glass of lemonade before taking a seat next to me. I take a rather large swig to calm my nerves. As I go to place it down on the table in front of me, I almost knock it over. I quickly recover and wipe my sweaty palms on my pants. Damn, did they crank the heat up in here or something?

"Sweetheart, are you okay?" My mom places a hand on my jittery leg.

Okay, it's now or never, before I completely ruin our day with anxiety. Just as I go to open my mouth, the front door flies open.

"I'm sorry I'm late, everyone."

I look back out the front window and see Haylee's car parked next to mine. How did I miss the sound of the car in the driveway or the driver's-side door shutting? I am quick on my feet, rushing to her as the front door closes. I reach for her, and she comes willingly into my embrace. I hold her tight as she buries her head in my chest.

"Oh, thank God you're okay. I'm so sorry, baby. I wasn't thinking. I was a fucking idiot."

I pull back and take that time to run my hands over her face, brushing her hair out of her face. My girl is perfect, though when her eyes meet mine, I see that they are puffy and red-rimmed. It breaks my heart a little more knowing that I upset her so much.

"Are you okay?"

She smiles softly at me and, just barely above a whisper, says, "Yes. I'm okay now. I just had to step away from the situation for a little bit."

"Where did you go? You had me so worried."

"You had a chance to talk to your sibling; I needed time to talk to mine. It's okay though. I came up with a plan. I'll explain it all later, but I think first thing's first: we need to tell everyone she's coming home."

I run my hands over my face, expelling a loud breath, knowing everyone is just in the other room. Haylee steps close, pressing her body against mine. She rises on her toes, her mouth now inches away from my mine.

"It'll be okay. I'm here. We're going to do this together. You and me against the world, okay?" She presses her lips against mine.

We pour so much emotion into that kiss, as if I'm apologizing for my words earlier and she's giving me strength to do this. When we break apart, I grab her hand and lace our fingers together. I bring our joined hands to my lips. Pressing a soft kiss to her knuckles, I tilt my head toward the living room.

"Come on. Everyone is waiting for us."

We walk hand in hand to the living room, and I expect to see everyone deep in conversation except everyone is staring at us with mouths open. The silence and tension in the room is ready to explode.

My father is the first to speak. "I'm sorry. Could you repeat what you said, Haylee?"

I swallow hard, and my grip on Haylee's hand tightens.

Oh, fuck.

CHAPTER 31
Haylee

Well, I'm not sure how Zach planned to tell them that Dani called, but I don't think it was them overhearing it from my big mouth. At least the secret is out now. Silence fills the room as our parents try to process what Zach just told them. Zach and I are currently sitting on the couch across from our parents.

My hand hasn't left Zach's since we walked into the room. I run my thumb over his skin, trying to reassure him. Nerves and anxiety surround him.

"My baby girl is coming home?" Kelly asks. Her voice is shaking, and Adam tries to comfort her with his arm around her.

Zach's leg bounces nervously, and I place my hand on his thigh.

He briefly looks up to me and smiles weakly before turning back to his parents. "Yeah, Mom."

All at once, questions come flying out of nowhere.

"Is she safe?"

"Is she okay?"

"Where is she?"

"Why didn't she call us?"

"Does she need anything?"

"How long will she be staying?"

My head is spinning from everyone speaking at once. My grip tightens on Zach.

I interrupt the slew of questions. "Okay, slow down. One question at a time."

I rub Zach's back in a circular motion. I'm not used to being the one put together. He is usually the strong one. But that's just how we work; if he needs my strength, I will be there for him, and vice versa.

"Go ahead, babe."

Zach clears his throat. "She called last night. She said she is living in some New Hampshire town and is tying up some loose ends there before heading this way. I offered her the guest room for as long as she likes."

The tears are falling steadily down both my mom and Kelly's faces. This is a conversation we all have only dreamed of the past four years. I would never have thought this would become a reality; I am sure that is how they feel too. Adam squeezes Kelly's shoulder, bringing her closer to his chest.

"When is she supposed to arrive?" my dad asks as he rubs his hand up and down my mother's arm.

"Monday."

Kelly jumps to her feet. "Well, we should be there when she arrives, right? We have to be."

Oh, no.

Side conversations begin, and I can hear my mom and Kelly making plans to come to the house. No, this just won't do. This is not the right way to go about this. Smothering her is only going to make her run again. Like Emmett reminded me, Dani and I were a team. This isn't what she would have wanted.

My voice is stern and direct. "I'm not sure that's the best idea."

I Never Expected You

Everyone turns their attention to me, confusion all over their faces. Kelly sits back down.

"I just think there's a reason she reached out to only Zach." I hate it just as much as everyone else that I haven't heard from her either, but now is not the time to hash out those feelings. "But I know my best friend, and there's a reason she chose *now* to come home finally."

"Did she indicate any reason?" Adam runs his hands over his face in distress.

At that moment, it's as if I see a glimpse of Zach in the future. Not only do they look alike, but Zach and his dad's mannerisms are so similar.

Zach, who has grown quiet yet again, responds, his voice just above a whisper. "No."

I chime back in. "All I'm saying is that we have no clue where her mind is now. If she's still in the same mindset as when she left, we don't know. I think if we bombard her or smother her by us all showing up, she may just leave again. And I, for one, am going to do everything in my power to keep her here. I think it should just be Zach."

"Well, how will that work? She's going to see that you live there too obviously. How *did* Dani react to the news of you two?" My mother's words sting a bit as I flash back to our fight this morning.

My gaze turns to Zach. He exhales loudly. "I was so shocked that she called, it didn't actually come up."

"What didn't come up?"

"Me."

Their expressions go from sadness to shock.

"I know. I know. But I couldn't believe I was actually talking to my sister—I didn't mean to overlook that."

He turns his body to face mine on the couch and reaches up

to cup my cheek, and I lean into his touch. "I'm so sorry, baby. I know I hurt you, and I'm sorry."

The tears I've been holding back this entire conversation begin to fall.

"You are the most important person in my life, and I'm not going to keep us a secret. We're going to tell her."

Okay, Haylee, time to tell him the plan. Just rip the Band-Aid off. He might not like this, but it's for the best.

"No, we're not."

This time it's Zach who flies off the couch. "What the hell are you talking about?"

"Zachary Jacobs, you watch your tone, young man," his mother scolds.

He holds up his hands in defeat, but he doesn't sit back down.

"We're not going to tell her. At least not yet."

"Are you insane?" I can see the tension rippling through his body.

Out of the corner of my eye, I catch our parents rising from their seat and exiting the room. *Assholes.* But I'm glad they did leave. This wasn't exactly how I had planned to tell him.

I pat the couch next to me for him to sit down. He continues to stand, holding my gaze.

Deep breaths, Haylee. He will understand.

"Do you trust me?"

His head snaps in my direction. His brows furrow and his forehead scrunches.

"What? Of course I do. Why would you ask me that?"

"Sit."

I adjust myself on the couch so I am now facing him. "So, remember how Cami was going out of town?"

"Yeah, for a few weeks, right?"

I nod. "Well, she asked if I would just check in on things while she was gone and said it was cool that I just stay there instead."

Zach goes to protest, and I hold up my finger at him before continuing.

"It's not for forever, just at first. Cami's apartment isn't that far from the house, and we can pretend that it's back in our early dating days when I still lived in the dorms. It'll be okay, I promise." I plead with my eyes to accept this.

Zach reclines back on the couch, stretching his legs out, and runs his hands over his face. I pull his hands down from his face.

"Let's just let her adjust."

He leans forward, placing his elbows on his knees. "I don't like this."

"I know, baby. I know." I rub circles on his back to soothe the tension.

I push to my feet and hold out my hand for him. He takes it, wrapping his long fingers around mine, and rises before pulling me into his arms. I melt into him. It's hard to believe it was just this morning we were fighting. I look up at him and rise on my toes to brush my lips gently against his.

"Are you sure about this? I think my sister will understand."

"I'm sure. And I'm sorry that my big mouth is the reason they found out."

A devilish smirk erupts on Zach's face. "Hey, I *love* that big mouth of yours."

I whack him in the chest and groan. "Perv!"

I turn in the direction of the kitchen, but am quickly pulled back into Zach's arms with my back to his front. I feel his stubble against my cheek.

"And it's fine. Honestly, I still hadn't figured out how I was going to tell them, so thanks for saving me."

Zach and I enter the kitchen to find everyone around the island quietly talking. Kelly is holding a photo. Once I'm closer, I see that it's a photo of all of us at graduation, the last picture we have of Dani. She looks up from the picture with tears in her eyes.

"So now what do we do?"

Zach goes to open his mouth, but Adam speaks first. "Now we wait."

Now we wait.

THIS HAS BEEN THE LONGEST DAY EVER. AS I PULL INTO the driveway, I just want to curl up in bed with Zach and sleep for days, but I know that is not an option. I somehow beat him home, but I know he is just minutes behind me. Once inside, I throw my purse and keys on the coffee table and begin taking down the photos of Zach and me over the years, leaving the empty nails in their place.

"So you're really doing this? You're just going to pretend that, what, this isn't our life? That we aren't together?"

I turn to face Zach, and distress is written all over his face.

"Zach, it's not like that."

"Please, Hails, tell me what it's like, because I'm having a tough time understanding this."

I step up to him and brush my knuckles along his cheek. I thought we had settled this back at his parents' house. I love him so much more though, knowing that he doesn't want to hide us.

"This isn't something I want, but…"

"Then let's not do it. Let's just put these back on the wall." He reaches for the photos in my hand. "And when she arrives in a few days, we are both here, ready to face the world."

"Baby, I just need you to trust me, okay? Can you please do that? This isn't easy for me; trust me. I've spent the past few years without my best friend, and as much as I love you, sometimes I just needed her. For all the moments we missed, I need to give her time and not give her a reason to run." My voice begins to break.

Zach sets the photos down on the end table, and his arms encompass me. "All right, Hails, we'll do this."

He dips his head, claiming my lips eagerly. When we part, I am breathless. He scoops me into his arms and carries me to the bedroom.

"What are you doing? I need to pack up my stuff."

"Nope. If you're going to make me spend my nights alone in bed, then I better make this night count." He kicks the door shut.

I'm greedy for his touch, and who am I to deny him what he wants? I've spent almost three years sleeping next to this man. I know it'll be an adjustment for both of us, but I need to remember this is for the best and it's not for forever. I'll be back in our bed before we know it.

CHAPTER 32
ZACH

I roll over and reach out in hopes of pulling Haylee closer to me only to find her gone already. She was serious, wasn't she, about this. I can't believe she just woke up and left. Why didn't she wake me? I push up on my forearms, and something on her pillow catches my attention—a note.

Hey,
See what this is? A note! You should learn about those sometime, so when people wake up and you're gone, they won't freak out. :-P

Years later and we are still not past this one mistake I made? True, it almost cost me everything, so yeah, I guess we are still bringing it up. I cringe at the memory of that asshole Chad's arm around her and start to crumple up the note. Oh, shit. I read on.

I left early before you could try to convince me more to stay. Just kidding. I met Cami to get her key and get her to show me a few things.

Here, I thought you could sleep with this shirt, maybe put it on your pillow and snuggle with it. Just don't do anything weird with it. Anyway, I'm not far, and I promise you one day you will understand why this is for the best. Wow, I wrote a damn novel. Turn the page over so I can finish this up. How are you still sleeping while I write this anyway?

I turn the note over and laugh at her sad attempt at humor.

I love you.
XO,
Hails

I bring the T-shirt to my face, and fuck, it does smell like her. It totally wouldn't be weird if I put that on her pillow and snuggled it, right? My dick aches for release, but that can wait—coffee first. I need to set up the other room for Dani, and I guess I should probably let Ky know what's going on and see if it's cool that she stays here. I stand and throw on a pair of gym shorts over my boxers and grab a shirt from the dresser.

When I enter the living room, Kyler is standing there with the most confused look on his face.

"Hey, you wanna explain to me why I just helped Hails pack her car up with her shit earlier while you were asleep? Did you guys have a fight or something? Were you a dick to her?"

I throw my hands up in innocence. Of course he would assume that, if something like that had happened, it would be my fault. Hell, who are we kidding, it totally would have been.

"We had a fight, but no, that's not actually about that." I tilt my head in confusion while I think. "Well, it's kind of about that. Fuck. I need coffee first though."

Kyler follows me into the kitchen.

"Everything okay? You're kind of freaking me out here, Zach."

I fill my mug with coffee and extend my hand to the stools at the island.

I sip my coffee and can feel his eyes burning a hole through me.

"My sister called."

CHAPTER 33
ZACH

As if my nerves weren't already shot today, basically anything that could go wrong today has.

Sleep through the alarm. *Check.*

Get caught up in a late meeting. *Check.*

Sit in traffic. *Check.*

I contemplated taking the entire day off to make sure I was home when Dani arrived, but I had a few meetings with clients that I couldn't reschedule. Staying busy at work was a good idea though, that is until now.

My nerves were high all day as I anticipated my sister's arrival home. It's been three and a half years. What is she like now? Is she different? Will I even recognize her?

All of these questions and more ran through my head, keeping me awake till four in the morning, only to finally fall asleep and sleep through my morning alarm two hours later.

When I spoke to Haylee earlier today, she reassured me that it would all be okay and just to breathe. She is my rock in life, keeping me sane and together. I just wish she would be at home with me when Dani arrives.

"Shit!" I yell as I slam on my brakes once again.

I hate that people don't know how to drive in traffic. I look down at the clock on the radio. Dani should be arriving soon.

Just what we need—Dani arrives and no one is home. What's keeping her from running then?

I grab my phone from the cupholder beside me and dial Kyler's number. I pray that he is home. The phone rings and rings before his voicemail picks up. At the beep I leave a message and cross my fingers he gets it in time.

"Hey, Ky. I got stuck at work, and traffic is a nightmare. If you're home when my sister arrives, can you let her in and I don't know, entertain her? I should be home soon. Thanks." *Click.*

I'm sure he can hear the stress in my voice.

Over the weekend, Ky proved how epically awesome he is by being cool with Dani staying with us for a little bit. He even helped me make the guest room a little more comfortable for her. He didn't pry about our phone conversation and what prompted her to decide to come home. I think he could tell that alone was overwhelming to me. He has been here from the day she left and has seen what we all have gone through.

My grip on the steering wheel tightens as I drive through traffic. My mind races, wishing Haylee would be there to calm me down. My sister. My sister will most likely be at my house when I arrive. I have dreamed of this day for so long.

How long is she going to stay? What happens if she leaves again? How will she react to Haylee and me? Can I really keep this from her?

My thoughts keep me busy, and before I know it, I'm turning onto our street. My heart jumps out of my chest as I see Dani's SUV parked in front of the house. I pull in to the driveway next to Kyler's truck, thankful he was home and hopefully got my voicemail and wasn't caught off guard by her arrival.

My phone buzzes as I turn off the ignition to the jeep.

I Never Expected You

HAYLEE: *Hey, babe. Ky texted that she was there. It'll be fine. I love you.* XOXOXO

Could this woman be any more perfect? I send a quick response, anxious to get inside.

ME: *Wish you were here. Love you too. I'll call you later.*

I grab my workbag and jacket and make my way up the pathway. I take one last breath before opening the front door. In front of me, I finally see her. Dani is standing in front of the wall Haylee had decorated with a bunch of photos from over the years. She hasn't noticed me standing in the doorway yet, so I take this time to take her in. She looks the same, just thinner, and from her profile, still sad. It's when I notice the photos she is staring at that I choose to break her from her trance.

"Holy shit, Dani, you're actually here!"

She turns around, surprised, and I race to her, scooping her up in my arms. I thought maybe I might have dreamed the entire thing, from the phone call the other night to Haylee moving out to now, but as I hold my sister in my arms, I know that it wasn't a dream. *She is here.*

I pull back and place my hands along her cheeks to look her over. Still the same sister; I just notice the emotion written all over her face. I want to remember everything about the version of the girl in front of me, just in case this is only temporary. *God, I hope it's not.*

I pull her over to the couch and take a seat. "Have you been here long?"

She shakes her head. I notice how she still looks around the room—guess it might be weird for her realizing I'd grown up while she was gone.

"Your *roommate* let me in."

I don't miss how she accentuates the word roommate. I guess she figured out one of the two pretty big details about my life now that I had left out.

"Oh, you met Ky. He's a good dude. We met freshman year of college. We hit it off right away."

Of course, if she had stuck around, she would know that. In the few months she was actually here, she was so closed off that I felt like I would crush her should I try to talk to her about my personal life. Not that I think she would have even paid attention.

Dani's lip visibly begins to tremble, and I fear that I said the wrong thing. Her focus goes back to the wall, and I realize where her mind has drifted. *Emmett.* I go to say something, but thankfully Kyler chooses that time to walk into the living room.

"Hey, man, you're home."

I nod.

"You headed out to—"

I quickly cut off his asking if I was going to see Haylee tonight since I had been over at Cami's the last two nights visiting. "Nah, I'm home tonight to catch up with Dani."

I shift on the couch to face my sister. "Pizza for dinner work for you?"

She nods.

"Ky, you want to join?"

Since we're all going to be roommates, they can spend some time getting to know each other. However, Ky reaches for the keys on the coffee table and heads toward the front door, slipping his shoes on.

"Thanks, rain check. I'm headed out to meet the twins. I'll catch you both later."

I remember a time when I was jealous of his relationship

with his sisters; it was something both Haylee and I missed out on these days, a relationship with siblings. Of course, she didn't have a choice with hers leaving; mine did.

"Nice to meet you, Dani. Welcome home." He closes the door behind him, and I catch the disgusted look on my sister's face.

I can't help but laugh. "The twins are his older sisters, Lauren and Kate. They live here in town. They usually meet once a week for dinner. Sometimes they come out for karaoke night, so you might be able to meet them soon."

My sister's eyes go wide, but I'm unable to get a read on her. Is she overwhelmed with finding out that I have a roommate or that I want her to get out and meet people? Maybe I should have kept my mouth shut about that part. Fuck, if she's overwhelmed with the idea of Kyler living here, I wonder how she's going to be once she finds out Haylee lives here too.

I slap my thighs and rise off the couch, extending my hand to help her up. "Come on, I'll give you the tour and show you the guest room. It's yours for as long as you like. I'll order a pizza, and we can get you settled and catch up. Still prefer ham and pineapple?"

"Sounds great."

As I make my way around the house, showing Dani around, my heart breaks a little as I take notice of the few of Haylee's things that are missing: the photos on the wall Dani was observing earlier—I'm surprised she didn't question the empty nails; the blanket on top of her favorite chair; and whatever crazy romance book Lauren has got her reading now, both gone.

"Well, here it is. Feel free to do whatever you want with it. And then next door is your bathroom that you'll share with Kyler. I hope that's okay."

She nods, but I see the apprehension on her face.

"Let me run and change out of these work clothes, and I'll help you unload the car." I leave her sitting on the bed, looking around.

Once safely inside my bedroom, I breathe for the first time. My sister is finally home.

CHAPTER 34
Haylee

In an attempt to distract myself from things out of my control, I lie on my stomach across Cami's bed with my textbooks open and a rerun of *How I Met Your Mother* playing in the background. But no distraction can keep my gaze fixated on anything but my phone. I haven't heard from Zach since he had gotten to the house. That has to be a good sign, right? I wonder how things are going back home.

Is she comfortable?
What does she look like?
Is she going to stay?
How did things go when she met Ky?
Did she ask about me?
Did Zach slip up about us?

I hate that I'm not there, but this was the right choice. I just have to sit and wait to hear from Zach. He and I are a team, through the good times and the bad. No matter what, we are always there for each other, but this is turning out to definitely be more difficult than I thought it would be when we came up with this plan. Maybe we should have just been a united front from the beginning.

Fingers crossed that the curveball of having a roommate doesn't spook her into running again. I adjust myself on the bed, ready to dive right back into homework, when my phone rings.

Even after almost three years, my heart still skips a beat when I see *his* name appear.

"Hey, I didn't expect to hear from you for a while."

"Hey, baby." The tension in his voice from earlier is long gone, and I breathe a sigh of relief. "Yeah, Dani went to bed early, so I'm just sitting here on the couch."

I roll over onto my back, and I imagine my teenage self laughing at me for being in almost the exact pose that I would have been in talking on the phone back in the day, just this time it's with a different Jacobs.

"She's really here? This all wasn't a sick joke?" My voice catches.

"Yeah, she is. Of course, I was running late, and Ky let her in." He snickers before letting out a small sigh, and I picture him relaxed on the couch, legs stretched out and running his hand over his face. If it were any other situation, I would be curled up on the sofa right there with him.

"And how did that go?"

He chuckles. "Well..." He pauses. "That seemed to go okay, but she totally called me out on not telling her that I had a roommate."

Oh the irony, that Kyler isn't the only roommate and surprise there. I wonder how she will react.

"Luckily, he was going out with Lauren and Kate, so I got some one-on-one time with her."

"What did you guys do tonight?"

"Just ate pizza, and I helped her get settled a little. She doesn't have many boxes, so honestly, I don't know if she's planning to stay that long. I told her she could stay as long as she wants, and she seemed to be okay with that. I'll tell you this, she loved the kitchen."

I grinned. "No doubt. I bet her wheels were turning for sure at all the delicious things she could make." My stomach starts to grumble at the thought of her baking treats.

"Yeah, I have a feeling that if she does stick around, we might need to up our gym time."

I roll my eyes at his comment. Like he would ever be anything but fit. The man lives at a gym. I'm just about to ask the million-dollar question of *why now* when I hear muffled talking in the background. *Shit, is he talking to her?* I freeze at the thought.

"Hey, man, how was dinner?"

Okay, clearly not Dani. Must be Ky.

Zach laughs in the background, and I pull the phone back from my ear. "Hey! What's going on? I'm missing everything."

"Ky sends his love, babe."

Yeah, why do I have a feeling that is not actually what he said? Those two are something else. I hear some more mumbling into the phone and take that time to close my books and set them back on the nightstand. I think it's safe to say that I won't be getting any more work done.

"You still there?"

I stretch out on the bed against the pillows. "Yeah, I'm here."

Cami's apartment is nice, but it's not home.

Silence takes over the call as we both listen to the calming sounds of our breathing. There's nothing more I want now than to be wrapped up in Zach's arms.

He's the first to speak. "I miss you."

I choke back the emotion trying to fight me. "I miss you too."

"Hey, hold on." I wait, and moments later Zach returns. "Sorry I heard a commotion in the hallway, but when I got there both the bathroom and the guest room doors were closed, so I don't know what it was. Weird. Anywho, let me walk to the bedroom." I hear the door click.

Rolling to my side, I prop my head on my elbow. "So, did she say where she's been, what she was up to, and what brought her home?"

"Yeah, it's kind of an interesting story actually. She said there had been a few times over the past few years that she thought about coming home and had even gone as far as packing up her apartment, but just couldn't do it."

I hate that my best friend was in such a dark place that she felt couldn't reach out to us. We would've helped her through it —hell, we still all have our moments. It definitely has not been easy, that's for sure.

"So, what changed about this time? What made her call?"

"Well, she had a dream that gave her a feeling she couldn't shake, and remember that Bruno Mars song we were all obsessed with that last Thanksgiving we were all together? She said she kept hearing that everywhere. After hearing it for like a week straight, she finally decided to press 'send,' and well, here we are."

I shoot up from the bed, my hand covering my mouth in disbelief.

"What? Did she say that?" My voice raises.

"Say what?" He seems a little panicked by my extreme reaction.

How do I explain that of all songs she kept hearing, I heard it too? Was that my brother's way of bringing her home? Okay, those are goose bumps up my arm. I squeeze my eyes shut and allow the tears to fall.

"Hold on. Zach, say that again. You said that she kept hearing 'Count on Me' by Bruno Mars, and *that* made her call home?" I begin to breathe heavily.

Is this really happening? My hand runs through my hair before clutching to my chest.

"Hails? What's wrong? You're kind of scaring me, baby girl."

"No." I shake my head as if he can see me right now. "It's just that the morning we fought after you had spoken with her and I went to the cemetery to talk to Em, I heard that song."

"Woah, what the fuck?"

"Right? What are the odds? That's just a coincidence, right?"

He blows out a deep breath. "I don't know, babe. That's pretty crazy."

I just can't wrap my head around this.

"Maybe it was my brother's way of finally bringing her home to us."

CHAPTER 35
Zach

"Whoa! What happened in here?" Entering the kitchen, I find Kyler dumping a dustpan of broken glass into the trash can. I set my keys and workbag on the counter before stalking to the fridge.

Jackpot! Leftovers of my sister's veggie lasagna. I hadn't planned to miss dinner tonight, but I got caught up with files on my desk after another day of nonstop meetings. Nothing better to relax with after a long day than good food, cold beer, and snuggling with my girl. The first two I can easily accomplish especially with my sister's talents in the kitchen. The latter? Well, Haylee has a late class tonight anyway, so I couldn't even stop by the apartment to see her.

I open two beers and hand one to my best friend. I wonder what broke?

"Care to explain?" I ask as I tip my fork in the direction of where the dustpan and broom sit next to the trash can. I shove the fork in my mouth and have to bite back a moan as to how good this is, even cold. I sure have missed my sister's cooking and baking. Hmm, speaking of Dani. Where is she? I know she's home because one, her SUV is outside, and two, she never goes anywhere.

Kyler shakes his head as if he is unsure what happened.

"Honestly, man, I don't have a clue. I mean, your sister and I had a nice evening chatting, she was standing there doing the dishes, and I just had to try one of those amazing cupcakes she made. That shit is heaven, like borderline orgasmic."

I mentally high-five myself at the thought of my sister's cupcakes. I'm going to have to step it up at the gym with her living here. But that still doesn't explain the broken glass.

Ky continues. "I even confessed my undying love for the damn thing, telling the cupcake how much I loved it. The next thing I know, Dani dropped the Pyrex dish, and it shattered everywhere. It scared the shit out of me. I ran over to her, but it was like she was paralyzed. It took me a few minutes to drag her out of the state she was in. She ended up cutting her hand."

What the fuck? I set the leftovers container on the counter.

"What? Is she okay?" My heart begins to race.

"Yeah, it was just a little cut. I tended to the wound, and she ended up going to bed." Okay, that makes sense why it's so quiet. "I guess it just slipped out of her hands, but her reaction to it...it was strange."

I'm not sure I'm following him. I tilt my head in confusion, but this whole situation is a little weird.

"What exactly did you say to the cupcake?" I chuckle while taking another bite of lasagna.

Kyler joins in my laughter. "I don't know, man. 'I love you, cupcake' or something."

I exhale loudly, placing my elbows on the island and my head in my hands.

"Shit. No wonder she dropped it," I mumble under my breath.

"Am I missing something here?"

My eyes meet his, and once again I'm reminded of the fact

that Ky doesn't know things of our past. I see the same innocent look when he asked me that first night who Em was. How was he supposed to know that the exact phrase he said was what Emmett used to tell Dani? She was his Cupcake. I should go check on her and make sure this isn't a setback and she is planning to run.

"It's not your fault, Ky. You didn't know."

"That she doesn't believe in love at first bite?" Kyler asks jokingly.

More pieces of our crazy life are put together for him.

"Emmett. Emmett used to call her Cupcake." I pause, biting back the emotion this memory brings. "He used to say 'I love you, Cupcake,' and she would respond, 'Forever and always.' God, they were sickening."

He snickers. "Hmm, sounds like another couple I know."

I bellow out a laugh and roll my eyes. Shaking my head, I mutter, "Nope, not even close."

Kyler settles onto one of the stools at the island. "She must think I'm the biggest asshole ever."

I don't know why he's so worried, but I'm thankful for his concern.

"Hey, don't worry about it. How could you know? She won't even talk about it, about him." I take a swig of my beer. I wonder if while she was away, she *finally* talked with someone. "I guess I should be happy she came home, huh?"

I take one last bite of food before placing the container in the sink and throw away the empty beer bottle. I wince as the bottle clanks against the broken glass already in there.

I turn back to Ky. "Sorry about all that, man. Thanks for cleaning this whole mess up and taking care of her hand."

I slap him on the back in gratitude. I am thankful he has

been so cool with all of this and accepting of my sister staying here. I'm sure it can't be easy for him. All he does is nod.

I grab my workbag and head toward my room the same time my phone buzzes. I reach for it in my pocket and smile at the photo of the beautiful blonde bombshell who always makes me feel at peace. Well, if I can't snuggle with her tonight, at least hearing the sound of her voice will be the next best thing.

CHAPTER 36
ZACH

I am quickly jolted awake from a nightmare, drenched in sweat. I wish I was one of those people who can't remember their dreams, but this is one too close to reality that it's embedded in my brain. This time when I got the call from my mom and ran back to the apartment, Dani was nowhere in sight and had been in the car with Emmett at the time of the accident. It felt so real. I'm not sure I would have survived had she been in the car with him.

I get up from the bed and walk to the guest room where my sister is staying. It's been eight nights since she arrived at my front door. I slowly open the bedroom door and see her sound asleep, headphones in her ears and clutching a photo which I don't even need to look at it to know it's Emmett. She's home, and that's all I need to keep telling myself, but she's not the same person she was when she left. Or maybe she is, but she's not the same Dani from before Em died. I'm worried that one morning I'm going to wake up and she'll be gone. It was hard enough getting through all of this with us as a family; I have no idea how she managed it for years completely alone. My heart breaks for her even more.

The other night when I came home to find Kyler cleaning up broken glass in the kitchen and he explained what happened, it scared the shit out of me. He had no clue that

I Never Expected You

would have triggered her, but is that how she's going to be from now on? Do we have to walk on eggshells around her? I already hate that Haylee and I are hiding our relationship from her—what else do I need to hide? I push the thoughts from my mind as I close the door and quietly pad back to my room. This isn't the first time I've snuck to her room to check on her.

I sit back on the bed against the headboard, running my hands over my face. I turn to the side of the bed usually occupied by Haylee, expecting to see her lying there. I completely forget for a moment that she's staying at Cam's apartment for the time being.

I reach for my phone on the bedside table and dial the only person I know who can calm me down.

"Hello?"

Oh, fuck, her voice is full of sleep. I didn't even look at the time before I hit "send." I pull my phone back from my ear to see the time. Shit, it's 3:30 a.m.

"Hey."

"Baby, it's 3:30 in the morning. Are you okay? Is Dani okay?"

"Yeah, she's fine. I just... I just..."

"Hey, talk to me. Did you have another nightmare?"

That's one of the many things I love about this girl; she gets me. Over the years, Haylee has always been there to calm me down when I wake up from these nightmares. It's been a while since I've dreamed of that night. It's always the same—reliving the night of the accident. Her voice and touch help keep away the ghosts of the past that I know will forever haunt me.

The first time it happened when we were together, I had woken up screaming, and she brought me down. I lay there with my head in her lap crying with no judgment from her. She knew the pain I felt; it mimicked hers. She just sat there, stroking my hair. She brings me peace. These past few days without her have been more of a struggle than I realized.

"Yeah, but I don't want to talk about it. I wish they would go away. It's bad enough living with the guilt of knowing I let her down."

"What are you talking about?" Her voice raises, no longer showing signs of exhaustion. I can imagine her sitting straight up in bed, her face full of concern.

"I promised Dani when we left for college that I would take good care of him, and look what happened."

"You listen to me. We're not going there again, okay? You are here. I am here. Dani is home. None of it was your fault." I hear her voice filling with emotion, and I hate that I'm not there to hold her.

Great, now I feel like an even bigger asshole for not only waking her up in the middle of the night but upsetting her.

"Hails, this is stupid. I miss you. You should be here lying next to me. I can't go another night with you not wrapped in my arms."

"I know, but we agreed—"

"No, you agreed."

"Okay. Okay. Are we seriously going to argue this again at 3:00 a.m.? Are you really all right?"

"Yeah, I think I just needed to hear your voice. Still okay if I swing by tomorrow after work with dinner?"

"Isn't your sister getting suspicious that you always come home late?"

"Nah, she thinks I work long hours. I guess you could say that is a perk of her not being around all this time; she has no clue about my schedule." I guess that's a weird positive to find in this scenario, that she can't call me out on my bullshit. "Ky hasn't slipped up or anything. He knows the deal. I'm sorry for calling and waking you up. I know you have a big exam in the morning."

"It's okay. But for the record, I prefer it when you wake me up with your tongue, but hearing your voice helps too."

Oh, so we're going there, huh? I let out a soft laugh, and my dick starts to stiffen at the thought of her waking up with my head between her thighs.

"Fuck waiting until tomorrow—can I come over now? Or maybe some phone sex?"

Haylee lets out a loud laugh, one that I know if she were here making that noise, she would be waking someone in the house up. The sound of her laughter goes straight down my spine to my balls. It wouldn't take much for a release.

Still laughing, she says, "Good night, Zach. I love you!"

I grumble, knowing that she knows exactly what she's doing.

"Love you too. See you tomorrow."

CHAPTER 37
ZACH

I don't know whether it was because I heard my sister singing in the shower this morning, something that hasn't happened in years, or just the fact that Emmett is always on my mind, but I found myself on the couch watching the home movies my parents put on a DVD for us—a time when our biggest problems were balancing a social life and lacrosse schedule.

If only we knew then how much or how little time we had left with Em.

"Hey, man." I jump when I hear a deep voice from behind. I turn to find Kyler standing in the hallway.

"Oh sorry, didn't see ya there. Have you been standing there long?"

"No, I just got off the phone with mama dukes." Ky takes a seat on the other side of the couch. He lets out a loud laugh, turning my attention back to the TV. "Dude, what the fuck is in your hair? Is that shit flammable?"

I roll my eyes. "Fuck off." I punch him straight in the arm. "That used to take me an hour to perfect the rolled-out-of-bed look."

I'm grateful now though that I wear my hair short. Kyler continues his laughter as we watch the video of us leaving for prom.

I Never Expected You

It didn't matter that I looked hot as fuck, a definite James Bond wannabe, but I preferred being out of the suit.

I watch as Emmett playfully shoves me on the screen. I can remember it as if it were yesterday.

"Knock it off, dude. Melissa isn't going to stand you up. She should be here soon."

"Ha! I'm not worried about that. She'll be here. She wouldn't miss what I have planned for us after prom, if you know what I mean."

Wow, I was something else back then.

"Un-freakin'-believable. Keep it in your pants, Jacobs."

"Whatever. I know you have something planned. Don't act like you don't. Just keep that shit to yourself."

There is a throat clearing in the background of the video that ends our shoving contest and draws our attention to the front porch. Whenever my sister walked into the room, she was all Emmett saw. I guess that's exactly how Haylee and I are now. That girl is my world. While all eyes were on my sister and best friend, I focus on the girl in the background. *My girl.* Although, back then, she wasn't my girl. She had gone with that douchebag; I don't even remember his name. He made me look like a saint.

Damn, she is so beautiful. How did I seriously not notice it back then? I hate hiding this—hiding us. If my sister can't be okay with Hails and I being happy, then we have more significant issues. We both stood by for years watching our siblings and best friends fall in love, and we both only wanted them to be happy. It was all that mattered. I would hope that my sister would have the same decency.

I prop my elbows on my knees and run my fingers through my hair, releasing a loud breath. "This is so stupid. I need to talk to her."

I need to bring my girl home.

Kyler and I are both caught up in the moment watching Dani and Emmett on the screen, my sister wearing a smile that I wonder if I will ever see again. It's not until a loud noise in the hallway where Kyler had first startled me from, that I pull my eyes from the screen.

"What the fuck are you doing?" my sister demands from where she stands.

I stare at her, watching the tears stream down her cheeks. She does not attempt to wipe them.

"I said, what the fuck are you doing? How dare you?"

Is she fucking serious right now? *Oh no, this bullshit, woe-is-me ends right now.* My sister stomps over like a child to me and reaches for the remote, but I refuse to give it to her.

"How dare I? Are you kidding me right now? How dare *you*?!" I rise to my feet, anger pouring off me. "You act like you're the only one to have ever lost someone they love. You think you're the only one who lost someone that day? I lost my best friend, Haylee lost a *brother*, Natalie and Brian lost a son. I am so sorry that you lost the love of your life, I truly am, but what about the rest of us?"

I begin to pace the living room.

"Fuck! Danielle, I didn't just lose Em that day—I lost you too. I lost my sister. Haylee lost her best friend. We needed you, and you were so fucking selfish living in your own world that you cut us all out too. We were all grieving, but you didn't care —it didn't matter. For fuck's sake, Dani, you fucking abandoned us! You just left us behind to put back the pieces of our broken world and try to move on. Do you think that's been easy?"

My voice roars, and I don't even care if the neighbors hear me. What is it going to take for her to understand what I'm saying? She. Left. Us. She is not going to show up after all this time and expect sympathy when we had to manage life on our own without only him or her.

"I miss him—I miss him every godforsaken day. He was my best friend, my brother. Some days, I have to just force myself out of bed, in hopes that when I walk into the kitchen I'll see him sitting at the island drinking out of that ridiculous Batman mug, that when my phone chimes it's a text from him seeing if I want to get a beer after work, or that I would've gotten a chance to give a kick-ass best man speech at yours and his wedding so that I could spill all the stupid embarrassing things over the years. I started planning that speech at thirteen because somewhere deep down I knew you two were the real deal. Sounds ridiculous, doesn't it?"

Does she really have nothing to say? Fine. I'll keep talking while she stares at me.

"I can't say that I know what you're going through because I don't know exactly, but I hurt too. You can't even say his name. Emmett. Say it... *Em-mett*." I'm sure to enunciate each syllable of his name.

"You, Dani, are still here. For some fucking reason that I'm still trying to figure out, he isn't. He was denied all his dreams and plans. He wouldn't want you to be living this bullshit excuse for a life that you are. He would want you to live, to move on. You can do that without forgetting. I do it every. Fucking. Day. You say you want to start over and move on, but look at you—have you even gone home to see Mom and Dad, visit the cemetery, or hell, even call Haylee?"

I know the answers to all of them, especially the last one. It breaks my heart every time I see or talk to Haylee, knowing that my sister hasn't reached out. Sure, she asked about her once, and I was vague with details when all I wanted to say was that she is the woman I plan to marry. Her silence is deafening.

"Yeah, I didn't fucking think so. So, dear sweet sister, if you want to talk about selfish, I suggest you look in a fucking mirror." I stalk over to my keys and storm out the front door with only one destination in mind.

F*UCKKKKKKKK*! I can't believe my sister is so fucking selfish and trying to act like the shit we went through only affected her. In what fucking world does she live where she is the only one who lost someone that day? I lost my best friend, and Haylee lost her brother. I needed to leave before I said something I'd regret. I almost told her to get the fuck out. When I grabbed my keys, I knew where I was headed. I knew that when I slammed the door so hard that I was grateful we no longer lived in the apartment because we definitely would have gotten a call from the building or worse, the cops.

This is fucking stupid, Hails and I living apart to be careful of Dani's feelings. Well, guess what? We're done with that. If she doesn't like it, then she can get the fuck out of my house. The apartment Haylee is staying at isn't too far from the house, and I make it there in record time. I pull into a parking space and shut the Jeep off when my phone vibrates.

Ky: *You okay, man?*
Ky: *Please don't do something stupid.*

I'm pretty sure I owe Kyler a beer or two, or possibly even a case of beers for having to witness that explosion. Maybe letting Dani move in was a bad idea. Just thinking about her makes me angrier. I quickly respond to the text and get out of the car.

I Never Expected You

Me: *Yeah, I needed to get out of there. Sorry to blow up like that. I'm heading over to Haylee's. I'll be back later or maybe in the morning. Idk.*

As soon as I'm in the building, I start running to the stairs. I also fucking hate this building. It's okay for Cam and whatever, but I don't want my girl staying here anymore. The damn elevator has been broken for months, and I'm guessing they have no intention of fixing it anytime soon. I am having her shit packed by morning, and she is coming home with me. Enough is enough. By the time I reach the apartment door, the anger has not only grown, but I'm covered in sweat, and my heart is racing. It doesn't matter that I live in the gym—that was a lot of fucking steps to run up.

I knock on the door and can hear her footsteps on the other side of the door. There is a pause—I assume her looking out the peephole—before I hear the sound of the lock unlocking. She opens the door in black booty shorts and a T-shirt—*my T-shirt*. Oh, fuck! She knows what those booty shorts do to me. As if I wasn't wound up enough. I let out a growl after taking her all in.

There's a look of her surprise on her face. "Hey, baby, what are you do—"

I cut her off, claiming her mouth with mine, my greedy tongue pushing into her mouth. I push her into the apartment and kick the door shut with my foot before spinning her around and hoisting her up in my arms, and she wraps her legs around my waist. I don't break the kiss. This kiss is anything but sweet; it's demanding, powerful, and messy. Teeth are clashing, and hands are roaming. I bite her bottom lip before swiping my tongue over to ease the sting and doing it again. Her moans go straight to my cock. I press it into her hot center, already feeling her wetness against my leg.

She is the first one to break the kiss, her cheeks pink and her lips swollen from my kisses. "Zach? What are you doing here?"

Instead of answering, I grind against her, resulting in her nails digging into my shoulder, and she lets out another moan.

"Sweetheart, what happened tonight? I thought you were staying in tonight? Is everything okay?"

With her pressed up against the door, legs still wrapped around me, I reach for her hands on my shoulders and press them firmly above her head. "Shut up."

She leans back and blinks at me, trying to figure out if I seriously just told her to shut up. I tighten the grip on her hands and press into her core. She closes her eyes, taking in the moment, probably wishing I was already slamming into her—well, that makes two of us. I'm done with the words. I'm still so fucking angry, and I want her so fucking bad.

In a firm tone, one she has heard me use plenty of times over the years, I look deep in her eyes so she sees my seriousness and say, "You're done talking, Hails. I just want you to feel my cock deep inside you."

I can see her breathing change. I release her hands and unwrap her legs, setting her back down to the floor before I spin her around

"Put your hands in front of you."

She's a good girl and does what she's told. I place my hands over hers before slowly dragging my hands down her arms and sides before reaching around the front and rubbing her slick folds over her booty shorts. She inhales sharply.

I waste no time yanking down her shorts to her ankles and unbuttoning my jeans before freeing my cock. I don't hesitate before thrusting inside her. I fuck her fast and deep. It doesn't take long for her pussy to start contracting around my cock. I am going to send her over the edge, making me feel the full force of her orgasm.

My grip on her hips tightens as I follow her orgasm with my own.

With both of us spent, Haylee leans her forehead against the door, and I against her back. She is the first to speak.

"Now do you want to explain what happened?"

I scoot up closer behind her and kiss her shoulder, up her neck, and nibble behind her ear, the spot I know instantly turns her on.

In a husky tone, I answer, "Nope! Now I'm going to carry you to the shower and clean my dirty girl up and then take you to the bedroom where you're going spread your legs for me. Then I'm going to lick you until you're begging me to stop. Is that what you want, baby girl?"

"Yes." She breathes it out rather than speaking.

I swoop my arms under her legs and carry her to the bathroom, and I plan to honor every promise I made her.

CHAPTER 38
Haylee

Oh. My. God. I may not walk for a week. Sex with Zach is amazing, especially after we had decided last year to rely only on my birth control, but that was next-level. My clit is still pulsing from orgasm after orgasm. I don't know what happened tonight, but I'm waiting for my brain to be able to function again and my heart rate to come down to a normal level.

Zach walks back into the bedroom with two glasses of water, only wearing his boxers. This man is fucking gorgeous. I don't know what I did to deserve him or all those mind-blowing orgasms for that matter, but he is mine to keep. He climbs into bed, handing me the water, and I find the strength to push myself up against the headboard.

"Thanks." It's the only word I can manage.

I take a sip of the cold water and set the glass on the nightstand. Zach does the same before pulling the covers over us. He wraps an arm around me, tugging me closer to his chest and kissing the top of my head.

"You okay?" he asks while running his fingers up and down my spine.

I nod. "I was thinking I should be asking you the same thing."

He lets out a low chuckle.

"You're not going to avoid the question by fucking me again. My poor vagina needs a break before you go anywhere near it." I put my palm on his chest and push him back as he tries to squirm away. "Nu-uh. You're going to talk, babe, about what got you coming in here like a damn Neanderthal." I lay my head on his chest and wrap my arms around him, giving him a chance to gather his thoughts.

"I'm done hiding us, Hails. We're telling her tomorrow about you and me. You're coming home."

"Baby, slow down. Just tell me what happened tonight." I cup his cheek and smooth my thumb over his stubble, trying to keep him calm. I can see the emotion rising.

"Okay. Tonight, Dani and I got into it. She caught me watching the home videos of Emmett, and she called me selfish. Lots of words were exchanged, ones I don't really want to repeat."

I settle back into his arms and trace the lines of his stomach muscles as he continues to talk.

"She acts as though she is the only one that lost someone. I'm sorry, but it's bullshit. She up and ran and left us all behind to pick up the pieces, and she has the fucking nerve to call me selfish. I'm done pretending that things are different than what they are. It's been two weeks, and she hasn't even reached out to you. I'm done keeping us a secret from her; I'm done living this lie. You are my life, and if she can't handle it, then I hate to say this—seriously, I do—but maybe she has stayed long enough."

I freeze in his arms. He can't be serious. We just got her back. He is not giving her a reason to run again. His heart rate has picked back up but not in a good way. I tighten my arms around him in hopes of him finding comfort to relax again. He brushes the fallen strands of hair out of my face before settling on the back of my head and gripping my hair between his fingers. He pulls my face to his, claiming my mouth in a searing kiss. I relish in the feeling of his tongue against mine. I reluctantly break apart from him so that I can say what I have to say to him without any distractions—well, any more distractions, including the growing bulge in his boxers.

"Okay."

"Okay what, baby girl?"

"Okay, we tell her tomorrow, but on my terms. I do it how I want to do it because I swear to God, Zach, I just got her back. I'm not going to lose her again." I fight back the tears forming behind my eyes as he pulls me swiftly back into his arms, protecting me from my feelings.

He kisses the top of my head before placing his cheek against it. "Okay. We will do it your way. And then we are going to pack your shit up, and you're coming home. *End of discussion.*"

I giggle at how fast his tone changes at the end. The man has made up his mind.

"Oh, really?" I love to tease this man.

He rolls me over onto my back, settling between my legs. "Really. And you know I usually get what I want. I might have to spend some more time convincing you, that's all."

PULLING BACK UP TO THE HOUSE, I DON'T KNOW IF I'M more nervous to see my best friend for the first time in years or to see how she reacts to me and Zach being together. We agreed this morning over coffee that we would come home first and talk to Danielle—that is, if she hasn't run off after their fight—and then we could finish packing up my stuff from the apartment and bring it all back over. First things first though. We stop on the front porch as Zach moves in to put the key in the door. The hand that is not linked with his, I place gently on his arm, bringing his attention to me.

"Are you sure you want to do this?"

Zach steps closer to me, cupping my cheeks and placing a sweet kiss on my lips. "Yes, Hails. I'm sure. It'll be okay. Like I said last night, I'm done hiding…hiding this. Us." He holds up our conjoined hands, placing a brief kiss on our knuckles. "You ready?"

I let out a breath and nod as he puts the key in the lock. We hear raised voices on the other side of the door. Zach and I look at each other, confused—maybe the TV is just too loud. As we open the door, I stand behind Zach, nervous again. The voices belong to Dani and Kyler. Zach and I look back and forth at each other and then back to Dani and Ky. Dani is standing while Ky is sitting on the couch. Zach's hand tightens in mine.

Dani looks very confused, her gaze going back and forth between Zach and me and our joined hands. She's here! She is *actually* here. I knew she was, but seeing her with my own eyes is something else. Part of me wants to run and slap the shit out of her for leaving the way she did and ignoring us all, but the other part wants to take her in my arms and make sure she promises never to do it again.

"Dani," Zach begins before turning his gaze to me and smiling, reassuring me that this will be okay. "Hails and I are together. We've been dating for almost three years. I was waiting for the right time to tell you."

The look of surprise on my best friend's face is priceless as she plops on the couch. I squeeze Zach's hand before I let it go and head over to where she sits. Kneeling in front of her, I reach for her hands. My eyes fill with tears as I realize how much I had missed her.

"Hey, bestie, it's been a while. About time you got your ass back here."

CHAPTER 39
ZACH

The older I get, the quicker Mondays get here. Making my way to the kitchen to grab a cup of coffee, I am startled to find Dani already up and in the kitchen, standing at the stove, sipping on a cup of coffee, and stirring something in a pan.

"Morning, sis."

She startles.

"Shit, you scared me. Morning, Zachy."

I instantly feel the caffeine rushing through my veins with the first sip. I lean against the counter and watch my sister make herself at home in the kitchen.

She stiffens before turning to face me.

"So I was thinking about maybe joining you and Haylee at brunch this weekend."

I push off the counter and stare at her. Is she serious?

"Really? Are you sure? I don't want you to feel pressured or anything."

She shakes her head. "No, it's time. I can do this."

"If you're sure, I'll let Mom and Dad know. They'll be so excited. I know it's been difficult."

Her smile falters, and I step up to pull her into my arms. "Hey, they understand. It's okay. I'll set it all up. Okay?"

She wraps her arms around me and nods against my chest.

"Sounds good. Do you want any breakfast before you head to work?"

"No, I gotta hit the road, but Haylee was in the shower; I'm sure she will eat something before she leaves."

I press a kiss to the top of her head before I make my way out the door. My parents are going to be thrilled. I mentally go over my schedule today and figure I'll call my mom on my lunch break.

Well, lunch ended up being two hours later than usual and eaten at my desk. I place the phone to my ear and wait for my mom to answer.

"Hello."

"Hey, Ma, how's it going?"

"Well, wonderful now that you called. It's not like you to call during the workday. Everything okay?"

"Oh yeah, everything's great actually. I mean, completely swamped at work, but I have some news."

"You finally proposed? Oh, Zach, that's so wonderful."

I rub my hands over my face. "No, Mom, it's not that." I exhale a loud breath. Wow, way to put a damper on this positive phone call. "But I think this will make you happier. Mom, Dani wants to come to brunch this weekend."

Thump.

"Mom? You still there?"

"I'm here. I'm here. Sorry, I dropped the phone."

I snicker. "I was wondering what that noise was."

"I... I... I don't know what to say. I've been waiting for this day for so long." I can hear the tears forming and the emotion choking her.

"It's okay, Mom. She brought it up this morning. She said it's time."

"We'll have to make this weekend extra special, go all out."

"Mom, slow down. Don't make such a big deal of this. Just relax. Make it like any other brunch, just one with both of your kids."

I hear her gasp. "Oh, Zach. I can't wait to tell your father."

A calendar reminder pops up on my computer screen, alerting me I have a client meeting in five minutes.

"Hey, Mom, I have a meeting soon that I need to prepare for. I'll call you later, okay?"

"Of course, thank you for calling. Natalie and I are going to have to go to the Amish Market on Thursday and gather the best for my baby girl."

Oh man, the mention of the Amish Market makes my stomach growl even though I just ate a burrito bowl. Nothing tastes more like home than a pretzel cheese dog and Barq's root beer from the Amish Market. I make a mental note the next time I am at home and have the time, we are swinging by there.

"I love you, Mom. Talk to you later."

"Bye, Zach."

CHAPTER 40
ZACH

I guess I shouldn't have been surprised that Dani had invited Kyler to brunch today. I mean, it's still a little strange, but whatever, he's family, and they seem to have been spending a lot of time together. I was shocked when he even convinced her to join one of the Lawson family dinners. How the hell he did that, I have no clue. Kate and Lauren are definitely two of a kind, but Dani survived to tell the tale and even got a job offer to help out at Lauren's school. Between that and Dani finally agreeing to go back home to see our parents, I would say we're moving in the right direction. I'm not one hundred percent getting my hopes up, but I think it's safe to say she is planning on sticking around.

The breeze feels nice with the windows down as we head down the highway in Kyler's truck. Not that I mind driving, but it's nice to be able to relax. The girls are sitting in the back seat, and I glance back at my sister. She looks lost in thought and keeps quiet most of the ride while Haylee, Ky, and I keep up constant conversation.

Before we know it, we are getting off our exit on Route 50 and turning into my parents' driveway. I stare up at the house once I shut the truck door behind me. I've always loved this house. One day, it would be nice to have one just like it. I could see myself sitting on the front porch swing with Haylee

I Never Expected You

enjoying a drink after the kids have gone to bed or having family cookouts out back and enjoying each other's company.

Woah, did I think of having kids? With any other girl that might have been a terrifying thought, but with Haylee, I want that future. Now if only I could get that one question out and we could move forward with our future.

My sister approaches slowly, also taking in the house. Her memories of this house I'm sure are different than mine.

She looks as if she is either ready to throw up or run out of here.

"It'll be fine. Let's go." She reassures us that she's ready to do this.

I take Haylee's hand in mine and caress the top of her hand

"Stop worrying, babe. Listen to your sister. It'll be fine," she whispers as we walk through the front door.

The four of us follow the sounds of our parents' favorite band, the Beatles, to find all our parents dancing around the kitchen. It's not anything unusual for them to be dancing in the house. I have plenty of memories growing up with my dad coming up behind my mom while she would be cooking and spinning her around and sweeping her off her feet.

I glance back at Dani to make sure she hasn't run off, and her eyes are glassed over and set on my parents and the view in front of her. I think about pulling her into my arms to tell her she is strong and brave to do this, but I choose not to, so I focus my attention back on my parents.

As the music ends, I clap my hands together, yelling, "Encore! Encore!"

My mom jumps and turns around, placing her hand on her chest. I feel Dani grip the back of my shirt, standing out of view. My mom first notices me before her eyes move behind me to see Dani.

"Hey, Mama," are the only words Dani can get out before my mom pulls her into a big hug.

"I missed you so much," my mom cries into Dani's shoulder, and I can't help but feel the tears beginning to burn my eyes at watching this. "When your brother said you were coming today, I almost didn't believe him because I didn't want to get my hopes up."

Haylee taps my arm and nods her head in the direction of her parents. We quietly walk over to where Natalie and Brian stand. They both pull us into a welcoming hug. Tears stream down Natalie's face as she takes in the scene in front of her.

My dad moves behind them.

"Hey, baby girl," he says as he pulls Dani out of our mother's arms and into his. I watch as her arms wrap tightly around his waist.

Kyler sets down the tray of whatever he has been carrying around and joins us and the Hanks. My father releases Dani from his hug but keeps his arm around her shoulders.

"I hope you don't mind that I invited Kyler."

Kyler walks up to my mom, and she pulls him into a hug. "Of course not. What a wonderful surprise." He then turns to my dad to shake his hand.

Haylee and I make our way around to say hello to Mom and Dad as Dani makes her way over to the Hanks. She slowly approaches—I can't even imagine what is going through her head. Natalie yanks Dani into a hug, almost knocking her off her feet.

"About time you came home, sweetheart, don't you think?" Natalie says with a smile.

Brian comes up behind Natalie and Dani, but Natalie gets defensive, not wanting to let my sister go. "Get your own Jacobs to hug—I've waited four years to hug this one."

I wish I could blame her, but that's exactly how we all feel.

So, he settles for kissing the top of her head before backing away and giving the girls more time. "Welcome home."

We all laugh in the background as Natalie pulls back but doesn't let go of her. Still in her embrace, Dani continues to cry.

"No more running, right?" Natalie asks, and Dani nods. "Because we're your family here, and I'm tired of just your mom's help in the kitchen. Haylee's useless."

"Hey!" Hails yells from my side.

I put my arm around her, kissing her temple tenderly. "Babe, I love your cooking, but..."

Before I can finish, she puts her forefinger in my face. "Don't even think about finishing that sentence, Zachary Jacobs!"

Even though she narrows her eyes at me, I see the playful smile across her lips, so I bite her finger gently.

Mom claps her hands together. "Okay, who's hungry? We've got a full brunch spread made."

Mom walks over to the tray Kyler set down on the counter, unsure what to do with it.

"Oh, I brought cinnamon rolls; they just need to be warmed up," Dani interjects while wiping away her tears as she lifts the foil.

Kyler coughs and raises his eyebrows at her. A weird exchange occurs between him and my sister, and I'm not sure what that's all about.

"Kyler made them."

"Well, then I'm definitely not eating them." I grab a strawberry from the bowl on the counter and shove it in my mouth.

Ky punches me in the arm and mumbles, "Asshole."

"Kyler! Language, please," my mother scolds.

I throw back my head in laughter and stick my tongue out at him.

My mom hands me a plate of food to carry out to the dining room. "Go make yourself useful, Zachary. Shoo, get out of my kitchen."

She swats me with a dish towel, and I race out of the kitchen.

"Damn, dude, these are delicious," I tell Kyler as I pluck my second cinnamon roll from the plate and shove it in my mouth. I haven't even finished chewing before I shout at him across the table. "I can't believe you've been holding out on me with your skills in the kitchen all these years."

Damn, if I knew he cooked this good, we wouldn't have ordered so much takeout over the years.

"Zachary Brian Jacobs, I know I taught you better manners than to talk with your mouth full," my mother scolds.

I look down at my lap as Dani and Haylee say, "Ooooooooooo," at the same time followed by their typical giggling. I find myself smiling at how easy we all have fit back together; it's as if no time has passed.

"Nice to see you girls back to your ways," my dad adds.

Kyler grins at me. "Nah, man, I just had a good teacher." He then turns toward Dani, wearing that same grin. "Dani even told me that next time she would teach me how to make that amazing veggie lasagna."

"Oh, now that sounds delicious." Brian leans back in his chair across the table.

"It's no chicken parmesan that Ms. Natalie makes, but it's

definitely a top contender," Dani adds before taking a sip of her drink.

Natalie leans over with her elbows on the table. "Dani, we're all adults now—I think we are old enough that you can drop the Ms. and just call me Natalie."

I used to think my sister made me look bad with all these manners, but once officially an adult, I got the same talk from her. Hopefully one day, I will just call her Ma as my mother-in-law. I push those thoughts aside. Today is not about that; it's about my sister finally having the strength to come home, and everything feels as though it is back to normal, although one major piece is missing.

"Okay," Dani responds shyly down at her hands.

Is it weird to realize that we're all adults now?

"I'm happy to hear you're still creating in the kitchen though." Natalie wears a proud expression on her face. My sister was the only one who picked up their talent for cooking and baking.

"Of course, it's my happy place. I found myself spending hours in my apartment creating new recipes and perfecting the ones you taught me over the years. I even used to make baked goods for two local coffee shops back in New Hampshire while I was waitressing."

"I would love to see these new recipes you've been working on." My mom sits up straight in her chair, wiping her mouth with her napkin.

"Maybe next time you guys can come to visit us, and I'll make something."

Look at that—my sister is already discussing the next time she wants to see my parents. I would say that's progress.

"I'd love that." Mom reaches over and grabs Dani's hand.

I can't believe that neither my parents or the Hankses had

driven to the house and barged through. If I were them, I'm pretty sure I would have.

As small talk continues throughout the table, we are all back in our groove until in a flash my sister has pushed her chair back, knocking it over and rushing right out the back door onto the deck. *What the fuck just happened?* We all look around, unsure what to do. Kyler goes to get up, but my mom rises and puts her hand on his arm and smiles.

"I've got this." Placing her napkin down on her plate, she gets up and follows Dani.

Quiet and awkwardness take over the room. Haylee reaches over and squeezes my thigh, giving me a reassuring smile.

My dad is the first to chime in. "Why don't we finish up here and you guys go relax on the couches while we clean up."

Ky, Haylee, and I look at each other before nodding. I try to focus on what's going on outside, but I see that my mom and Dani have made their way down off the deck, I assume either for a walk or to sit down by the pool.

I can't find the appetite to finish the plate in front of me.

Haylee leans over, forcing me to look in her direction. "Hey, you okay?"

I shrug because honestly, I'm not sure. "Maybe this was all too much, too soon."

Maybe we had forced this all on her without her being ready.

"She's going to be okay. She's so strong and has a heart full of love. Just like you."

I turn from looking outside at nothing back to my beautiful girlfriend and lean in, pressing my lips against hers. When we part, she blinks, staring up at me.

"What was that for?"

I smile at her, a genuine, honest smile that she is responsible for putting there. "For being you."

Once the three of us are done at the table, Dani and my mom still have not arrived back inside, so we move our conversation to the couches. Haylee and I take our usual spot while Kyler sits across from us. Not long after, my sister returns from outside, halting the side conversation Haylee and I were having. Her eyes are red, a visible sign of crying, but she has color in her cheeks and doesn't look broken. Kyler leans in and whispers something, and she nods. She turns away from the conversation with Kyler to rub her hands over the couch.

She's going to be okay, and damn it if I'm not going to do everything in my power to make sure that statement is true.

CHAPTER 41
Haylee

Cami: *One more week till I'm back. Get excited biAtch!*
Me: *Yay, I've missed you.*
Cami: *I've missed you, too.*
Me: *How's lover boy?*
Cami: *He's not a boy. *winkface**
Me: *How's lover man? Lol.*
Cami: *Things are great. So much to fill you in on. His family is interesting, to say the least.*
Cami: *Oh by the way, thanks a lot for ditching house sitting. *Eyeroll**
Me: *Whatever. When you originally proposed the idea, you just wanted me stopping by anyways. I stop by and get your mail after class.*
Me: *It's great being back in my own home though.*
Cami: *Fill me in on what's been going on?*
Me: *There's way too much to text, but here's the cliff notes.*
Cami: *You know I prefer cliff notes over the real thing anyways.*
Me: *I think something might be going on between Kyler and Dani. They hang out a lot.*
Cami: *No shit! Sex on a stick and the long lost sister? Damn, I miss everything.*
Cami: *But how do you know they're not just being friendly?*

Maybe she just doesn't want to be a third wheel with you two – hello! Been there done that, so Ky is the only other option. Remember, Ky has been rocking the whole third wheel thing since the beginning so maybe he's just tired of you guys.
Me: *I mean, I guess that could be, but it's the little things I've been picking up on that have my wheels turning.*
Cami: *Like what?*
Me: *Well, she never left the house, yet all of a sudden, he convinced her to go to dinner with him, Lauren and Kate.*
Cami: *OMG! Did the Lawson twins eat her alive?!*
Me: *No, that's the thing. They hit it off great. Lauren even offered her a job at her school.*
Cami: *Wow, I'm impressed. What else?*
Me: *Dani invited him to brunch back in Annapolis when she was finally ready to go home and see her parents.*
Cami: *I can't believe I missed the big reunion.*
Cami: *Maybe just for moral support?*
Me: *No, something was weird about the little touches I picked up on.*
Me: *Drinks when you get back?*
Cami: *You betcha.*
Me: *Well I need to get ready. We are going to Lucky's for dinner and karaoke.*
Cami: *And...now I want margaritas and tacos from there. Thanks a lot.*
Me: **wink face* Anytime.*
Me: *Tell the professor I say hi.*
Cami: *Will do. Tell Zach the same. Love you.*
Me: *Love you too!*

CHAPTER 42
Haylee

"That was a cruel joke you played on your sister. You know that, right?" I ask Zach once he and I are alone at the table at our favorite dive bar, Lucky's.

Kyler, Zach and I discovered this place not long after we moved into the house. We all have a love for tacos, tequila, and karaoke. And that's where their joke on Dani comes in. When we brought Dani here tonight, she apparently didn't know that tonight was karaoke night. Her eyes nearly popped out of her head, and the color drained from her face when Scott got on stage and announced they were ready to start karaoke. Dani has a fantastic voice, but it's been years since I've heard her sing.

Earlier tonight, Kyler and Zach tricked Dani into agreeing that she would get up to sing if they did. She easily agreed to it. I had to fight back the laughter as she thought she'd won; they'd played her so well, having convinced her that they didn't do this regularly. I have seen these two perform songs such as "Islands in the Stream," "You're the One That I Want," and "Ain't No Mountain High Enough."

The joke was on her when they got up on stage and had the crowd pumping as they sang "When the Sun Goes Down" by Uncle Kracker and Kenny Chesney.

"Hey, she got up and sang, didn't she? And you heard her—she said she hadn't felt that alive in so long. So ha!" A smug

I Never Expected You

smile spreads across his face as he sits back in his chair, crossing his arms. After a moment, he reaches for his drink from the table and sips the last of his margarita. "And look she's even dancing," Zach says while looking around for the waiter to order another round.

I look over to the makeshift dance floor where, just moments ago, Kyler led Dani, and my eyes go wide at what is unfolding in front of me. If I had had a drink in my hand, I definitely would have dropped it.

Would you look at that? I so should have called that. There was no way those flirty looks exchanged between them earlier were just my imagination.

"Yeah, babe, I don't think dancing is the only thing on in her mind at the moment."

Zach finally turns to see what I mean by that only to see our best friends wrapped up in each other, and yep, his tongue is totally in her mouth. *Sweet Jesus, they keep this up, and they'll be fucking in the middle of the bar.*

"What the..." Zach leans forward on his chair. He looks over at me in shock before looking back at his sister and Kyler again.

I lean over to Zach and whisper in his ear, "Go pay the bill."

"What?"

I raise my eyebrows at him. "I said go pay the bill. Come on —I want to spend our last night at Cami's, just us. And clearly..." I nod to the couple just a few feet ahead of us. "...they should get some alone time."

Zach cringes, and with the tequila flowing through my veins, I let out a loud snort.

Zach goes off to pay the bill and returns just as Dani and Ky are making their way back to the table.

Zach helps me into my jacket as Kyler approaches. "Leaving already?"

"Yeah, well, I found myself ready for bed all of a sudden," Zach responds before turning to me, a grin all over his face.

Nice cover, babe. I decide to go along with it. I let out a fake yawn and giggle. Kyler keeps looking at us as if he's trying to figure out what's going on.

"We're gonna head out. Bill is paid—you got next time."

Kyler nods. "Thanks. See you at home?"

"Nah, I think we'll be staying at Cami's tonight. She gets back in town tomorrow, so we're going to take advantage of her place for one more night." Zach waggles his eyebrows.

Not to mention if what we witnessed on the dance floor is any indication of what is about to happen at home, we want to be nowhere near the house.

"See you both in the morning." He points between the two of them, and that's my cue to get us out of here before he does or says something stupid.

I reach for his jacket and pull him out of the bar. Before we get to the front door, I look back toward the table and see Ky whispering something in Dani's ear from behind. The smile on both of their faces puts a smile on my face. It's nice to see both of my best friends happy.

I WALK OUT INTO THE KITCHEN AND FIND ZACH HALFWAY in the fridge. Since I moved back home, I haven't restocked the refrigerator, so I have no clue what he's going to find. I hop up on the counter wearing only the button-up shirt Zach wore earlier tonight to Lucky's. He hasn't noticed me yet.

Zach finally backs up out of the fridge with a jar of jelly in hand.

"Whatcha planning to do with that?" I ask.

He spins around, clutching the jar of jelly to keep it from falling. "You scared the shit out of me."

"Seriously? It's a studio apartment, babe. How did you not hear me?"

"I don't know. You know how I get when I'm hangry. There's like no food here."

I throw my head back in laughter. This man is always hungry; if it's not for food, then it's for me.

"Um, yeah. Maybe because you showed up here all caveman-like demanding I come back home and I haven't been here to restock it. I didn't have a reason to leave food here when Cam wasn't living here. I still don't know what you're going to do with that jelly since I'm pretty sure there's no bread… that's at least not growing something on it."

Zach has since moved over to the pantry. "Aha!"

He brings the jelly and peanut butter over to where I am sitting on the counter. Setting the jars down, he nudges my legs open and slides between them. Reaching up, he brushes the hair out of my face before leaning in.

I can feel his hot breath against my lips as he says, "I love seeing you in my clothes. You are so sexy, Haylee Hanks."

I run my hands up and down his sculpted chest. A growl erupts from his throat moments before slamming his mouth against mine. After a few minutes of kissing—damn, I will never tire of kissing this man—we part, entirely out of breath. His hands seductively trail up my thighs. I wonder if he will take me right here on the counter.

His voice is deep and full of need. "You know what I want, baby girl?"

I place another brief kiss on his lips before I lean back on the counter. The shirt rides up, and a deep groan emits from him. I look up at him through hooded lids and bite my lip.

Reaching between my legs, I open the drawer under where I'm sitting and pull out two spoons. His eyes light up, and his smile widens.

"Damn, I love you."

This man seriously has no idea how much I love him back.

Passing the jars back and forth, Zach and I sit on the counter enjoying each other's company, eating peanut butter and jelly with spoons.

"You know, I'm going to miss this little apartment," Zach says, looking around.

I look at him with shock. "What? You hate this place."

I take a spoonful of peanut butter before handing him the jar.

"No, I hated you living here."

"What's the difference?"

Zach sets the peanut butter down on the counter and hops off before settling back between my legs. "The difference, baby, is that you belong with me. You being here meant we weren't together."

I go to interrupt telling him just because I wasn't living with him didn't mean we weren't together, but he presses his fingers against my mouth to stop me as if he could sense what I was going to say.

"What I mean is, I'll miss having a place of our own. Maybe one day soon, it'll be just you and me. Ky and Dani might get their own place. Kyler doesn't really date, so this must mean something to him. They both looked pretty happy with each other. Speaking of which, did you have any idea they were a thing?"

"No. Yes. I don't know."

"And you didn't tell me? What the hell, Hails!"

"No, I mean, I didn't know anything, but I kind of picked up on something. You didn't?"

"What? When?"

Is he seriously that oblivious that he missed all the looks they gave each other when they thought no one was looking or the way that he touched her leg at brunch? Hell, he got her to join him and the girls for dinner when we've been trying for weeks to get her to come out with us.

Zach shrugs. "I guess it makes sense. Now that I think about it, how did we not see this coming? I don't know why I didn't think of it first."

He pouts toward the bed. I hop off the counter and quickly put the food away. I can't wait to go home tomorrow and get the scoop from her. And if Dani thinks she's staying quiet…oh, that girl has another thing coming.

CHAPTER 43
Haylee

There is no sign of Dani or Kyler when we return home the next morning. Zach and I are sitting at the island sipping our coffees when they finally emerge. No one says anything as they fix their coffee.

Zach is first to break the ice. "Well, I'm headed to the gym this morning. You up for a workout this morning? That is unless you already got a workout in."

I almost choke on my coffee. Dani's face turns the reddest shade I have ever seen.

Ky steps up to Dani and kisses her forehead.

Damn, who knew Kyler Lawson was so adorable? You better believe I will be getting details of whatever went down later.

"Sounds good. Leave in five?"

Zach nods, and Ky walks out of the room, along with Dani. I turn to face Zach and raise my eyebrows.

"What?" he asks, pretending to be innocent.

"You're such an asshole."

"You always have known this." He laughs, stepping into my space. "I promise to be on my best behavior."

It's now my turn to laugh. "Zach Jacobs on his best behavior? I never thought I'd see the day."

Zach goes to lean in to kiss me when a throat clearing

behind us pulls us apart. We both turn to find Kyler standing there with his gym bag.

"Ready to go, man?"

"Yep."

With a quick peck on my lips, Zach leaves with Kyler, and I am headed to Dani's room to get the scoop. I find her rummaging through her closet, trying to find clothes. I first look at the pile of clothes spread out all over her bed and smirk. I know what's going on—someone has a hot date and nothing to wear. I've waited so long to do this with my best friend.

I clap my hands together. "Looks like we need to go shopping."

I grab my keys, and we are out the door.

"So..." I start as we climb into my car.

"So..." she responds as she buckles her seat belt and places her hands in her lap.

Oh, hell no. She is not going to play all innocent with me.

"You and Kyler, huh?"

A goofy grin and a blush appear on her face. *Oh, this is going to be good.*

"Mmmhmm." Did she moan?

I throw my head back in laughter as I start the car. "Oh, I think lunch might need to added to our shopping date, and that lunch may need to include cocktails because you better damn well believe you are spillin' all the details! But first things first, we need to set the mood."

I have waited years for this moment. Her face lights up as bright as the sun as Katy Perry begins to play through the speakers.

"What!" Dani squeals.

"You have no idea how long I've waited to be able to jam to this CD with a Jacobs and not feel like I'm being judged. I have watched your brother and Kyler do some crazy and stupid shit over the years, but there is some serious judgment in his eyes when I play this in his presence. It's like he didn't even know who I am, even though he's seen us perform these songs all the time. I guess it was different once it was his girlfriend doing them? I had to channel my inner Katy, all by myself. Now...let's go get you all hot for your date!"

We make our way to the mall, singing and dancing to all our favorite songs. This feels good; it's us against the world again.

After a full morning of shopping, Dani and I make our way to the cute little bistro on the waterfront. It's one of my favorite places to eat. I usually bring my mom here when she comes to visit. We both order a mimosa and a salad. I order my typical chicken Caesar salad, and she orders a steak salad. It's cute—that's usually what my mom orders too.

Once the waiter leaves, I place my hands on the table and stare at Dani. I eye her up and down, and she looks confused.

"What?"

I smirk. "I'm trying to figure out who you are and what you did with my best friend?"

She laughs. "What the fuck is that supposed to mean?"

She doesn't say it rudely, as a smile is still on her face from ear to ear. That smile hasn't left all day.

"Well...it means, look at you, Dani! Look at how far you've come recently. You're opening yourself up to not only us, but to Kyler. After all that time away and shutting us out, you actually saw your parents and mine—my mom has not stopped talking about how excited she is about having someone to help her in the kitchen, so thanks."

It's a never-ending story of jokes about how bad I am in the kitchen.

Dani giggles and shrugs. *Smug bitch.*

I continue. "But in all seriousness, D, I'm proud of you. I mean, look at you, actually going on a date, and hello, that kiss last night."

I fan myself because it was H-O-T.

She nods, and I don't miss the blush on her cheeks.

The waiter brings our drinks and salads. I take a bite and moan. *Oh my God, this is heaven in my mouth.* I look up to see that Dani is just pushing food around on her plate.

"To be honest, Hails, I'm not sure how to feel. There is something about Kyler that, I don't know how to put it in words…"

I'm not sure where this is going, but I cut her off instead of letting her continue. "You don't need to put it in words, because you just smiled when you mentioned his name, and that, I think, is enough."

"Can I be honest?" she asks while taking a bite of her salad. I nod, so she continues. "I have no idea what I'm doing. I mean, I've only ever been on one first date, and that was when we were thirteen. What if I'm no good at it or Kyler realizes how much of a mess I am? Then it'll just be awkward."

I hate that she is doubting herself right now. This stops now. I raise my glass at her and nod so that she picks hers up too.

"I know you are scared, but that's how these things go." I think back to how nervous I was before Zach and I's first date. "I knew Zach my whole life, but I almost threw up from nerves before our first date."

She giggles. I narrow my lips into a straight line.

"What I'm trying to say is just take it one day or date at a time, okay? Now cheers, bitch—to us being back together and being able to gossip about boys and it not be my brother."

She grimaces and opens her mouth as if she had a smart-ass comment, but quickly shuts it. After setting my drink down, I prop my elbows on the table and rest my chin on my fists.

"Now spill all the juicy details of Lawson, because I'm dying to know."

CHAPTER 44
ZACH

"I don't think life can get much better than this, do you?" Haylee asks, snuggling into my chest as we enjoy our morning coffees in my favorite chair in the living room.

The house is quiet; Dani and Kyler must still be sleeping because we haven't heard a peep from them yet, and both of them are fiends for caffeine first thing in the morning.

I lean down, kissing her temple. Haylee is right; life is perfect at the moment. My girl is in my arms, a smile is back on my sister's face, and my best friend is happy. We even spent the weekend home for my mom's birthday. It was perfect having everyone back together. I know it made my mom's night.

My fingers trace up and down Haylee's arm. I can think of one way life can actually be better—if she agreed to marry me.

What am I waiting for? This is the perfect moment. It's now or never. I tap her leg so that she hops up off my lap, and she stands with a look of confusion.

"Don't go anywhere. Stay right there."

As I head toward our bedroom, I hear her say behind me, "Where are you going?"

Before I back out or some sort of karmic accident happens yet again, I am doing this. I am going to ask Haylee to be my wife. I should have done this a while ago, but then life got in the way. I'm done waiting. Like she said, life is perfect, but as we know, that can change in an instant. I *am* going to make her my wife. I reach into the closet and pull out the box of ties. I open the small velvet box one more time and take a deep breath.

You got this, Jacobs. Go make her yours forever.

Haylee

Zach disappears into the bedroom, and when he returns, I notice something in his hand. Before I have the chance to ask what he has, he strides over to where he left me and drops to one knee.

Holy shit, is he...?

"Oh my God, Zach..." I shriek, my hand flies to cover my mouth as I take in the view in front of me.

Zach Jacobs is on one knee in our living room. He opens the velvet box, and I am met with the most stunning ring I have ever seen. It looks like my grandmother's ring yet different.

My eyes fill as he begins to speak.

"Haylee Grace Hanks, I have had the honor of knowing your love and friendship for twenty-two years. Throughout those years, I have watched you go from the silly, nerdy girl next door to this incredibly beautiful and charismatic woman. We had to go through an earth-shattering tragedy to find ourselves."

I choke out another tear as he continues.

"Your love and comfort put me back together. You make me laugh, smile, and feel complete. I look at you and not only see my past and present, but also my future. I am so head over heels in love with you. Please let me spend the rest of my life making you as happy as you make me. Hails, will you marry me?"

Is this happening?

"Yes! Yes! God, yes!" I shout as he slides the ring on my finger and stands, pulling me into his arms and crashing his lips to mine.

My hands wrap around his neck and pull him closer to deepen the kiss. When we break apart, I hold my hand out to admire the ring.

A noise in the hallway turns our attention to find Dani and Kyler standing there. Tears are running down Dani's face; Kyler next to her rubbing her back. He leaves her side and walks toward us.

"Congrats!" He first pulls me into a hug. "I'm so happy for you both."

I somehow manage a "thank you" in between tears.

"It's about damn time, man." He and Zach hug their manly hug, slapping each other's back over and over.

Once they separate, Zach puts his arm around me, and I instinctively wrap my arms around his waist. I look down at my ring finger one last time before my eyes meet my best friend's.

I see it in her eyes—something is wrong. Dani has still not moved from where she's standing. I tense, and I feel Zach's arm tighten around me.

The smile has left Zach's face as his eyes narrow at his sister. "Dani, say something."

"Are you fucking kidding me?" Dani shouts.

Her brother and best friend get engaged, and the first words out of her mouth are "are you fucking kidding me"? My heart begins to break. I suck in a breath, and the tears continue to fall down her cheeks. My eyes travel back and forth between Dani and Zach. The atmosphere in the room changed drastically from love to...I don't even know the words to describe what is happening right now.

Kyler cautiously walks to his girlfriend, glancing back toward us before he places his hand on her arm. "Aren't you excited for your brother and your best friend?"

"Are you seriously going to lecture me right now?" Her eyes are full of rage now, and I can't hold back my tears.

A sob rips from my throat. This was supposed to be the happiest day of my life—just a moment ago it was.

Zach steps in front of me, his arm wrapping around my waist as I grip his shirt and continue to cry. Is she not happy about me and Zach getting married or us being together at all? Maybe we read her being happy for us all wrong.

"Fuck, Dani! Why can't you just be happy for Haylee and me? Huh? It's always just about you still, isn't it?" The anger is radiating from my fiancé's body.

Dani leaves the room for a moment, then returns with her purse and keys in hand. *Oh, no. This is not happening again.* I am not going to watch my best friend walk out that door again.

"Oh, please. Love is for assholes. All it brings is pain, and anyone would be a fool to believe in that shit...that happy ever afters can actually happen."

Emmett. My heart sinks in my chest when I realize this is another moment my brother is missing. That's it. She thought of him too. Of course she did. Even though she has been happy lately, a new version of her old self, in fact, and I can tell that she loves Kyler, her mind drifted to the one she always thought she would see in front of her. I need to stop her.

I go to step forward to stop her, and Zach puts his hand in

front of me to stop me as Kyler approaches her first. He reaches for her hand, and she snaps.

"Don't touch me. What, you think you can fix me? That we can just play house and live out our happy ever after bullshit? You're nothing but a replacement. You may have replaced Emmett in my brother's world, but you won't in mine. This is… This is…"

Kyler's face goes white. Zach falls back as if her words punched him. My arms wrap around him to hold him up. I can't believe this is happening. Can I pinch myself and wake up from this nightmare?

"What, baby… It's love? It's real? It's raw? Because it's all of those things, Dani! Why can't you just let me in?" Kyler's voice is full of anger and hurt.

I have known him for years now, and I have never seen him like this.

"It was a mistake, Kyler. You can't make me happy, and you're a fool to believe you can. I'm incapable of loving or being loved. I'm just broken," Dani fires back at him, giving us one more glance before she leaves, slamming the door.

Silence fills the room as we all just stand there, unsure how to react. Did she just leave for good? Is she coming back?

I know what she said hurt, but I know her more than she knows herself and she didn't mean those words only out of hurt. By the time Kyler finally comes back to reality, her words have left a brand on him.

He rushes to the front door, opening it to find her already gone. "Fuck! Where did she go?"

Zach turns in my arms, his hands cupping my cheeks to rub the tears away. "Baby, I am so sorry."

For the second time today, Zach gets on one knee in front of me, this time begging for forgiveness, only there is nothing to forgive.

"It's okay; we need to find her. I told you once before that I have her back—I'm not letting her go." I nod over to my fiancé's best friend, who is sitting on the floor with his head down.

Panic of the reality that his sister just walked out the door finally hits, and Zach's eyes go wide and he rises.

"Fuck." He looks over at Kyler and sees that his phone is in his hand. "Is she answering?"

The look on his face has devastation written all over as he shakes his head no.

Zach crouches down in front of his best friend and puts his hand on his shoulder. "Hey, we're gonna find her okay?"

He nods, but doesn't say anything as he hits "send" again.

I back up to the couch, pull my legs to my chest, and rest my head on my knees as I try to think like Dani. She just witnessed me and her brother get engaged. I replay her words over and over again. Where would she go when her family is out of town? She wouldn't have really left, would she? I mean, all she took was her purse, keys, and phone. She left all the rest of her belongings behind. I look down at the ring on my left hand and stare at the combination of diamond and amethysts—my brother's birthstone.

Oh my God. Emmett. That's it!

I ignore the conversation going on in the background between Zach and Kyler, and I hop off the couch and gather my things. Crap, where are my keys? I see the keys to the Jeep on the table and grab them before heading to the door.

"Woah, Haylee, where are you going? You're just going to leave?" Zach rises to his feet.

Concern is written over both Zach and Ky's faces.

"Call it best friend's intuition, but I know where she went. Give me some time to get there, okay?"

"I don't get it. Where did she go?" Kyler asks.

Instead of answering, I step up to Zach, press a brief kiss to his lips, and give Kyler a small smile, reassuring him I am confident.

As I close the door behind me and head to Zach's Jeep, I pray to God I am right. Pulling out of the driveway, I take a deep breath and put the vehicle in drive, then head to the same place I go when I'm upset—Glen Ridge Cemetery.

CHAPTER 45
Haylee

I hold my breath as I pull through the cemetery gates, hoping my intuition was right, and finally release it as I turn onto the hill and see her SUV parked there. I pull out my cell phone to call Zach. We spoke for most of the drive, mainly me reassuring him and Kyler that this is where she would be.

The phone doesn't even ring before he picks up.

"Hey, baby." His voice, while calm, is laced with panic.

"Hey."

"Please tell me you have some news. Ky and I are going crazy here."

I get out of the Jeep and make my way toward her. I see that she is sitting next to Emmett's grave with her knees pulled into her chest, resting her chin on them.

"Yeah, I found her. She's okay. We'll be home soon."

"Oh, thank God. Ky, she found her." Instant relief floods my fiancé's voice.

I hear Kyler mumble something in the background, but can't fully make it out.

"Bring her home. I love you."

"Love you too." I end the call and put my phone away as I approach her. I take a seat next to her on the grass.

"I figured this is where I'd find you. I come here when I

need a moment too." I turn to face my brother's headstone and place my hand over his name, *Emmett Adam Hanks*. "Hey, big bro. About time she visited, huh?"

I know that this is the first time she has been here since the funeral. I think of all the times I have been here since then.

Silence consumes us. I just sit and stare at her. There is so much emotion written all over her face. Her eyes are swollen and red. All of the years of pent-up grief finally unleashed. I just want to pull her into my arms and never let go, but I need to give her the lead with this.

I hate this for her. I hate this for us. Her eyes turn heavy with guilt as she looks to me and begins to speak, but I cut her off.

I reach for her wrist. "It's okay, Dani."

She shakes her head. "No, it's really not. I'm not sure how to do this. I'm a mess. I ruined this morning, and then I said some very hurtful things to Kyler."

Her shoulders are tense as if she is carrying the weight of the world on them. The things she said to Kyler hurt all of us, but he loves her enough to know she didn't mean them. He just wants her home and safe. I can see how upset this whole situation has made her, and it kills me to see her like this. This is a shell of the girl she used to be before Kyler brought her back to life. Yeah, I can honestly say that she is a better person and healing because of him, not because of anything Zach, our parents, or I did, but it was all Kyler. I can see how much they mean to each other.

"Then I come here for the first time since the funeral, and I scream. Like seriously at the top of my lungs, wake-the-dead-style scream. I'm surprised no one called the cops to haul my ass out of here. I'm just still so angry. Where do you find the strength to move on?"

I think about what she just said. *Move on?* Is that what she thinks we did? I could never "move on" from the loss of my brother; I just learned how to deal with it since it's something that I can't change. I tighten the grip on her wrist as I fight back my own tears.

"It's not easy. It's honestly a lot of work, but I take it one day at a time. Some days I am so angry that he's not here, and others I use the anger I have that he's not to power me through the day. I'm angry for all the big events he has missed and will continue to miss."

Give me strength, Em.

This was a big moment today that he missed. I hate it that he isn't here to see me happy, to see Zach happy. Who would've thought it would've been us?

"I'm upset that he isn't here to celebrate my big news. I hurt for my parents, for you, for Zach. I use it to make something of my life—a life he didn't get. I was in a bad place after he died...I not only lost my brother, but I lost my best friend. I felt like I had lost everything. I mean, I did. So did Zach. He had lost his best friend and his only sister."

Dani looks down guiltily. When she looks back up to me, I have to fight the feeling of wanting to just pull her into my arms and cry.

"Zach and I started hanging out and were just friends, but then it turned into something more—we drew strength from each other. Moving on doesn't mean I'm any less sad or miss my brother any less. It just means I'm living."

I adjust myself on the grass so that I'm closer to Dani. "Please don't think that I'm not dying on the inside, all because I appear to have my shit together on the outside. There have been plenty of nights that I have cried myself to sleep, and Zach will just hold me and let me fall apart. I cry if I see something that reminds me of him or when I see something that I think he would've liked. But I also know that he wouldn't want me to be sad and not live my life. I know that I get to spend the rest of my life living for my brother and have a man next to me who I love so much.

"Through Em's death, I found Zach. Yes, I've known him my whole life, but it wasn't until we were both so broken and lost in the darkness and consumed by our grief that we found light in each other. We healed each other. It's still a process, but we are facing it together. He would be so happy for us…well, after he thoroughly kicked your brother's ass, of course."

We both laugh. That has to be a good sign, right?

I take a deep breath and look into her eyes so she really hears what I'm about to say. "He would want you to live too, Danielle. He would hate you like this; you and I both know it."

"But I feel guilty…" she attempts to say before I raise my hand to cut her off.

"I know how madly in love my brother was with you and vice versa. I know the dreams you guys planned and the life you both wanted together. I was there for both of you. I saw both sides of your love as his sister and your best friend. And then life stepped up to the plate and gave a big fuck-you and destroyed them, all of them—your dreams, mine, my parents', and anyone who ever did or would have known Emmett. I know that Em wouldn't want this for you. He told me once that all he wanted was for you to be happy—it was why he did stupid shit like the singing and dancing in public or verbally proclaiming his love for you as if he just discovered new land. He said his sole purpose in life was to make you smile. Yeah, he actually said that—big, bad Emmett was pretty whipped. I never understood any of that until Zach."

Maybe Kyler is Em's gift to Dani, to always keep her smiling.

The corners of my mouth curve upward, and I feel my cheeks warm as I think about how lucky I am to have Zach in my life. My thumb plays with the new gorgeous ring on my finger. Oh my God, I can't believe I'm engaged. I get to spend the rest of my life with a man I genuinely adore and who loves me. I close my eyes and look up at the sky.

"Ya know, I don't know exactly where my brother is right now, but I hope that he is at peace. And of course, if he chooses to haunt me, I hope he at least doesn't do it while Zach and I are, well..." I wiggle my eyebrows and giggle as Dani holds her hand up for me to stop.

After all that she and Em put us through with PDA over the years, I am half-tempted to finish that sentence.

"But what I do know is that he would hate you not being happy. He would hate knowing that the smile that he made sure he saw every day was gone. He would understand and want someone to be able to put that smile back on your face if he can't. We know that if he were here that you both would be together and hopefully, by now, I'd be spoiling the shit out of my nieces or nephews." My smile quickly fades. "But he's not. He's never coming back. So, Dani, I need you to live, for you, for Emmett, for the dreams, and for the memories. You can't live your life carrying the weight of my brother's death, you just can't. I won't allow it. We let you walk away once before, and fuck if we are going to let you do it again. Prove that my brother's death wasn't for nothing but his dreams dying with him and yours as well. We can't change your dreams together falling apart, but you can still do something about yours—make new ones."

Dani begins to fully break down again, tears running down her cheeks and shoulders trembling. "But I just feel so guilty that I get to live and he doesn't."

I pull Dani into my arms, not holding back, both of us sobbing. After a moment, I pull back and place my hands on her cheeks to force her to look at me.

"I know, I know, but I need you to fucking stop. Don't let your guilt get in the way of being happy. You did not cause that accident. That's what it was—an accident. A wrong place at the wrong time. I need you to make the decision to stop feeling guilty. To make the decision of living your life. You only get one, and how amazing is it that in that one life you get two great men who love you when most people don't even get one?"

Dani gasps and pulls back in shock. I'm not sure what I said just now to earn that reaction. "Kyler doesn't love me."

My brows furrow. *Is she serious right now?* That boy is head over heels in love with her.

I try to hide back my laughter, but a giggle escapes. "Oh, yes, he does. I've known him for a few years now, and I've never seen him look at someone the way he looks at you."

"And how is that?" She cocks her head to the side.

I place my forehead against hers. "Honey, Ky looks at you the same way Emmett used to."

How has she not realized this? I reach out for her hand and squeeze it to show her it's okay to admit her feelings for him. Like I told her, my brother wouldn't want her not to allow herself to love again.

"It's also the same way you look at him."

She silently nods. *See, that wasn't so hard, D.*

She wipes under her eyes and laughs. "Shit, Hails, when did you become the smart and wise one out of the two of us?"

I smile. Well, she walked right into this one. "Probably around the same time I started sleeping with your brother."

I am mentally high-fiving myself as she jokingly gags. *Payback is a bitch.* But we end up just laughing more.

"If that's not the pot calling the kettle black, missy. Remember every time we talked about boys growing up and all your firsts? I had to hear about my brother, so bleh." I stick my tongue at her as we continue to get lost in our laughter.

Once we compose ourselves, wiping away tears of joy now, Dani grabs my hand to inspect my new bling. "So you're really going to marry my brother, huh?"

"Yeah, I am," I respond, my cheeks beginning to hurt from how broad my smile is. I turn to my brother's grave and hold up my hand that has the combination of the diamond and amethyst stones.

"Did you hear that, big bro? I'm getting married. Can you believe it?" Wow, I'm not sure I still believe it.

I turn back to my best friend. "But you know what's better than him becoming my husband?"

I roll my eyes at Dani as she brings her hand to her chin and dramatically thinks my question over. "A root canal? Maybe natural childbirth? Falling out of the tree and breaking your arm?"

This girl thinks she's so funny. And for the record, no, falling out of a tree and breaking your arm is *not* better, even if it's enjoyable getting your brother into trouble for it.

I playfully shove her. "Bitch! No, I was going to say, I still get you as my sister. See? *That* plan didn't change."

Not only am I marrying the man of my dreams, but I get my best friend as my sister-in-law. I had always hoped one day we would be real sisters, but I had believed that that dream had died along with my brother. That is, until Zach swept me all my feet and stole my heart.

Dani lunges toward me, almost knocking me to the ground. "I love you, Hails."

"I love you too, D. Now, what do you say we get back to the

house because I'm pretty sure Kyler has officially driven Zach insane and possibly paced the floor away."

I've felt my phone vibrating in my pocket multiple times while sitting here. No doubt Zach checking in making sure she didn't run again.

Dani nods, and we help each other up, brushing the grass off our clothes. I step forward and kiss the headstone, the same thing I do every time I go to leave here.

"I'll see you later, big bro. I promise I'll take care of her." I look back at Dani, who has her arms wrapped around her waist. "I miss you. Love you, E."

I step back, and Dani asks, "Can you give me a minute?"

I nod toward the cars and head in that direction. I look back one last time to see her bent down, running her hand over the stone.

I pull my phone from my pocket as I walk away, giving Dani the space she needs to say goodbye. As I predicted, I have eleven texts from Zach. I choose to respond to his texts rather than call.

ME: *On our way home. See you soon.*

My phone buzzes a moment later.

ZACH: *Be careful. I love you...fiancée.*

A smile appears on my face, and I am overjoyed with love as I type back.

ME: *You too. Xo*

I lean against the Jeep as I wait for Dani to be done. Once she approaches, we both nod as we get into our vehicles and make our way back to our guys. I follow her the entire way home, decompressing the day. Wow, has it seriously only been one day?

Fights.

Emotional breakdown.

Engaged.

Dani and I arrive home and stand in the doorway watching Zach and Kyler hug. We share a glance before looking back at them. I press my lips together to suppress my laughter. When another minute has passed, I clear my throat, and I must startle them because they both jump back. They both begin to make manly grunting noises. I guess to prove they're still macho.

Damn, boys are so weird. Am I sure I want to marry one of those?

I finally release the laugh I was holding in. "Ummm, we can always come back, but Kyler, maybe you should remember that this Jacobs is already taken, and I don't like to share."

I stalk toward Zach and wrap my arms around his waist.

Zach leans down, whispering against my lips, "I missed you."

His lips crash onto mine, staking his claim, as if the ring on my finger didn't do that enough. I get lost in his kiss just like I always do. I can kiss this man forever, and now I get to. I finally open my eyes.

"Hi."

"Hi," he says back, panting, and I notice his shorts are little too tight.

He looks up and then searches the room. I turn around and

I Never Expected You

see that we were so preoccupied that we didn't even notice Dani and Kyler leave the room. Oops.

"Should we go find them? I'm hungry."

When this man is hungry, he goes from zero to hangry pretty quickly, but I think it's best to give them time.

"I think we should let them talk first. It was a lot today. I think they have some things to talk about."

Zach pouts like a child, earning a giggle and eye roll from me. *My future husband, ladies and gentlemen.*

Zach plops down on his favorite chair and lasts all but five minutes before he jumps up. "Okay, I'm starving."

I chase after him. "Babe, I think you should wait or maybe knock first."

"I'm hungry, Hails," he shouts over his shoulder as he reaches the door. "You guys wanna go out or order piz...*fuck!* Not again," Zach yells before slamming the door shut.

Oh shit! He blocked me, but I did catch a glimpse of Dani's back, and I'm pretty sure she was on Kyler's lap. I think it's safe to say the two of them made up.

Zach continues to yell at them through the closed door. "Seriously, Dani, haven't you ever heard of a fucking door lock?"

I can hear their laughter on the other side, and as awful as it is, I can't hide my laughter either. The poor guy walked in on her sister in the act not only once but now *twice*.

In between her fit of giggles, Dani yells back, "Haven't you ever heard of knocking first?"

"I told you to knock first. Maybe you should listen to me more often," I add as Zach continues to curse and grumble.

By the time I reach the living room, he's already sitting in his chair again, probably wishing he'd listened to me in the first place, but I won't tell him "I told you so," at least not yet.

I crouch down in front of him. His elbows are propped up on his knees, and his head is in his hands.

"For fuck's sake. I'm going to need some therapy for this. I'm not even hungry anymore."

I raise my eyebrows at him.

His head moves in agreement. "Okay, okay. I *am* still hungry."

I stand and step between his legs and sit in his lap, wrapping my arms around his neck. His hands rest on my thighs. "What do you say we go get a pizza, and then we can come back and celebrate? Remember that whole thing that we got engaged today?"

His eyes go wide. "What? We did?"

He clutches his chest in shock.

I poke his chest. "Hilarious, asshole. You better watch it."

"Or what?"

I ponder it over. Hmmm...think quick.

"Or you don't get dessert after dinner." I stand and go to walk away when he pulls me into his lap.

"Dinner, then your dessert, babe. Let's go." He pushes me up and smacks my butt.

When I turn to face him, he gives that signature Jacobs wink and holds his hand out for me to take.

CHAPTER 46
ZACH

We had returned home with pizza and no sign of Kyler or Dani having come out of her room and nope, I was not about to go knock on the door. Haylee heads to our bedroom as I finish cleaning up the kitchen, putting the leftover pizza in the fridge.

I mumble under my breath, "If they want leftovers, at least they are there, *so you're welcome.*"

I lean against the doorway of our bedroom, staring at my beautiful fiancée currently sitting with one foot propped up on the bed, unlacing her Converse.

That beautiful woman right there agreed to be my wife. I have been carrying that ring around for what seems like forever and finally popped the question, and of all things, she said *yes*. This has been one of the longest days of my life. I may have decided last minute to finally pop the question to her, but I didn't plan, once she said yes, to spend it worrying about my sister, calming Kyler down, and definitely not walking in on my sister and Ky in a compromising position.

Thank God I wasn't just another second or two later. I shiver at the thought and focus back on Hails. I walk over to her while she is working on the other shoe.

I bend down to one knee and reach for her left hand that

already has my ring on it. My thumb drags over the ring. It seriously is a beautiful ring, and being a dude, I know absolutely nothing about jewelry, but this ring...it's personal. I would never have thought about adding Emmett's birthstone to the ring—that was all Brian.

"What are you doing?"

I look up from the ring to meet the most stunning pair of blue eyes I have ever seen. "When I decided I was going to propose today, I didn't expect the rest of today's events to unfold the way they did. That put a little bit of a damper on our celebrating, so I thought I would do a redo and then give you a proper celebration." The curves of her lips go upward in a smile as she looks down on me, still on one knee.

"In the last conversation Em and I ever had, he told me one day a girl would knock me on my ass. I laughed at him then. I never thought I would find a girl who would not only turn my world upside down, but would capture my heart completely. I found that in you, of all people. I knew early on that you were the one I wanted to spend the rest of my life with. In fact, I've had this..." I place my thumb and forefinger around her ring and slide it off her finger. "...for quite some time—since my graduation, actually. Your dad had this custom-made with your grandmother's ring. He wanted you to have a part of your brother for the rest of your life."

Her hands cover her nose and mouth as tears fill her eyes. *Shit, I made her cry. Get to the point, Jacobs.*

"There never seemed to be a right time to give you this ring, but if there is anything that we have learned over our years together, it's that nothing goes as planned, so this morning, I knew that there was only one thing that could make life even better, and that was you agreeing to be my wife. I didn't need anything fancy to ask you—just you."

I Never Expected You

Tears are running down her cheeks, and her body vibrates as she sniffles away the tears. I reach up and cup her cheek and run my thumb along her cheekbone.

"Haylee, I never imagined my life turning out the way it did, and that is all because of you. You are my life, my world, my everything. Thank you for never giving up on me and always being by my side. You're it for me, Haylee Hanks. I love you so much. Marry me?"

She nods. "Yes, baby, my answer is still yes. I love you so much."

I slide the ring back on her finger and rise up, cupping both of her cheeks and pulling her face to me. She draws in a small breath as my lips press against hers. I explore her mouth with my tongue, and when her tongue seeks mine, I lose all control. I wrap one hand around her waist and lift her closer to the top of the bed. Her hand slides to the back of my neck, and she deepens the kiss. This kiss tells her everything I didn't say or couldn't say. I'm not sure there are words that could adequately describe how much I love Haylee Hanks.

Clothes are ripped off in a flash; hands are grabbing, teeth clashing, lips consuming. This is the proper way I had planned to celebrate her saying yes today. I roll over to my back and bring Haylee on top of me.

I hiss out an elongated "Fuck!" as she sinks down on me.

As much as I love being in control in the bedroom, there is nothing sexier than this woman on top of me. My fingers press into her hips before she can begin to move, and I take a breath to commit this moment to memory. Her nails grip my chest, and we lock eyes. For just a moment we stare at each other. This woman has actually agreed to marry me, and I will love her until my last breath and then some.

Just as she goes to open her mouth to say something, I begin to move my hips, and whatever she was going to say is replaced with a moan. I bring my right hand to the back of her neck and pull her down to me as I grind into her.

"I love you so much, baby girl." I don't even allow her to respond by claiming her lips again.

CHAPTER 47
Haylee

1.5 years later...

"Hey, how was your night with Kyler?" I ask Zach as he closes the front door.

I grab the remote and hit Pause on the rerun of *How I Met Your Mother* I was watching. It still feels weird that Dani and Kyler don't live here anymore. It's been four months since they got a place of their own, just down the street. Of course, it has a fantastic kitchen.

Zach leans down and the moment his lips touch mine, I feel electricity shoot through my body, my nipples pressing against the inside of my bra. Don't even get me started on the butterflies he causes down below. The contact breaks too quickly, and I let out a groan in response.

Zach sits down next to me, smirking, throwing my legs over his and extending his arm along the back of the couch.

"Well..." That Jacobs smirk overtakes his face, and his features light up. Guess he had a good time. "Tonight was interesting."

"What do you mean? Everything okay?" I begin to worry and sit up straighter.

Zach leans over and steals a sip of my ginger ale, prolonging telling me what happened on boys' night out.

I gently shove him. "Come on, don't hold out. What happened?"

"Patience, young grasshopper."

"You know damn well that patience was not a virtue I was born with. Now spill, Jacobs!"

Zach throws his head back in laughter. "This is very true."

Enough with changing the subject damnit. I'll call Ky and ask him. This is getting ridiculous. I throw my hands up in frustration

Zach reaches for my hand and brushes his hand over the ring he gave me a year and a half ago, and his smile widens.

"Ky is going to ask Dani to marry him. He's already spoken to my dad, and tonight he wanted to make sure I was okay with it too. I can't believe he asked for *my* permission. Oh, and he wants you to help him pick out the ring this week—that is, if you're free. I told him you would call him."

"What? Oh, my God! That's amazing!" I jump up off the couch in excitement.

I only get a moment to celebrate before my stomach has other plans. My hand rushes to cover my mouth, and I spin on my heels and race to the bathroom.

"Hails?" Zach calls out from the hallway. "Are you okay? I know my sister had a crazy reaction to us getting engaged, but don't you think throwing up is a little extreme?"

I turn to look at him, now standing in the bathroom doorway, and narrow my eyes before my stomach turns on me, and I continue to the porcelain throne. When I finish, I sit back and exhale a loud breath, trying to blow the fallen strands of hair out of my face.

The humorous side of Zach leaves, and his face turns

serious as he crouches down in front of me, tucking the fallen hairs behind my ear.

He brushes his lips against my forehead before he stands. "Come on, let's get you cleaned up and into bed."

"I'm fine, really, Zach. Dinner must not have settled with me."

I wash my hands and splash water over my face. I reach for the hand towel and find the ring empty. As I lean down to reach under the sink for a new towel, I see the unopened box of tampons and instantly freeze. *No, wait...when was my last period?*

The color from my face drains.

"Are you about to get sick again?"

"No, I think I'm okay." *But am I?*

"Are you sure, because you don't look it."

With the tampon box in my hand, I sit down on the closed lid toilet and stare at it. *Come on, Haylee, when was the last time you needed one of these?* Things have certainly been stressful lately with wedding planning, and there is no shortage of sex in this house.

As if Zach and I were in tune enough and he could read my thoughts, he mutters, "Oh shit."

My eyes meet his, and he visibly swallows before running his fingers through his hair. I worry that I am going to need to move from where I'm sitting to allow him to lose his dinner with the way he's looking. Finally, he shoves his hands in his pocket.

"Okay, wow. Talk about a crazy turn of events tonight. Hey, it's okay."

Zach sits on the edge of the tub, removes the box from my hands, and places it on the floor. He laces his fingers with mine. "Hey, come here."

I hesitate at first, but then I rise from where I sit and settle into his lap. His hand rubs circles on my back.

"Okay, here's the plan. *Tonight*, we go back into the living room and curl up on the couch and watch some more *How I Met Your Mother*, I tell you about Ky's plans, and we worry about *this* tomorrow. Deal?"

I nod in between sniffles.

"Plus, I'm pretty sure there are some cookies and cream ice cream still in the freezer."

My eyes perk up at the mention of ice cream. Nothing a little time with my favorite five can't fix.

Zach leans in to kiss me, but I press my hand to his chest and push him back.

"What's wrong?" He tilts his head in confusion.

"I have vomit mouth. It's gross."

Zach cringes and suppresses a laugh. "Well, I kiss you after you have my dick in your mouth, so I don't think it really matters to me."

"Jesus! You are insane."

He goes in for another attempt, and I wiggle out of his arms and stand. I turn around and press my hands against the counter, knowing that he could quickly hoist me up on to the counter and wrap my legs around his waist.

I kick the fantasy out of my thoughts. "You go change and meet me back on the couch—*with the ice cream*, or no snuggles for you."

Zach settles for a kiss to the top of my head and exits the bedroom.

Slowly turning around, I bring my hands to my stomach. Could I be pregnant? I can hear the sound of my heartbeat pounding through my ears. I close my eyes and take three deep breaths. *One. Two. Three.*

I Never Expected You

Whatever the outcome, we're in this together. I try to push those thoughts aside, but that's like telling someone afraid of heights not to look down when they are high up. I put the box of tampons back under the sink and say a silent prayer that it's just the stress of wedding planning that stopped the visits from Aunt Flo and not something that will be solved in nine months.

Fuck. Fuck. Fuck. That can't be right. One word in front of me that changes our lives.

Pregnant.

Holy shit. I walk out of the bathroom and join Zach on the bed. The bedroom is so quiet. I'm not used to the house being so quiet after four adults living here—then again, I guess the silence won't last long with a little one on the way. *Holy crap! I'm pregnant.*

"Well, what did it say?"

I hand Zach the pregnancy test and watch his reaction as he sees the results. Zach hops up from where he was sitting and paces the floor back and forth.

"You're... We're gonna... I'm gonna be..." He stutters his words.

I honestly can't tell from his expression if he's happy or mad. I mean, he can't be mad, right?

I place my head in my hands and begin to cry. This isn't part of our plan. We're supposed to get married first.

Zach places his hands on mine as he crouches down to his knees. He pulls my hands away from my face and reveals my watery eyes. I don't even try to fight the tears from falling.

"Baby, what's wrong?"

"This! It's all wrong. It wasn't supposed to happen like this.

We're supposed to get married first and then have a baby. We're not ready for this."

He takes my hands in his and sits back next to me on the bed, pulling me into his lap. "Hey. It's going to be okay. Yeah, we didn't expect it to happen so soon, but what can I say? The Jacobs sperm is strong, especially with this weapon of mass destruction."

I shake my head and laugh through my tears as he points to his dick. "You really need to stop calling it that."

He brushes off my comment and continues. "It may not have been part of our current plan, but if you haven't noticed, our families and plans don't usually work out. All I know is I want to have kids one day, and I want them with you. If it happens a lot sooner than we thought, then so be it. Either way, you are going to be an amazing mom, whether it be now or down the road."

I can't believe him right now. I thought he would have been freaking out.

"Why aren't you freaking out right now? You're scaring me."

He places a kiss to the top of my head before resting his against mine. "To be honest, I have no fucking idea. When you first mentioned that this was a possibility last night, I was freaking the fuck out internally, but I couldn't stop thinking about it all night. After all the bad we've endured over the years, now look at all the positive things happening in our lives. First my sister is going to get engaged, and now we're going to be bringing a baby into this world. You and me." He places his palm over my stomach. "We did that. We made a baby; how freaking cool is that? Like seriously."

Ha! Leave it to Zach to bring humor to a serious moment; it's one of the many reasons I love this man. He is right though—

I Never Expected You

having a baby would come eventually, but who cares about a timeline.

"We're really doing this, huh?"

"You bet we are." Zach looks down and bites his lip. "Damn, your tits are going to get so big. It's going to be fucking awesome. I need to go call Ky and tell him the news."

"About my tits?" I raise an eyebrow in question.

"No—you know those are all mine." He winks and looks down at my chest before bringing his eyes back to me. "I want to tell him about the baby."

"No, don't do that. He has enough on his plate right now. I can't believe that he is going to ask her, or even more that he is such a romantic that he asked you to for permission too. That's just so sweet."

"Like I would have even thought about saying no to him."

"So let's let them have the spotlight for now, and then we'll give it some time before we make any announcements, okay?"

Zach thinks it over but finally agrees. First thing's first: help Ky pick out a ring, while I soak in the idea that I'm going to be a mom.

CHAPTER 48
ZACH

Sitting at a table close to the front of the stage seems weird. For all the years we've been coming to Lucky's, we have always sat at the same place, except tonight, per Kyler's request. Tonight is the night: he plans to ask my sister to marry him. The difference between him and I is that he hasn't waited for months and months to ask her.

I lean over and brush Haylee's hair behind her ear. "You know, with our family all here tonight, it would be a great opportunity to tell them about the b-a-b-y."

Haylee turns to me, and her eyes darken. "Don't even think about making this about us. Tonight is about your sister and Ky. We can tell them all later."

I lean back into my chair and grumble, "Yeah, well, payback would be sweet since she made a scene with our engagement."

She whips her head around. "Are you serious right now?"

I shrug jokingly. "I'm just saying. I know this is about them. I can't even believe he's doing it."

"Right?" Haylee takes a sip of her drink.

We wanted to get here early to order a nonalcoholic beverage for her so that people wouldn't question anything.

"Do you think she'll say no?" It's an honest question.

"Nah, she loves him. He's hers forever." Haylee turns to me with so much love in her eyes.

I Never Expected You

Kyler is currently near the stage hiding out and waiting for Dani to arrive. I look up to see her headed in our direction. I glance over to where our families are seated, hoping she doesn't notice them.

Dani shakes her coat off and places it on the back of the chair. Luckily the chair she picks has her back to our families.

"How come we aren't at our regular table tonight and stuck up front by the stage?"

I look at Haylee and bring my drink to my mouth to hide my face. Yep, I'm a total coward, choosing to hide behind my glass as I lie right to my sister's face.

"Oh, well, we were running late, and the table was already occupied."

Well, your boyfriend is about to make some big romantic gesture and wanted you to be close to the stage, was what I wanted to say.

"Oh," she responds, taking a seat. She glances around but never fully turns around, thank God. "Where's Kyler? I thought he was meeting us here?" She looks down at her phone.

Just then, the spotlight on the stage appears, and Scott takes the microphone. I settle back into my chair, wrapping my arm behind Haylee. *Here we go.*

He waves his hands in the air to quiet the crowd down. "All right, all right, everyone. Tonight we are doing something a little different—our favorite dynamic duo is flying solo. Let's everyone give Kyler a warm welcome and see if he is actually any good without his partner in crime. Thank God this is just one night and one night only."

He steps aside and claps his hands together. Kyler appears on the stage.

"Tonight, I'd like to dedicate this song to my girl, Dani. I love you. Here it goes."

Hmm, this sounds familiar—singing in front of the crowd to the girl you love. *You're welcome.*

Kyler begins singing "Danny's Song" by Loggins and Messina. *That's cute, but wait...* I furrow my brows as he continues singing and listen to the lyrics. Is he singing a song about becoming a dad? *Shit, does he know?*

I glance over at my sister and see her taking large swigs of her margarita, and I can't help but laugh as I see Haylee staring at her too. I'm sure she is jealous, but at least we got here early enough to order her a nonalcoholic drink so that no one would figure it out.

The song finally ends, and we all applause, including Haylee giving one of those crazy whistles. Pretty sure I might be deaf in the ear closest to her. Kyler takes the microphone off the stand and heads toward our table, stopping right in front of Dani. He takes both of her hands in his, and both are smiling stupidly.

I pull Haylee into me, and she looks up at me, her eyes so full of love and unshed tears. I love that he has included all of us in this big moment.

"Dani, I have possibly been in love with you from the moment I met you—or at least since the first time I tasted your cupcakes. When you walked into my life, I didn't realize that something was actually missing. Even though you claim that I saved you and put you back together, I know that it was really you. You saved me by showing me what it meant to really love someone and to be loved by someone. Maybe, in a way, we saved each other. You bring out the best in me and I in you. You are the light in my darkness. Life is never going to be easy as we both know that from the journeys that brought us here, but with you, I feel as though I can face anything and everything that is thrown at me. I love you so much. I know you hate my jokes and my apparent bad taste in movies, but I want to spend the rest of my life proving to you that *Office Space* is, in fact, a funny movie."

Dani laughs through her tears, and I can't help but wonder what the hell she has against *Office Space*—it's a great movie.

Kyler gets down on one knee and pulls out a small velvet box with the ring. Damn, Haylee did good helping to pick that out.

"Danielle Kathryn Jacobs, I love you with all my heart. Will you marry me?"

Dani looks around, and her eyes go wide as she must finally notice our families sitting in the back. When she turns to face Kyler again, she nods.

"Yes, baby, a million times yes!"

Wow, I don't think I have even seen Kyler move as fast as he does then when he stands, sweeping my sister into his arms, and kisses the shit out of her. Our family has gotten up from their seats and moved toward us.

"You do realize that that song is about having a baby and we —" Dani turns to our family, throwing her hands up innocently. "—are *not* expecting, just to clear that up."

Everyone laughs, but I see this as a sign to make out the announcement. I look at Haylee with raised eyebrows; she can't deny this moment either.

She speaks first, shouting, "No, but we are!"

So much for the waiting part.

I wave my hands in the air. "Surprise!"

Well, so much for not stealing the thunder from the newly engaged couple. Oopsie.

Everyone stares at us as if they are trying to process what we just said before bursting out in celebration again.

Kyler steps beside me and pulls me into a hug, slapping my back. "Holy shit, you're gonna be a dad!"

When we pull apart, I see Dani and Haylee jumping up and down in excitement. The Lawsons, Hanks, and my parents all hug everyone. I'm sure anyone that just happened to be in here tonight is probably like what the fuck is going on.

While the moms, Kate, Lauren, and Haylee inspect the shiny new ring on my sister's finger, the men all pull extra tables over to join ours.

I take a seat next to my fiancée, who is glowing even more now that the news is finally out in the open. A weight lifts from my shoulders as well.

I sit back and look around at where our lives have ended up. My sister is happy in love and engaged to my best friend, and I couldn't be happier for the two of them. They deserve all the love and happiness in the world.

Haylee and I will one day tie the knot, and the craziest of all is that there is a little Jacobs baby growing in her belly. I did that. I'm going to be a dad. Something that should be terrifying isn't because I know that I have the love of the most amazing woman next to me. At that moment, she glances over at me and smiles that perfect smile, and I know that life is good.

CHAPTER 49
ZACH

"Hails!" I call out, emptying my pockets onto the dresser. She isn't in the kitchen or living room, but her car is in the driveway.

"In here." I follow her voice to the bedroom that used to be Kyler and Dani's. We haven't figured out what to do with it just yet, so it sits completely empty still.

"What are you doing in here?"

I find her sitting in the middle of the floor, legs extended in front of her and crossed at the ankle, her hand rubbing over her still-tiny belly. She says that she sees it growing already, but she still looks small to me.

"Just thinking."

I prop myself against the door, trying to keep the gift bag hidden from her view.

"Care to share with the class there, future Mrs. Jacobs?" My smile widens at her with the knowledge that she will one day be my wife.

Wife—nothing makes me happier than calling her future Mrs. Jacobs. Wait, nope, I will be happier when I can drop the "future" and she is just Mrs. Haylee Jacobs, my wife and the mother of my child. *Wow, when did I, the manwhore, as my fiancée called me many times, become romantic and whipped?*

Probably about the same time I fell in love with this girl in front of me.

"About the nursery. I want to turn this room into it." The corners of her mouth turn up.

Anytime the baby is mentioned, the sweetest smile takes over her face. It's a nice change from the look of shock and panic that was on her face when we first found out. I don't blame her, though; it came as quite a surprise.

I look around the room and laugh to myself. When we first looked at this house when we were just about to graduate college, I never pictured this room one day as a nursey.

"I think the crib should go there..." She points to the far wall. "...and a dresser and changing table there, and a rocking chair right there in the corner."

"Wow. How long have you been sitting there, babe?" I joke, earning a judgmental look from my girl.

I laugh and shift against the doorframe, and the pink gift bag in my hand catches Haylee's attention because her eyes grow wide with excitement. Not long after we had found out about the baby, I had gone online and ordered these.

"What's in your hands?"

"What?" I say, playing innocent.

"Zach." She goes to stand, but I quickly stop her, bringing the bag into her full view. "Oh this bag, you mean?"

I ended up having the package delivered to the office because I knew that if it arrived here, she would have snooped. I'm proud of myself for keeping this from her. And I'm even more proud of myself for wrapping this myself. *Okay, so shoving items in a bag with just tissue paper isn't rocket science.*

I settle next to Haylee on the floor and set the bag next to me on the opposite side of her. She goes to reach for the bag, and I pull her into my arms.

"First thing's first." I lean in and press my lips against hers. When I pull back, her eyes are still closed.

"Hi."

As if my voice finally brings her back to reality, her eyes pop open. "Hi—now give me my present. That is for me, right?"

"Well, it's for *that* one in there." I point to her belly. "And since they're in you, I guess you get to open it."

She reaches over me and grabs the bag. "I don't care even if I win by default."

I laugh and settle back on my hands while watching her tear through the tissue paper.

"Oh my God, Zach… These are…these are…" She pulls out the onesies I had ordered and sighs in awe as she reads each one.

There are a total of four, each with a different phrase: "Daddy's Drinking Buddy," "My Daddy had fun making me," "Sorry, ladies, my daddy's taken," and "My Daddy is Jealous I had Boobs for Breakfast." The last one earns a loud laugh from Haylee.

She places them all on her knee and turns back to me. Her eyes are brimming with tears. I cup her cheek with my palm and swipe my thumb over the tear that falls. Her voice is barely a whisper.

"I love it—it's the baby's first present." Her smile widens. "She's going to love them."

My back quickly straightens. "Wait, what? You already know it's a girl?"

Haylee places her hand on my chest to calm me down. She rises to her knees in front of me and places both hands on her belly. "No, I just feel like maybe it is. We won't know for a little while."

I place my forehead against hers. "You wanna know something?" I pull her into my lap, and she rests her head against my chest. I put my hand over her belly. "I feel like it might be a girl too. And I hope she looks just like you. Absolutely beautiful just like her mama." I kiss her forehead. "Now how 'bout you tell me what else you were thinking in this pretty little head of yours about this room. I want to hear it all."

CHAPTER 50
Haylee

*L*ately, our weekend brunches have turned into wedding- and baby-planning central, and the Jacobses' house is home base. Today is no different. Mom, Kelly, Dani, and I are sitting at the dining table surrounded by color swatches, guest lists, and catering menus. I swear, between our wedding, the baby shower, and Dani and Kyler's wedding, our moms are in planning heaven. Dani and I already set our dates, just six months apart. Zach and I decided to wait until after this little peanut is born to get married. We've waited this long; what's a few more months? He already knows I'm his and he is mine *forever*—this is just a formality making it legal.

I sit back in my chair and rest my hands on my growing stomach. The first trimester was rough with morning sickness, but so far, I feel great during my second trimester. Things are totally normal—just add a growing stomach, huge boobs (which Zach loves), and a sex drive that is out of control (also something Zach loves). Don't even get me started on the cravings. I crave carbs constantly. We buy macaroni and cheese like it's going out of style. We also buy Yoo-Hoos in bulk—I drink chocolate milk with just about every meal.

"Anything for my girls," he always says.

Yep, that's right—our intuition was right, and we are having a girl. We just found out a few days ago. It's been hard to keep it a secret from everyone.

I'm off daydreaming of pink dresses and tutus when my mom touches my hand, pulling me back to reality. "What do you think of this?"

I snap my head to her. "Huh?"

I realize I must look like a deer in headlights. Oops, I'm caught not paying attention because I have no idea what she asked me. A giggle escapes Dani as I shrug.

"My bad."

My mom rolls her eyes. "I was saying, during the ceremony, your dad will be on the end and then me, followed by your grandparents."

"No, that doesn't work for me."

Mom looks back and forth between Kelly and Dani before turning her attention back to me.

"Well, I mean it all works, but I want an empty chair on the end, and then Dad can sit next to that."

A gasp escapes Dani, and she quickly covers her mouth as she understands what I want the empty chair for.

"An empty chair?" Kelly asks.

I nod and cross my arms; this is one thing I am not willing to compromise on. "Yes, I want to leave a chair for Em." The emotion threatens to come up just like many of my meals did during the first trimester. "It's important to me. All I want is for my brother to be there, and since he..."

I try to fight the tears, but it's a never-ending battle these days with my pregnancy hormones so crazy. I back up from my chair and begin to pace the kitchen, and the room starts to shrink in size.

"You know what? No, that color doesn't work for me either." I point to the color swatch we had just decided on. "And why the hell can't we have macaroni and cheese at the reception? It's my wedding, and I can do whatever I want." I don't mean to raise my voice, but I can't help it. At this moment, I am thankful our dads, Kyler, and Zach are downtown at the boat show and not here to see my outburst. "And if I want to have an empty chair for my brother? Then I'm going to have an empty chair." I stop in my tracks, and my breath quickens.

It all begins to hit me at once. I need air. I turn on my heels and quickly run out the front door, leaving my mom, future mother-in-law, and best friend in my wake. Once on the front porch, I attempt to catch my breath. I feel a hand grip my shoulder.

I look over my shoulder to see eyes so much like the ones of the man I love.

"Hails, are you all right?"

I turn away. "I'm sorry, I just needed some air. Can you tell my mom and Kelly I'm sorry—I just need some time to myself."

She gives me a brief smile, but it doesn't reach her eyes like it usually does these days. Before I know it, I hear the door click, and I am alone on the front porch to drown in my own thoughts. I look up to the sky. *Damn it, Emmett, why did you have to leave?*

I SIT ON THE FRONT PORCH SWING, WITH MY HANDS ON MY belly and eyes closed as I rock back and forth. I've since managed to get my breathing under control, but I wish Zach were back from the boat show already.

As if he had appeared out of nowhere, I hear, "Hey baby, what's going on?"

I open my eyes and meet his, instantly feeling better. I hop off the swing—or, well, as quickly as I can, and rush to his arms. His arms are around me, and my lips are on his as soon as we are close enough. A moment later, I pull back, confused.

"Why aren't you at the boat show? Where's everyone else?"

"My sister called me. She's worried about you—they all are. She said you had an anxiety attack. I left and came straight home. Talk to me, Hails. What's going on?"

He leads me back to the swing, and I settle next to him. The emotions threaten to come back up, and I swallow them down.

"It's just too much. All this planning. I was just overwhelmed by it all." I look away toward the driveway.

Zach furrows his brows and draws my attention back to him. "Did something happen?"

I exhale and blink, letting the unshed tears spill. "We were talking about food and colors and seating arrangements and it just really hit me that Em won't be there. I know we talk about it all the time, but it's just so real."

Zach cradles my head to his chest, running his hands down my back.

"Shhh, it's okay. Just breathe."

He lets me break down and cry in his arms. This man is everything I never knew I wanted, never knew I needed, yet he was always standing right in front of me. When the pain of losing my brother gets to be too much, Zach is there to pick up the pieces of my broken heart and mend them back together.

With his head against the top of mine, he presses a kiss to my hair. "I wanna take you somewhere."

"Where?" I sit up, brushing the tears away.

"Do you trust me?"

"Of course." Why would he ever think otherwise?

Zach stands and reaches for my hand, pulling me to my feet.

As we make our ways down the steps and toward the Jeep, I look back at the house.

"Should we let them know where we're going?"

Zach opens the passenger door for me. "Nah, they'll be okay."

Once I'm seated, he closes the door before running around to the driver's side. *Where are we going? I know better than to ask him again. I know he won't tell me.* Zach reaches for my hand and presses his lips against my knuckles, sending sparks up my spine.

"Ready to go?"

I nod.

CHAPTER 51
ZACH

On the way down to my parents', I was excited to see the sign that the carnival, the same one we always went to as kids, was in town. This was what we needed—an escape. It has been so stressful for both of us, preparing for the wedding and the baby. It has brought up plenty of emotions for both of us with the realization that one significant person will not be present for both big events in our lives. I miss Em every day, but it hurts more around the big moments. My daughter will never get to know what it's like to be spoiled by her uncle Em, Haylee will never get to dance with her brother at her wedding, and I will never get to hear what his best man speech would have been—I know it would have kicked ass. I know both of those weigh heavy on my fiancée's heart, as it does mine.

"What are we doing here?" Haylee asks as I escort her out of the Jeep.

"You'll see, baby girl." I lace my fingers with hers, and we make our way toward the entrance.

I watch the color flow back in her cheeks, and I know I made the right decision bringing her here. As we pass the funnel cake stand, her eyes widen.

I lean down and whisper in her ear, "Don't worry, there is plenty of time for that, but first thing's first."

I stand behind her in line at the Ferris wheel and place my

hands on her hips, pulling her slightly back toward me. "I wanted to remind you of where it all began."

When the cart stops and the attendant waves us over, I let her take a seat first before sitting next to her. I wrap my arm around her and transport back to the first time we were on a Ferris wheel when we both trying to figure out what was happening between us. She snuggles into my chest.

"I promise to protect you." My words to her from that night replay in my head. I will always protect her. There are moments, like the one today, that I know we cannot avoid. I hate that it feels like I can't do anything to help her. This was the best I could come up with—an escape from the overwhelming feeling of everything going on in our lives.

We are silent on the ride up, and of course, we stop at the very top again. This time, Haylee relaxes more into my arms.

"Thank you. I needed this." She peers up at me with her blue eyes.

I brush a stray piece of her hair behind her ear before my thumb strokes the soft skin of her cheek. "Sometimes, we need to take a moment and escape the chaos to remember that it's just you and me. Never forget that."

Haylee rests a hand on her belly, and my heart warms.

"Well, I guess it's not just us anymore," I add, realizing that in just a few short months we will become a family of three officially with the arrival of our little girl. A smile spreads across my face at that thought—*our little girl.*

"Nope. You ready for a family?" She looks back up at me.

"More than ever." I press a kiss to her forehead.

We sit in silence and look at our surroundings, but the peacefulness is over when Haylee clutches her stomach, a look of panic across her face.

"Oh my God! Hails, are you okay?"

The look of panic fades, and the brightest smile appears. "I'm more than okay. I think she just kicked."

My eyes grow wide. "Really?"

She nods, her eyes filled with tears, this time of joy, not sadness. She reaches for my hand and places it over her belly. I'm not sure what I'm supposed to feel for. Does it—

"Woah! Was that it?"

"Uh-huh." I stare at Haylee in amazement.

Could my girl be any more beautiful, the way the sun reflects off her? She is a vision, an angel. *My angel.*

Wow, now my eyes are filling up. That's my baby girl in there. I feel the warmth of Haylee's palm cupping my cheek, her fingers spread while her thumb brushes away a fallen tear. Shit, look at me being the one all emotional.

"Baby, are you okay?" she asks, and I place my hands over hers.

I can't hide back my smile. "More than okay. I mean…" I choke on my words. *Get yourself together, man.* "I know that's my baby in there, and I know we've seen pictures of our peanut, but actually to feel her. It just…it just feels so real." I press my lips to hers as the Ferris wheel begins to move.

I place my hand back on her belly as the ride makes its way around to the start, but instead of stopping, it continues for another loop.

With my forehead against hers, I tell her, "I love you, Haylee. You too, baby girl."

"Emme," Haylee says just above a whisper.

Who? Did she say the name Emme?

I pull back with my brows pinched together.

She places both her hands over her growing bump and continues. "Emme. I want to name her Emme after my brother. I've been thinking about it for a while, and then

I Never Expected You

when we found out it was a girl...I just thought it was meant to be."

I crash my lips to hers and kiss her just as the cart comes to a stop. I extend my hand, and when she links her fingers with mine, I feel the same spark I felt all those years ago. Once out of the way of the people boarding the ride, I lead Haylee through a clearing in the crowd. I turn to face her once we find an empty spot. I crouch down to my knees. Haylee grabs my shoulders in an attempt to pull me up, but I don't budge.

"Zach, what are you doing? People are staring."

"Let them," I respond before closing the distance between me and her baby bump. I don't even care if people stop and listen.

"Hey, Emme. It's Daddy." I feel Haylee's grip tighten on my shoulders as if I were holding her up. "I just want to tell you I love you very much. Your mom and I both do. Just a few more months, and then we get to meet you."

The sound of sniffling brings my attention back to Haylee. I look up to see her wiping away fresh tears. I turn back to the bump to place a sweet kiss on her stomach before rising.

"You like the name?" she finally asks.

"It's perfect. I have an idea, and if you hate it, then we move on from it."

"Okay." She draws it out, unsure as to what I am about to suggest.

I smile at her and tuck a stray hair behind her ear. "What if we name her Emme Danielle?" She doesn't say anything, so I continue. "I know it's stupid to think about, but I'd like to believe that they brought us together. The beauty of *us* came from the ashes of our loss."

"Wow."

"I know it was a crazy suggestion."

"No, it's just that that was beautiful and so deep."

"So what do you think?" I am more than happy to go with whatever name she wants, but silently I hope she likes this one.

Rising to her toes, she whispers against my lips, "I love it. Emme Danielle Jacobs."

I close the space between us, pressing my lips against hers, having her as close as she can be with her stomach.

I break the kiss and lean my forehead against hers. "Now how about we go share the news? I don't know about you, but it was killing me not to spill the beans that we know it's a girl."

She nods and takes my hand. We start to make our way back to the car—of course, not without stopping for two funnel cakes. Yep, Haylee ate her entire cake and even some of mine. I'm sure everyone is beginning to wonder where we are and if we will be back. I think we'll end up just staying over.

CHAPTER 52
Haylee

When I slowly open my eyes, my heart skips a beat as I take in the view in front of me. Zach is sitting in the rocking chair in the corner of the hospital room, rocking our baby girl back and forth.

Stubborn like her father and two days after my due date, our precious Emme Danielle Jacobs arrived at 7:43 a.m. this morning after twenty-two hours of labor.

"You did this to me. You're never coming near me with that thing again." I rested my head against the pillow after another contraction passed.

I could finally breathe. They were getting stronger and closer together.

"Sweetheart, you're doing so great. You look beautiful," my fiancé spoke sweetly, brushing the sweaty hair out of my face.

I turned and narrowed my eyes at him.

"Shut the fuck up, Zach, or I'll chop that thing off and feed it to you for dinner," I said through gritted teeth. I was exhausted and ready for this to be over.

"You can't cook, Hails."

Another contraction hit, and I reached for Zach's hand, nearly crushing it.

"It'll be a burnt penis then!" I roared.

I threw my head back, looking over at Zach after releasing his hand. I stuck my bottom lip out at him. "I'm sorry, baby, I didn't mean it."

Zach's eyes were focused on his hand that just felt the wrath of a woman in labor. "You're a monster, Hails."

I ignored his comment. "Can you hand me some ice chips?"

Zach cautiously walked over to me with a cup of ice in one hand and his other covering his dick.

I almost laughed, but another contraction hit the same time he handed me the cup, causing ice chips to fly everywhere...

Throughout the day there has been a constant flow of visitors in our room from our parents, Dani and Ky, Cami, and even Ky's sisters. Zach won fiancé of the year when he somehow convinced everyone that mom and baby needed some rest time. Okay, so maybe our family won family of the year too by actually agreeing. Although I thought we would have to pry that sweet baby out of her aunt and uncle's hands. I can already tell that Emme has her aunt Dani and especially her uncle Kyler wrapped around her finger, even at only a few hours old.

I don't even remember falling asleep, but I needed it. Sleep the last few days of pregnancy has been basically nonexistent, and don't even think about resting during labor.

I try to push myself up and wince at the sharp pain in my abdomen. I have to suck in a breath as I take it at a slower pace. Now sitting up, I have a full visual of Emme sleeping in her father's arms. I already know she will be a daddy's girl; there is no doubt about that.

Watching them together, I am reminded of the moment we first heard her cry once she was born, and tears had run down both of our cheeks. It was seriously the happiest moment of my life when the doctor laid Emme on my bare chest. I never knew instant love at first sight until I looked into my daughter's eyes for the first time, eyes that mirrored my own. Her crying calmed as I introduced myself as her mommy and Zach as her daddy.

Zach's voice is soft, just barely above a whisper as he talks to her. I think I just fell further in love with this man. I relax back into the bed and close my eyes in an attempt to rest again, but my eyes shoot open as his voice grows a smidge louder and I hear what he is talking to her about.

"And your mom showed up with this douchebag Chad, so I had something to prove she was mine and that I had fallen in love with her."

"What the heck are you telling our daughter over there?"

Zach's eyes shoot up as if he was just caught red-handed in the cookie jar, but as his eyes meet mine, his features soften before he returns his attention back to our baby girl.

"I'm telling her the story of us, how her awesome parents came to be."

While that is adorable, the story is far from appropriate. I hold back my laughter to keep from feeling the pain.

"Zach, you can't tell her that story."

"Why not? She should know how romantic her daddy is and how her mommy almost made a big mistake where this little one's dad could have had a microdick instead of this." He points to his pants, and I groan.

"Okay, for starters, babe, can we not mention microdicks around our daughter? Or really any dicks for that matter. I just popped a 7 lb 12 oz baby out of my hoo-ha." Zach's ears perk up at the mention of my ladybits. I hold up my finger in protest. "Oh no, don't even think about it. The candy shop is closed for six weeks—you heard the doctor."

I choose now to change the subject. Sleep deprivation and cohesive conversations do not mix.

I straighten up. "Now bring that baby over here before

everyone gets back and I have to fight off baby snuggles with our moms and your sister."

He chuckles. "I think you'd have to fight off Ky more. Who knew he was so good with kids? He's a natural. They'll start popping out kids soon, I bet."

"Why don't we let them get married first?"

"Where's the fun in that?"

Zach gets up slowly, still with a tight hold on Emme, making sure not to drop her. I've never seen him walk so slowly or carefully in his life. He finally makes it to the side of the bed and gently places Emme in my arms before taking a seat in front of me on the bed. We sit there, a family of three, soaking in the moment. I lean down and press a kiss to the top of her head, and she squirms but doesn't wake up.

"She's perfect," I whisper and fight back the tears.

"Just like her mama." I lean forward, and Zach meets me halfway till our lips are touching.

This kiss is sweet and simple yet still full of so much love. Our kiss ends when there is a knock on the door. Yep, I knew that wouldn't last long.

Zach announces, "Come in."

The door opens, and in strides our family for the second time today. A familiar scent fills the air, and my smile widens and my stomach growls. I realize I haven't eaten in hours.

"Okay, whoever has that bag of french fries, I'll trade you this precious baby for them."

Dani grabs the bag from her fiancé's hand and rushes to the side of the bed, reaching for her goddaughter. A few weeks back, Zach and I asked Dani and Kyler to be godparents, and of course, they accepted.

My dad sets a chocolate shake on the table next to the bed, and I am seriously in heaven.

I Never Expected You

Zach gets up from his seat and presses a kiss to the top of my head before joining the rest of our family over on the other side of the room. Our moms have settled in on the couch by the window that Zach had slept on last night.

I slide over on the bed, allowing room for Dani next to me, and I pass this little bundle of joy over to her aunt. Dani is a natural holding her, not that I would expect anything less. One day, my best friend will make a great mom.

"You know, you look pretty good holding one of those."

Never taking her eyes off of Emme, fully captivated by her, she responds, "Yeah, Kyler said the same thing when we left here earlier. I think if he had his way, he'd be putting one of these in me tonight." She pauses and looks up, locking eyes with me and smiles. "You're a mom."

I laugh, shoving the salty-sweet goodness of french fries dipped in a chocolate shake in my mouth—the ultimate comfort food when funnel cakes aren't available. They also make me think of mine and Zach's first date.

"I know, right? It's crazy."

Dani shakes her head. "Nah, it's not crazy. It's amazing. You and Zach made this perfect little angel." She leans down, inhaling the sweet baby scent. "Oh, the stories I'm going to tell you one day, sweetheart, of the trouble your mom and dad used to get into all the time."

Zach perks up from his current conversation with his dad and Ky. "Hey, don't act like you were all innocent. We've got plenty of stories."

Dani rolls her eyes, but a few stories come to mind.

"Yeah, yeah, yeah. Let's hope this little one isn't like her parents and can refuse a dare."

"Ha, like the time Zach ate a five-gallon bucket of Cheese

Balls at seven in the morning." Kyler laughs, and I cringe at the thought.

"Or the time you tried to explain to me as to why you had to drive with a leopard-print bra hanging from the rearview mirror in your car." My mom raises her eyebrow at me.

Zach and Kyler high-five. "That was a good one. Totally forgot about that one."

"There's always my personal favorite," Dani begins, but I hold my hand up, knowing exactly what she is about to share.

"Oh no you don't. We get it. Ha. Ha. We've done some crazy things." I change the subject by directing my attention back to the precious little angel in my best friend's arms.

Ky steps up the bed. "So are you going to give that baby up or what?" Dani turns away from him, cradling the baby closer to her, but eventually allows him to take her from her arms. I look around at the smiling, happy faces around the entire room and feel overwhelmed with joy and love. All of the people we love are here right now celebrating at this moment. It's in that moment a heavy cloud fills my mind that this is yet another moment my brother is missing.

Zach's eyes focus on me when he steals a french fry from the tray and mouths, "You okay?"

I nod, afraid that if I speak, I might get too emotional.

CHAPTER 53
Haylee

It's been a week since we brought Emme home from the hospital. A week of little sleep, nonstop feeding, diaper changes, and visitors. If I had my way, I would have done this sooner, but Zach had a point that it wasn't worth arguing and I shouldn't push myself.

"Hey, big bro, there's someone I want you to meet."

Zach bends down, unbuckles the straps of Emme's car seat, and reaches in to pull her out. She's dressed in one of the onesies Zach had bought her—"Sorry, ladies, my daddy's taken." I take a seat in front of the headstone with my legs crossed as Zach hands her to me before sitting next to me. I press a kiss to the top of my daughter's head.

"Emmett, I want you to meet your niece, Emme Danielle Jacobs. Emme, I want you to meet your uncle Emmett."

A stray tear runs down my cheek, and Zach reaches up and brushes it away with his thumb. I give him a brief smile.

We sit and chat until Emme releases a loud cry, and it may have only been a week, but I already know that this is a hunger cry. Call it mother's intuition.

"What do you say we get this little one back to my parents' house? I think she's getting hungry, and I don't really wanna whip out a boob here."

Zach's eyes go wide as he takes Emme from my arms to settle her back in her seat.

With one last kiss on the top of the stone, Zach and I walk back to the car, his arm around my shoulders and the other looped through the carrier handle.

When we get to the car, Zach places Emme's seat in the backseat and closes the door. I settle in the passenger seat as Zach rounds the car to the driver's side. Zach starts the vehicle but doesn't move. The familiar sounds of "Golden Slumbers" by the Beatles begins to play on the radio. I stare out the window at the hill where my brother's final resting place lies. Zach reaches for my hand and squeezes.

"You doing okay?" he asks as he links our fingers.

I turn to face him. "Yeah. I wish he was here, but a part of me knows he's always with me...us...her."

We both look back at Emme in the back seat, who has since calmed down. My heart warms, wondering if this is Em's way of comforting her.

"I love you, Haylee." He reaches down to my hand and brushes his lips against my knuckles, mainly the engagement ring on my left hand.

"I love you too."

I OPEN THE FRONT DOOR TO MY PARENTS' HOUSE, AND THE delicious smells of my mother's chicken parmesan hit my nostrils, causing my mouth to water and stomach to growl.

"Mmmm, it smells like heaven in here," Zach says, setting Emme's car seat down.

The house seems rather quiet. *Where is everyone?*

"Mom? Dad? We're here."

My mom strolls out of the kitchen. "Hi, sweetheart."

She kisses my cheek and Zach's before focusing her attention on her new granddaughter. Her face lights up when she sees Emme in her seat. This version of my mother is nothing like the version of her just after Emmett died. My daughter helped mend the pieces of her broken heart.

She reaches in to unbuckle Emme and cradles her in her arms, slowly rocking her back and forth. Emme begins to fuss, indicating that she is hungry.

"Someone's hungry. I'm just going to go take her up to my old room and feed her."

I reach for her, but my mom doesn't give her up. "Actually, why don't you follow me for a second? I want to show you something."

"Can it wait?" I look over at Zach, and he shrugs before I focus back on my mother, who has already begun heading up the stairs.

Zach leads his arm for me to follow, so I do.

"Do you have any idea what's going on?" I ask Zach as we make our way up the stairs.

"Nope, not a clue."

Once Zach and I are at the top of the stairs, I watch as my mother passes my old room and stops in front of the bedroom that used to be Emmett's.

My dad is standing outside the door. He gives us a brief smile before pressing a sweet kiss on my daughter's head.

"What's going on?" I ask nervously as Zach steps up behind me and places his hands on my shoulders.

With tearful eyes, my mom looks at my dad before returning her gaze to us. "Your father and I wanted to do something special for you guys so that when you are here visiting, Emme has a place of her own."

My breath hitches as my father opens the door, and they step aside, revealing what's inside. I fall back in shock, thankful that Zach is there behind me to keep me upright. His grip on my shoulders tightens as we make our way into the room.

My hands cover my mouth as I look around the room that was once decorated with lacrosse trophies, car posters, and pictures of my best friend. The walls are now covered in a pale pink. There is a rocking chair in the corner with a small bookshelf. I run my fingers along the worn wood. I can remember this same chair in my parents' room growing up.

"That over there is the same rocking chair I had from when you and your brother were babies."

Tears flow freely down my face as I notice the crib and beautiful bedding, but it is the lyrics on the wall that brings on the waterworks. Above the crib are lyrics to "Golden Slumbers" by the Beatles, the same song we heard at the cemetery.

My dad steps beside me, placing his arm around my shoulders. "I used to sing that song to you both. It's one of my favorite Beatles songs."

I don't even know what to say. I wrap my arms around my dad. "Thank you so much. This is perfect. I am at a loss for words that you guys did this."

"Well, it wasn't all us. Kelly and Adam helped too."

I look over my shoulder at Zach, who is staring at the photo of him and my brother on the wall.

"Brian and I will leave you three in here, and you can feed Grandma's little angel. But once you are back downstairs, I hope you know that I don't plan to give her up at all."

I laugh. "Yeah, I know. I'm chopped liver when you and Kelly or Dani are around."

My mom hands Emme off to Zach, and I pull her into an

embrace. "Thank you so much for this. You really have no idea how much this means to me."

"I'm so happy you love it. We'll see you downstairs. Dinner will be ready soon."

My parents exit the room, closing the door gently. I sit in the rocking chair and rest my head against the back, closing my eyes. When they open, Zach is in front of me, a smile from ear to ear.

I set Emme into an easy position for feeding before I adjust my shirt, revealing my nursing bra.

"Did you have any idea they were doing this?" I ask once Emme has latched onto my breast.

Zach puts his hands in his pocket and shakes his head. "Not a clue. This is seriously amazing, what they did. Who knew this room could look so good?"

I don't either. I love that my parents turned his room into a nursery. I know it took a lot of strength to do this, and I love them even more for that. I gaze down at my daughter. *Be brave and fearless, Emme. Your Uncle Emmett is always with you.*

CHAPTER 54
Haylee

Five months later...

"They're all set. You ready to go marry that goofball out there?" My best friend stands in front of me in her dark purple maid-of-honor dress.

The day is finally here: I marry my other best friend, my soul mate, my other half, some may even say my better half. The man at the end of the aisle waiting for me is the love of my life.

I smile at Dani and nod. "I am. It sure seems like it took forever to get here, but I'm ready."

With one last hug, she turns around, waiting for her cue to walk to the front.

Looking over her shoulder, she mutters, "I mean, technically it did, because someone had to go and get knocked up."

I hold back my laughter even though the expression on her face is killing me right now. "Don't make me trip you walking down the aisle, missy."

"Love you, bestie." She smirks.

"Love you too," I yell as the doors open and she disappears down the aisle.

My dad takes his place next to me. He holds out his arm, and I loop mine through his.

"You sure you wanna do this, baby girl?"

"Daddddyyyyy."

We both smile at my whine.

"I'm just kidding. I couldn't have picked a better man for you, sweetheart. That boy up there loves you to the moon and back. You and that beautiful grandbaby of mine are his world. But you say the word and we will blow this popsicle stand."

I throw my head back in laughter. I adjust my bouquet and rub my thumb against the photo dangling from the ribbon with a picture of my brother.

I tense and grip the bouquet tighter, fighting back the tears. I am about to walk down the aisle, and there is no time to redo my makeup.

My daddy pulls me into an embrace and kisses the top of my head. "I know you wish he were here, sweetheart, we all do, but just remember he is always with you, especially today. He's right there with you as we walk down the aisle."

My dad is right; my brother is always with me. I pull back and brush the tears away, hoping I don't look like a raccoon.

"You look beautiful. Let's go get you married."

The doors open when the music changes to play "Heartbeats" by José González. Everyone turns their attention to us, and as I take a deep breath as take my first steps to forever.

ZACH

"You may now kiss your bride."

My lips are on my wife's—wow, that is crazy to say— in an instant. The spark that ignites is as strong as the very first kiss we shared against her dorm room door. I smile against her lips and kiss the tip of her nose before we turn to face the crowd.

Kyler slaps me on the back as Haylee and I take our first step. We are just six months away from the roles being reversed and him and Dani making their first walk as husband and wife. We approach my in-laws, where my sweet little girl is resting in her grandma's arms, and stop to press a kiss to the top of Emme's head. She stirs, but doesn't make a peep.

Once in the back of the church, I pull Haylee into my arms and place my hands over her cheeks, caressing them with my thumbs. "Hello, Mrs. Jacobs."

I bring her lips to mine, sweeping my tongue across the seam of her lips to let me in. This kiss probably is a little too risqué for church, but oh well. This woman is now officially my wife, and I plan to kiss her as much and as long as I want from now till forever.

Kyler and Dani make their way to us, and everyone cheers.

"It's party time," I shout.

The reception is in full swing, and everyone seems to be having a great time. The hall is covered in beautiful shades of purple and gray. In one corner, there are photos of Haylee and me over the years and more recent ones that include Emme, while on the other side, there is an "In Memory" table with pictures of Emmett and us. There is a sign that sits on the table reading, "We know you would be here today if heaven weren't so far away." I'd give anything for him to be here today, but it's one of those weird moments where I feel like he is actually here.

Dani gave us a surprise when she decided to sing the song we had chosen for our first dance, "Can't Help Falling in Love" by Hayley Reinhart.

I sway side to side, holding Emme in my arms as I watch Haylee and her dad make their way to the dance floor for their father-daughter dance. I feel a hand clasp on to my other shoulder and look over to see my future brother-in-law standing there with his hands in his pockets.

"You're really a married man."

"Yep. Crazy, huh?"

"Nah, it suits you."

The music begins to play, a country song. Kyler's jaw tenses.

"You okay, man?" He stares out to the dance floor and then shakes whatever he was thinking away. A wrinkle forms on his forehead. "Dude, you look like you saw a ghost."

"No, it's just this song..."

"It's perfect, right? When Haylee first played it, I fell in love with it and pulled a page from my parents' book and ended up spinning her around the kitchen."

I turn my attention back to my wife and father in law, and they continue to sway to Heartland's "I Loved Her First."

When the song ends, Haylee makes her way over to me so that I can steal my mom away for our dance. I hand Emme off to her and kiss her cheek before making my way to find my mom.

As "In My Life" by the Beatles plays—of course, my mom picked a Beatles song—I twirl my mom around. I place one hand on her waist and hold on to the other one while she balances her free hand on my shoulder.

"I'm so proud of you, Zach."

"You are? For what?"

"Look at all you have—a beautiful wife and daughter who both adore you, a great job, a house. You have everything."

The corners of my mouth rise as I think as to how lucky I am with everything and everyone I have in my life. "Yeah, I guess I am pretty lucky, huh?"

"That you are."

I search the room as we continue to dance and lock my eyes on Haylee talking with our friends who traveled from New Orleans. When the music ends, I walk over to the DJ and make a song request before I stroll up behind my wife.

"Hey, guys, thanks for making the trip."

"Of course. We wouldn't have missed this, Zachy-Poo."

I roll my eyes. "Watch it, Benny-Boo, or I'll have my wifey here throw another punch your way."

He jokingly cowers. "No, thank you. I'm a changed man thanks to HailsBails." Turning to Kyler, he punches his arm, "Hey, MaiKy, you're next." Bennett wiggles his eyebrows and wraps his arms around Ky's shoulders.

I let out a laugh.

"You boys are coming to New Orleans for the bachelor party, right? Hunt and I will hook you up."

Before I have the chance to step in with bachelor plans as Ky's best man, a familiar '80s love ballad begins to play, and Haylee looks back to me.

"Are you serious?"

My mind takes us back to where it all started when I stood on a table in front of tons of fellow UPenn students and professed my love to this woman. To think, I almost lost her.

"When it comes to you, always. Dance with me, Haylee Jacobs."

She extends her hand to mine, and I lead my new bride to the dance floor.

CHAPTER 55
Haylee

Our Friday nights sure have changed— sort of. There is still food, margaritas (the occasional one for me, at least —you know, breastfeeding and all), and karaoke. So maybe it wasn't *that* much, but we now do it all at home instead of at Lucky's. We save that for special occasions, a.k.a. when we have a sitter who's not Dani or Kyler so that they can join us.

For an engagement present, Ky and Dani had given us a karaoke machine. The excitement on Zach's face was priceless. You would have thought he was a little boy on Christmas opening that one present that he had been asking for all year. I was not as excited, but it has grown on me. Those nights at Lucky's were a big part of our lives for the longest time that I would have been sad to give up the whole experience, so we decided to stick with it just at our house instead.

Dani and I are walking into the living room from the kitchen when we hear the familiar sound of the most annoying song I have listened to recently, "Baby Shark." However, as irritating as it is, it is very catchy and always gets stuck in my head. Zach is always playing it for Emme, and she just giggles. Dani stops abruptly and grabs onto my arm and chokes on her drink, almost spitting it all over the floor.

Zach and Kyler are standing with their backs to us, shaking their asses just like I have seen them start every routine for the past few years. When the lyrics start, they both turn around, and I see that not only is it Zach and Ky partaking in this madness, but Zach has baby Emme strapped to his chest. Oh my God, my poor daughter, I think even though I know she is such a daddy's girl that she loves this. She has the biggest smile on her face, showing her two little teeth.

"Wow, they are... I don't even have words." Dani continues to shake her head in awe.

"Hey, he's *your* brother!"

"Yeah, and your husband, which means you're here by choice! Not me! I'm stuck with him no matter what."

We both laugh.

"Touché. And on that note, that's also your fiancé over there, so doesn't say much about you either since you *choose* to be with him."

Dani watches Kyler dance and laugh with his best friend and goddaughter. She bites her lip as if she is lost in her own thoughts, and I see a blush creep up her cheeks. Oh Lord, it may have left PGville in that brain of hers. I'm not even going to ask. We are just about two months out from their big day, and I can't even put it into words the excitement and love I feel for my best friend and her man. I never thought I would see the day that she opened her heart again.

Emmett would want her to be happy, and I think once she realized loving Kyler didn't mean she loved Emmett any less, she opened her heart to move on. I know that my brother would want her to be happy, and as heartbreaking as it is that he can't be the one to do that, he would approve of Kyler being the one who does.

I let her enjoy her moment thinking whatever dirty thoughts she has in that head of hers before I jokingly punch her in the tit, bringing her back to reality.

"Oww!" she yelps, almost dropping her drink, and rubs her sore breast. I notice that the duet is now down to a solo, and I turn to see Kyler is now staring at his fiancée, his mouth hanging open.

"Fuck, Hails, what did you do that for?"

"Oh please, I barely hit you. Either way, your fiancé over there..." I point my drink in his direction. "...is staring at you like a raw piece of meat, ready to devour you, so I'm pretty sure he will make you feel better later."

She smiles that signature Jacobs smirk and makes eye contact with Kyler. Shit, here we go again. I give up! I roll my eyes, place my drink on the table, and stroll over to where my husband and daughter are currently standing. I will never be tired of hearing that—my husband, my daughter.

In my peripheral vision, I see that Kyler has walked over to Dani.

"Hey, you two," I say. They both whip their heads in my direction. "You cut that sh...stuff—" I catch myself from saying "shit" in front of Emme. I am determined for her first word *not* to be a curse word even though her daddy curses like a sailor. "—out. There are innocent eyes here that don't need to see all the things her father has."

I raise my eyebrows and laugh. Zach must be cringing at the awful memory of not only walking in once, but *twice,* on his sister. I personally find it hilarious; him, not so much. I turn around to see Zach's face, and he is so serious, staring at me. I know that look. I'm definitely going to get it later—in the best possible way, of course.

I bite my lip, and his eyes darken. Would it be appropriate to kick our houseguests out and tell them they have to take my daughter for the night? My breath catches in my throat as I remember last night when he had me bent over the side of the couch. *"Fuck, look at you so fucking perfect bent over for me. Your bare pussy on display begging for me. Tell me, baby girl, do you want my cock now, or do you want me to eat you like this?"* It took everything I had not to wake up Emme or the neighbors even with the way he made me scream in pleasure.

The moment breaks when Emme decides she's had enough being attached to Daddy and unleashes fury in her diaper, causing all of our attention to turn to her as her face turns extremely red while she poops. Dani and Kyler bust out laughing, and I try to hide my laughter knowing that she is attached to Zach and it's possible that diaper was explosive and he has shit on him.

Zach finally lets out a loud laugh and looks down at Emme, smiling. "See what your daughter thinks about that awful memory you bring up." His words are soft as he turns his attention to her. "Now what do you say we go change that nastiness in your diaper, sunshine? Daddy's got you."

It's so sweet to see him with her—the same man who has such a filthy mouth with me. I remember back when he was a big manwhore, and I never thought the day I would see him with a child, let alone *my child*. Zach takes Emme to her room to change her as the three of us take a seat in the living room.

In the middle of the conversation, we hear Zach yell, "Sweet Jesus, what did she eat?"

We all start to laugh as Kyler yells to his best friend, "Yep, she's all Jacobs!"

"Not cool, man. I never smelled like this before!"

Both Dani and I must have the same thought because we both say, "Umm, you sure about that?"

After a few moments, Zach and Emme walk out to join us, both sporting a new outfit. Emme is no longer strapped to her daddy's chest, but is in his arms. I think there is nothing that could make this moment better, being surrounded by the ones I love: my husband, my daughter, my best friend, and her fiancé.

My emotions have been over the place lately, especially since having Emme, and I have been missing Emmett more than usual. Not wanting to let my feelings get the best of me, I hop up from the couch and pull Emme into my arms.

"Why don't you boys go start the grill, and we will be right out with the sides?"

Zach looks at me, knowing me well—sometimes even better than I do— and can tell something is up.

Instead of making a scene, he walks toward me, cupping my cheeks, and whispers in my ear, "You okay, baby?"

I nod. He doesn't push the subject and kisses my forehead before kissing Emme's.

He leans to my ear one more time as he goes to pass and whispers, "I love you."

He winks and then walks off behind Kyler toward the kitchen, leaving just us girls in the room.

I hate when those moments come on. I miss my brother every day, but some days, it hurts more than others. I look down at my daughter, who has since fallen asleep on my chest. She loves my boob, just like her father. I guess making a massive mess in her diaper tired her out.

I turn to Dani. "I'm going to go lay this one down in her crib, and then I'll meet you outside."

She nods before getting up and heading into that direction while I take my sweet girl to her room.

I JOIN EVERYONE ON THE PATIO AND SET THE BABY VIDEO monitor on the table.

"So, Haylee, I have to ask. Will you explain to me the part in your vows where you promised to stay away from Zach's gym bag? Every time I ask this one over here..." Kyler nods in Dani's direction. "...she starts laughing until she can't breathe."

Dani laughs uncontrollably, further proving Kyler's point. Ugh, it was a horrible moment although now we can laugh looking back on it—at least I do; Zach, not so much. Zach groans over at the grill.

"You just had to put that in your vows, didn't you?"

With an ear-to-ear grin on my face, I defend myself. "Hey, I made up for it by buying you a new bag! And if I remember correctly, you brought up my shitty cooking, so it was only fair."

"Hello? Anyone going to fill me in on the story or what?" Kyler dramatically folds his arms and stomps over to an empty seat at the table.

Dani composes herself long enough to begin the story. "So it was the summer going into our sophomore year, and the boys had just gotten back from the gym. They smelled horrible."

"Horrible doesn't even cover it!" I interject.

"It wasn't that bad," Zach shouts over his shoulder.

"You smelled like roadkill!" I respond to my husband, glaring at him.

"Anyways," Dani continues, "our girl Hails here thought she had never smelled anything worse than the way the boys smelled post-workout. So, I saw an opportunity and took it."

An evil grin takes over her face, reminding me of the gif of the little girl who you know is up to no good. I throw a stern expression in her direction, and she waves me off.

"What! If you weren't just like my brother, where you can't refuse a dare, we wouldn't have had a problem, now would we?" She sits back in her chair, so proud of herself.

I close my eyes, and the memory is still as fresh as if it were yesterday. My best friend's voice is ringing through my ears. "*I dare you.*" I hear those words, and I refuse to back down. Maybe that had to do with growing up with such a competitive brother; I had to prove I could hang. More than one occasion though it has gotten me in trouble, and this one was no different.

"Without even thinking, Haylee accepted the challenge, and I had to race behind her to catch up as she went to where the gym bags sat by the front door. Now for the record..." She turns away from her fiancé to face me. "...yes I should've stopped you. I had been near those nasty things before, and let me say, they were N-A-S-T-Y."

"So, Haylee grabs *my* bag," Zach shouts.

I guess he still believes that I did it on purpose, no matter how many times I have tried to say I didn't know if it was his or my brother's.

I interject, "Hey, as I told you for the millionth time, I didn't know it was yours."

"Yeah, sure, babe."

I roll my eyes at him.

"Wait, so what happened?" The intrigue in Kyler's voice draws my attention to him.

He is like a little kid listening to this story. His elbows rest on the table, propping his chin up, and his eyes are wide as he waits for the rest of the story. I can't believe neither Zach or Dani has told him this before.

I go to open my mouth to continue, but Dani begins talking first, fully animated and full of life. "So Haylee picks up a gym bag, *not knowing whose bag it was.*"

She turns to her brother, whose attention is back on the grill. I mouth, "Thank you" in her direction, and she nods.

"She unzips the bag and stuck her face in it, her face

instantly turning green and gasping for air." She bends over in laughter.

I'm not sure who more entertaining to watch: Dani enthusiastically telling the story playing out the actions, or Kyler listening. It's sweet watching his full attention on her.

"Oh, shit!" Just when I thought Kyler's eyes couldn't get any bigger.

I press my lips together, knowing that her favorite part is coming. I had never seen Dani laugh as hard as I did at that moment in time when I would have much rather have been anywhere but the foyer of the Jacobses' house. Tears are streaming down her face, and she is trying to catch her breath. I swoop in to finish the story.

"After I stuck my face in the bag, my face turned green, and I immediately dropped it. All hell broke loose. I puked right into it."

Kyler chose the wrong moment to bring the beer bottle to his lips because at that moment as I continued the story, he turned his head and sprayed the beer that he had planned to drink, forcing more laughter from us.

"So Zach came running down the stairs to see what the commotion was and found me hunched over with his gym bag open and Dani leaning up against the wall laughing uncontrollably." I point in her direction. "Basically, how she is now."

"Holy shit!" Ky's face fills with joy, and he joins his fiancé in laughter, wiping the tears from his eyes. "Oh, man, that's fucking amazing. I can't believe you never told me that story before."

Zach sets the plate of cooked food on the table and walks over to where I sit. He pulls me to my feet before taking a seat and pulling me into his lap.

"Well, that's because it's not a fond memory to recall."

I Never Expected You

I poke his chest with my finger. "Well, Captain Smelly Bag, maybe you shouldn't have allowed something to die in there, and then it wouldn't have turned out that way."

He nuzzles his face into my neck. "But you still fell for me, stinky gym bag and all."

I turn to face him. "Maybe I should get my head examined."

I flinch when he pinches my side. "Okay, okay. Of course I fell for you—it's not like I had much of a choice, babe."

"That's right. You were always meant to be mine."

His lips crash onto mine, and we forget about our surroundings. It's just Zach and me, just like it was always meant to be.

EPILOGUE

HAYLEE

Four months later...

I walk into the bedroom, thankful that my parents have Emme for the weekend because I would never have been able to put this all together with her hanging all over me. Now that she is walking, she finds herself into everything and always keeping Zach and me on our toes. I carry the tray of Zach's favorite breakfast, coffee, four slices of bacon, and two blueberry waffles covered in syrup. I swear to God, if he gets syrup anywhere on the bed, he will be packing his bag and sleeping on his sister's couch. I'm sure he wants to be nowhere near their house with them still being in their honeymoon phase. Lord knows what places in that house they have not christened.

I'm impressed that I was able to hold the tray steady enough from the kitchen to the bedroom. My hands are sweaty and shaky, not to mention I am full of nerves to the point of nausea. This should feel like a typical morning, even though it is anything but. I've been keeping this secret for the past week while waiting for this customized coffee mug to come in from a shop I found on Etsy.

I set the tray down on the nightstand as I settle on the bed next to my sleeping husband.

"Good morning, handsome," I breathe against his lips before touching them with mine.

Zach reaches up, grabbing the back of my head, pulling me closer to him while deepening the kiss. Shit, my hormones have been raging lately, and I am so horny now, but breakfast first, sex later. He growls from the back of his throat as my tongue glides over the seam of his lips before pulling back. I sit back on the edge of the bed and pull my legs up under me.

"I made you breakfast." I point to the tray of food next to him.

"But I'd rather have *you* for breakfast." His eyes are now open and staring at me with a gaze that suggests this breakfast may just get cold after all.

Don't fall for it, Haylee. It's a trap. Be strong.

I bite my lip to prevent myself from launching my body over his and ravaging him. He sits up with his back against the headboard, his bare chest now on display. Maybe this can wait till after.

Zach looks over and sees the coffee mug on the tray. His jaw tenses as his brow furrows.

"Hey, where's my usual mug?"

Of course he would notice that. The man has been drinking coffee out of the same mug since Emme was born. It's blue and reads "World's Best Farter, I mean father."

"I bought you this one. It's cute. You don't like it?"

He inspects the mug, his face giving no indication if he hates it or not. He gives me the side-eye as he brings the cup to his lips. He makes a moaning noise, happy with the way his coffee tastes on his tongue.

"I miss my old mug." He makes a pouty face.

Lord help us when his daughter starts doing that. She already has everyone wrapped around her little finger.

"But at least you make the best coffee."

I may not be the best cook, but with Dani's help, I'd like to say I'm improving...sort of. My family hasn't been poisoned yet, so that's a start, right?

This is seriously taking forever for him to finish this coffee. Why of all days is he savoring this? Most mornings, he has already begun his second cup before I am even halfway through my first. What he doesn't realize is that this coffee mug isn't just any mug. When he reaches the bottom, it says a special message.

"Wow, babe. Not that I'm complaining, but what did I do to deserve this? I mean if this is a thank-you for the multiple O's you got last night, then I don't know why I don't get this morning often."

I punch his arm as I take a seat next to him and steal a piece of bacon off the tray.

"You are so cocky, Mr. Jacobs."

He shoves in another bite of waffles. "Yeah, but you still love me anyway."

"We all sure do." My heart begins to race as I notice the coffee mug is close to being empty.

With one last sip...*here goes nothing.*

Zach's eyes go wide as he brings the mug away from his lips.

"Umm, Hails?"

I scooch to my knees next to him and visibly swallow. There is no way he can't sense my nerves.

"Yeah?"

He looks deep into my eyes. I feel the sting of tears trying to

I Never Expected You

break through. He sets the mug on the tray and sets it all to the side.

His palm cups my cheek. "Baby? Are we…?"

He launches at me and has me on my back in seconds, hovering over me, his eyes glassy with unshed tears and a grin illuminating his beautiful face.

"Are we really? Are you? We're gonna have a baby?"

I nod, completely speechless and overwhelmed with love. His lips crash on mine before I could even open my mouth to respond.

He breaks the kiss, brushing the stray hairs out of my face. "We're really having another baby?"

"Yeah, we are. I just found out last week."

He presses butterfly kisses along my face and neck.

"I love you, Zach."

"Oh, Haylee, I love you so much. You have given me a life I never expected let alone dreamed I could have. I love you so much. Thank you for giving me everything."

How I got so lucky to call this man, my soul mate, I have no idea, but I will spend the rest of my days on this earth showing him how much I love him, starting with right now.

Later that day…

Dani and I are meeting for lunch at our favorite bistro downtown. I had gotten there a few minutes before her and am sipping on my water when I finally see her approaching the table. She quickly takes a seat across from me, setting her bag and jacket next to me.

"Hey."

"Hey. Nice to see you could separate yourself from your husband for a moment." I wiggle my eyebrows at her.

"Oh whatever, like you are any better."

Touché.

The waiter approaches. "Can I start you ladies off with something to drink?"

"I'll have a lemonade."

"Actually, that sounds great. Make it two."

"You got it, two lemonades coming up."

As the waiter walks away, I place my clasped hands on the table.

"So where is my wonderful brother today?"

"He went to the gym, and then I think he was going to your house. He had something he wanted to tell Kyler."

"Oh, yeah, what's that?"

There is no hiding my smile. I rest my arms on the table. "That we are expecting another baby."

"You're joking, right?"

My smile disappears at her response. Well, that was the last response I expected to get from her.

"No, I'm not. We're having a baby."

The curves of Dani's lips turn upward as she reaches into her purse.

"Well, one, that is amazing news. I am so happy for you guys. But also, I'm a little bummed that I can't have your maternity clothes."

"Wait, what?" And then it clicks. "Oh, my God, are you pregnant too?"

I cock my head to the side as I focus on the small photo she places on the table. I take in the way she is glowing.

"Yes. We just had our first sonogram. I wanted to tell you so much, but we wanted to wait until we confirmed it at the doctor's."

I cock my head to the side as I focus on the photo. "Oh my God! Dani is that…?"

THE END

ALSO BY AUTHOR

I Never Planned On You

Book 1 in the I Never Series

A Brother's Best Friend Romance

I Never Expected You

Book 2 in the I Never Series

A Friends to Lovers Romance

I Plan on Forever

An I Never Series Novella

COMING SOON!

PLAYLIST

1. Us - James Bay
2. Golden Slumbers – The Beatles
3. Fix You – Coldplay
4. Wait – M83
5. Wake Me Up – Tommee Profitt
6. Wasn't Expecting That – Jamie Lawson
7. Ashes – Celine Dion
8. Count on Me – Bruno Mars
9. You Make It Easy – Jason Aldean
10. Drink a Beer – Luke Byran
11. I Want to Know What Love Is – Foreigner
12. I'm Yours – Jack Savoretti
13. I Found – Amber Run
14. The Sound of Silence – Disturbed
15. Saturn - Sleeping At Last
16. In Case You Didn't Know – Brett Young
17. One Call Away – Charlie Puth
18. Let It All Go – Birdy, Rhodes
19. So Cold – Ben Cocks
20. I Love You – Alex & Sierra
21. Without a Word – Birdy
22. I Could Fall In Love – Selena
23. Remembrance – Tommee Profitt, Fleurie

Playlist

24. Everything Has Changed – Jasmine Thompson, Gerald Ko
25. Unsteady – X Ambassadors
26. Can I Be Him – James Arthur
27. Over and Over Again – Nathan Sykes, Ariana Grande
28. Never Say Never – The Fray
29. Baby Shark – Pinkfong
30. When the Time is Right – Griffin House

ACKNOWLEDGEMENTS

Thank you to the readers for again taking a chance on me. If I Never Expected You was the first book of mine you picked up, I hope it won't be the last. Your support means everything to me and *you* are the reason I continue to share these stories.

Amanda Carol: Thank you for letting our characters be friends. Of course, thank you to Bennett, Hunter and Aria for making the trip for Zach and Haylee's wedding. I can't wait to see what sort of shenanigans our characters get themselves into in the future. *Want to learn more about Bennett and the rest of Zach's New Orleans' friends? Be sure to check out "The Awakened" by Amanda Carol, available for free in Kindle Unlimited.

My facebook reader group: Thank you for being a part of Talk Wordy to Me. I love how excited ya'll get when I share new things, snip-its and the inside scoop before everyone else. I also love getting to know each one of you and look forward to what I have to share with you guys in the future.

The Chaddettes: Thank you for being my people. You guys are there for me when I need to be excited, w I need to vent or just need to just send an inappropriate meme. I never expected *winkface* to find such an amazing group of women to take this crazy journey with. I am so proud of all we have and all we have yet to to accomplish in life. A special shout out to Amanda, Becca and Claudia. You ladies helped shape the characters in to who they are today. All three of you at some point made your way into the story as a way to say thank you. Love you guys! Chicken wings for all at Steele Tobys.

My beta readers: I huge round of applause for Amanda, Becca, Claudia, Bibi, Jenny, Alley, Ashley, Laura, Katey, Jacinta and Kat. I couldn't have done this without you ladies. Each of you read this book in its various raw and ugly and WTF stages and you haven't unfriended me so YAY! Your feedback meant everything to me.

My fellow authors: Thank you for supporting and guiding me along this journey. If I could thank each one of you individually, I would but I only have so much room, just know how much I love you guys. I fangirl everyday as I get to know some of my favorite authors.

Chris Wood and Melissa Benoist: Even though I know they will most likely never read this, thank you for being the perfect muses for Zach and Haylee. Aren't they adorable? I had so much fun researching their characters.

The biggest thanks to Jeannette, Sandra, Carmen, Clara and the ladies of Give Me Books Promotions. Ya'll are the behind the scenes crew who helped make this book happen and share the word.

I can't go without thanking my real-life support team. These people are there to deal with my crazy day in and day out and still continue to love me; Travis, Jen aka my real-life Dr. Foster, Margaret, TK, Jesseca and Abbie Thank you for dealing with my crazy!

Lastly, to Ms. Carmen – I hope this book lived up to Chapter 33.

ABOUT THE AUTHOR

Stefanie Jenkins writes contemporary romance and lives in Surf City, North Carolina with her husband and two sons. Born and raised in Maryland, Stefanie brings her favorite parts of her hometown to life in her books. She is a coffee addict, wine connoisseur, hockey fan & lover of all romances.

Follow Stefanie on Social Media:

Facebook Page: https://www.facebook.com/authorstefaniejenkins
Facebook Reader Group – Talk Wordy to Me: https://www.facebook.com/groups/sjtalkwordytome/
Instagram: https://instagram.com/authorstefaniejenkins
Goodreads: http://bit.ly/grsjenkins
Website: https://www.authorstefanie.com/
E-newsletter Sign up: http://bit.ly/sjenewssignup